DINNER AT SAM'S

A Ruby's Novel

DL WHITE

DEDICATION

Dedicated to my Aunt Marilyn, whom I wish I would have known longer.
And, as always, my family— especially my parents, who never stop letting me know how proud they are.
I love you all.

CONTENTS

Acknowledgments	vii
Prologue	1
Chapter 1	7
Chapter 2	21
Chapter 3	32
Chapter 4	45
Chapter 5	61
Chapter 6	72
Chapter 7	83
Chapter 8	100
Chapter 9	118
Chapter 10	133
Chapter 11	142
Chapter 12	153
Chapter 13	170
Chapter 14	179
Chapter 15	188
Chapter 16	203
Chapter 17	212
Chapter 18	228
Chapter 19	246
Chapter 20	258
Epilogue	273
Thank You!	277
About the Author	279
Also by DL White	281

ACKNOWLEDGMENTS

Writing is such a solitary act, but many on the outside don't know that it takes a village to write a book.

Thanks to my village. I am indebted to you!

PROLOGUE

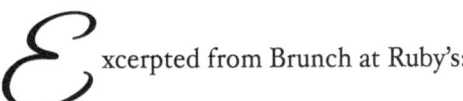

$\mathcal{E}$xcerpted from Brunch at Ruby's:

MAXINE

I PASS AN OPEN, LIT OFFICE AND DON'T THINK ANYTHING OF it. It's not unheard of for an agent to be working past six o'clock. After all, I'm still in, as is Virgil.

A sniffle and half of a sob makes me stop in my tracks. I'm late. I don't have time, but I double back anyway and stick my head into Vanessa's office. She's at her desk, which faces the door, but she's turned away, her head in her hands. She sniffles again.

"Hey. Vanessa. What's up?"

Her head pops up and she nearly jumps out of her chair. "Maxine! I didn't know you were still here."

"I was just leaving. Are you alright?"

Her face falls like she's going to start crying again. "I just got some bad news."

"Is there anything I can do?"

I've loved hearing her laughter waft down the hall into my office, but the chuckle she gives me isn't her usual fun and bubbly quality. It's sardonic and gritty.

"Unless you can work some kind of miracle? I'm fucked." She gulps, her eyes flying up to my face to see if I've frowned at her utterance. "Sorry."

I ease into her office and take one of the seats across from her desk. Her office is simple and tasteful, minimal without being plain. She's orderly and likes clean surfaces. Except for her computer, a file organizer, a three line office phone and a few framed photos, her desk and credenza are clear of clutter.

"You've been quiet, I've noticed. Is there something going on?"

She shakes her head, moaning. "My husband. Soon to be *ex-husband*, rather. He's been living... what do they call it? A double life?"

"What's that? A double life?"

"He's having an affair. Well, it's more than an affair. It's like he's with me and her. And here I thought I was his one and only."

She sniffles, leans over to grab the handles of her purse and rummages around in it until she produces a packet of Kleenex. She pulls one cloth from the plastic case and dabs at her eyes and nose.

"He's a salesman. Technology, cloud computing, all those buzz words. Business is booming, he says. He has all these business trips he needs to go on. Clients to schmooze. Deals to close. He's gone for weeks at a time and he's always on the phone, it seems like. I never even thought to question him. Everything was always taken care of."

Her lip quivers and her nose flares and tears fill her eyes

again. "They have a house together, Maxine. They take vacations together—vacations he and I planned but he could never get the time off of work. Meanwhile, our mortgage and our family and the life we built together—he left it all behind. I don't know which life is fake and which is real."

"How did you find out about this? About her?"

She sighs, wiping away the streaks of mascara from under her eyes and down her cheeks. "He always handled the finances. He opened the mail and paid the bills. He's just always taken care of everything. I never had to worry. I never thought to save any money. That was for me and the kids and fun things.

"Anyway, a few months ago, one of the kids picked up the mail. I happened to flip through it and some envelopes looked serious."

With bated breath, I wait for the dramatic reveal. Paternity results? A welfare check? STD Test?

"We were in foreclosure. Thousands in arrears, plus late fees and interest. I almost passed out." She pauses and sniffles, taking another swipe with the wad of Kleenex clutched in her palm.

I'm almost afraid to ask. "And the others? What were they?"

"Notices from the IRS for back taxes. We file separately. He said that made more sense because of his business expenses. It turns out it's because he doesn't like to pay taxes. He hadn't paid them in years. He's into the government for almost fifty grand. That's where I lost it. What if they come after me? I don't have fifty-thousand dollars!

"I confronted him and he swore on the bible, on our kids, on his mother's grave that it was a mistake. He'd take care of it. Well, I started snooping and finding things, stuff I hoped I wouldn't find and didn't want to believe, but it was right there in my face. He always said he didn't believe in Facebook, but he has a profile where he's connected to her. This woman. Jasmine.

"They have friends and a social life. Barbecues and couples nights and last spring, when our youngest had her kindergarten graduation and he said he had a conference he couldn't miss because he was the Keynote Speaker?" She huffs. "He was at happy hour with her and their friends at Davio's."

I'm floored. Jaw on the floor, limbs numb, speechlessly floored. "Wow. So bold."

"He was always too busy to do anything with me or our kids. He always had to work. Now I know what he was working on. How does he even live with himself?"

"His day planner must be serious." I instantly want to take back my snide comment but Vanessa laughs.

"He's mega organized, obsessive about planning. That's why I couldn't believe he hadn't paid the mortgage. You don't forget to pay the mortgage six months in a row."

"So today you got some bad news?"

She sniffles, the corners of her mouth pointing toward her chin. "Our house is scheduled to be sold at auction. I was hoping I could save it, but after the bank kicked me and the kids out, I've had a hard time getting back on my feet."

Vanessa sucks her teeth and sighs. "I love that house," she moans. My heart almost breaks. "It was the first piece of property I owned. We bought it together."

"The first piece of property you bought with this man and he let it go under? For some other hot thing? That's we call a sign. Now you get to find a place that's all your own, that you will love just as much or more because it's yours. And that will happen in no time at all because your listings are selling–"

She snickers. "None of that matters with this foreclosure on my credit. He shut off our cards, drained our accounts and he's gone... everything's gone. I sold everything I could, pawned my jewelry, put my nice clothes into consignment. The kids and I are in my aunt's basement. I don't know what to do."

She starts to warble again, but I reach across the desk and lift her chin so she can see me. "What's this bastard's name?"

"Warren."

"Is Warren Jackson is sitting around, crying because the house got sold and his marriage is over and his credit is bad?"

She shakes her head. "I know you want to drown your sorrows and feel sorry for yourself, but you don't have time for that. Good riddance to bad rubbish, Grandma Elise used to say. You get yourself together and get back on your feet. Show Warren he might bring you down, but he didn't take you out. You have children?"

She nods. "Two girls."

"They're going to need you to be strong and press on. You can do this. I might not know exactly what you're going through, but I've been through some things in my life. Tomorrow, we'll do lunch and I'll tell you all about it. And we'll work on a plan to get you where you need to be."

I stand and hook the strap of my bag over my arm. "For now, go wash your face and gather your things. Go be with those girls. There's more to life than work and they need you more than Donovan does right now."

CHAPTER ONE

anessa

"Sᴀᴍ's Bᴀʀ ᴀɴᴅ Gʀɪʟʟᴇ. Sᴀᴍ sᴘᴇᴀᴋɪɴ.'"

My uncle's voice, even over the phone, had always been a salve to my soul. Slightly soft, slightly gritty, like low grade sandpaper. He owned Sam's Bar and Grille, home of his popular, well-seasoned and fried-to-order chicken wings. Though we tried not to refer to his wings as *famous*— we'd never hear the end of it— people had been known to get hooked on his special spice blend and drive from far and wide to the heart of Decatur, Georgia, which made Uncle proud.

I would have smiled upon hearing him in my ear, but I was in a terrible mood.

"Hi, Uncle; It's Vanessa."

"Hey, Lil' Girl! You don't sound so good."

"The car died on me, in the middle of interstate traffic. I need to pick up the girls from the after-school program and they're going to charge me for being late and I don't even know what's wrong with this car but I know I can't afford to fix it and–"

"Hold on, hold on, hold on. I'm an old man, you know. Deaf in one ear and can't hear out of the other one. You say you're stuck somewhere? In this rain?"

"Yes, in this rain," I answered, watching the torrential downpour from inside the car. I had stood outside with my head under the hood, like I knew what I was looking at or how to fix it. I finally came to my senses and got back in the car.

Now I was wet *and* stranded. "I don't know what Roscoe did to the car the last time I took it to the shop, but whatever it was didn't stick. Now I can't get to the girls–"

"I said hold on, now!" Sam's tone was gruff but his bark was worse than his bite. He wouldn't even kill spiders. Out of respect for him, though, I pressed my lips together so I couldn't say another word. "Tell me where you are. I'll send Roscoe to you with the tow truck."

I gave him my location, with landmarks to help my cousin find me. I heard him growl out the order on a two-way radio he keeps at the restaurant for just such an occasion. A few squawks on the other end confirmed my rescue was en route, and even if it was my slow-footed cousin, I was relieved.

"We got that settled; now what about the girls?"

"They're at Kid Care on Claremont. They have to be picked up by six o'clock or they charge me extra." I glanced at the face of my watch and groaned. "If Aunt Marilyn could–"

"She'll pick them up. Have Roscoe drop you over to the house. Stay warm and dry. Help is on the way."

Help is on the way. How many times had my uncle uttered that phrase to me in my lifetime?

My head was heavy as I tipped it back against the headrest and watched rivulets of water squiggle down the windshield. Today's rescue would add another hash mark to the hundreds of hash marks I've counted over my twenty-eight years, a never-ending cycle of my aunt and uncle coming to my rescue. First when my mother died, later when I rebelled against their strict upbringing and did everything a respectable young lady shouldn't do.

And *much* later, when my husband left me and our daughters with a mountain of debt, a foreclosed home and a car that needed more than prayer and duct tape to hold it together, Auntie and Uncle had come to save us, moving us from a near palatial estate on the outskirts of town to a daylight basement in their house.

I was still an agent at Donovan Luxury Realty. Maxine Donovan— Glass since she got married— owner and principal agent, knew the whole story of how Warren was living a double life, somehow married to me *and* building a life with another woman. She'd given me a lot of leeway, but I could tell her patience was running thin.

Honestly, so was mine. I needed to get my life together.

A few months ago, I was able to move the girls and I to a two bedroom condo, not far from Auntie and Uncle, and a few blocks from Sam's, so we still saw them often. Once I divorced that son of a bitch Warren Jackson, the future would be bright.

The loud rumble of the tow truck startled me as it passed, then pulled off the interstate and backed up to my car. When the brake lights glowed and the driver's side door opened, I grabbed my bag and got out of the car. The downpour had eased, but raindrops still pelted us from above.

Roscoe wore his usual uniform, blue overalls permanently smudged with motor oil. "Go ahead and get in!" He yelled over the sounds of traffic speeding by. "I'll strap her up and we'll get going."

I ducked around the rear of the white truck with the

Roscoe's Auto Repair logo on the side and climbed up into the cab. I was relieved to be sitting in a heated vehicle, but regretted inhaling so deeply once I was in and settled. The truck smelled like old hamburgers and feet. I rolled the window down an inch to breathe in the fresh air from outside.

A few minutes later, my Audi was hitched up to the truck and Roscoe climbed inside. He put the truck in drive, waited for an opening and slammed his foot on the gas, shooting us into traffic. I braced myself against the dashboard with one hand while I pulled the seatbelt across my lap.

"Take it easy, Roscoe! Are you trying to kill us?"

He grinned, both hands gripping the large steering wheel, the radio crackling in the background. His other tow truck drivers were having a lively conversation over the airwaves. He reached above his head and turned a small dial, which quieted the cackles and rowdy conversation.

"So, what happened this time?"

"Same as last time. I lost everything. Engine, power steering...everything. I barely got it to the shoulder. I thought you fixed the..." I flapped my hand around in the air, gesturing toward the engine of the truck. "You know... the thing."

Roscoe laughed. "I thought I fixed *the thing* too. I told you I don't know nothin' about German cars. I did the best I could."

"I know," I grumbled, folding my arms across my chest. "I don't want to take it to the dealership but I might have to. What if I had a showing today? What if I had a closing? I can't be late to a meeting with DJ Fresh Beats because my car decided not to work."

"You sellin' a house to DJ Fresh Beats?"

Occasionally, I forgot who I was talking to and dropped a name. Dre Prescott, as he was known off-stage, was a DJ turned record producer who'd won a Grammy for his work on an R&B artist's debut single. He decided he needed a home large enough to house a studio. Since he was making royalties hand over fist, he wanted something over the top.

Of course, he called Donovan. And of course, Virgil, Maxine's assistant and office manager, assigned him to me. For no reason, other than my relative youth and proximity to popular culture, I was assigned to the clients who were around my age group and so rich they didn't know what to do with themselves. Unfortunately, Dre didn't make a move without the approval of his mother and girlfriend and between the three of them, I hadn't made any progress.

"Trying to. If his mama and his girl would stay at home, we could get somewhere. My point is, I need a reliable car." I sucked my teeth and propped my elbow up on the windowsill, glaring at nothing. "I think I'm going to have to break down and take it in."

"You know the dealership is going to rob you blind."

I bounced my glare from passing traffic to the pudgy, dimpled man in the driver's seat. "Getting it fixed for free isn't doing me any good, is it?"

"Guess not. But I was just saying; be ready for that bill. If I can't fix it, it's something fancy. And fancy means a fifty-dollar part and twelve hours of labor at *you can't afford that* prices."

He flipped his blinker and pulled off at an exit, then slowed as we entered a familiar residential area. "I'm taking you to mom and dad's, right?"

I nodded and rode along as he navigated the narrow streets in the wide truck, eventually stopping in front of a modest brick ranch with two magnolias shading the front yard and a red Cadillac in the driveway.

"You don't want me to do anything to the car, then?"

Under my breath, I cursed Warren, as I had a hundred

thousand times since I found out about his other life. I hated feeling helpless.

"Take a look, I guess. If it's not simple, don't mess with it. I'll have you tow it to Audi." I climbed out of the truck and walked up the driveway to the front door. Before I could reach for the knob, the door swung open and two little brown girls spilled out of the house.

"Mommy!" reached my ears and, for that moment, my terrible day and my wet bra and my dead car melted away. They made me smile when nothing or no one else would. I gathered them to me, letting them usher me into the house. It was cozy, lived in and smelled of beef stew. I was suddenly *so* hungry.

"I'm sorry I couldn't pick you up. My car broke down again. Did you have a good day?"

The girls pulled me further into the house to the den, where they'd already spread out on the comfortably worn furniture. The TV played a Disney show on mute. They chattered, almost simultaneously, about their day as second and third graders— spelling tests and math homework and permission slips until a figure wearing an apron stepped into the open doorway.

My aunt Marilyn was every definition of the comforts of home. Diminutive and plump, she always wore a smile so wide, her glasses rode her full cheeks.

"Have you girls even let your mama breathe for a second? She just got here and all I hear is chitter chatter coming from this room. Get on that homework and let me say hello to my niece."

The girls seemed okay with me slipping away, so I followed Auntie down the hall to the eat-in kitchen, where everything was ready to set the table.

"Is Roscoe going to look at the car again for you?"

"Yeah. But he's just tinkering around, throwing things at

it." I fell into a routine I knew well, grabbing a set of bowls and dotting them around the table. On the next lap, I laid silverware and set a glass at each spot. "I might have to take it to the dealership."

"Vanessa, you need to go on and get rid of that car. Get you something nice and reliable."

"The car I have is paid for, Auntie!"

"It's paid for, alright," she fussed, stirring a simmering pot. "It's costin' you what you'd pay for a new car every month. This is the second time it's broken down on you. What if the girls were with you today? What if you had some place to be?"

I lowered my voice so the girls didn't hear, planting a fist on my hip. "What am I supposed to buy a car with, Auntie? My pretty face? Warren left me with no options. Besides, I can't even afford a car right now. If it wasn't for Roscoe I'd be on the bus."

"Sam and I told you —"

"I know, Auntie. You and Uncle said you would help. But you've helped enough. And you never know when we might need that money later. Let's keep it where it is."

I sidled up next to her and dropped an arm across her shoulder, watching her ladle the savory stew into a stoneware bowl. She shook her head and pursed her lips and huffed like she always does when I refuse money. They couldn't bail me out forever.

"Your stew smells real good and so does the cornbread. I'm going to have the girls wash their hands."

GIBSON

"Gibson, are you with us? Come in, Gibson."

In no rush to return my attention to the meeting I was required, as an Associate, to attend, I slowly rolled my head to the front of the spacious meeting room, where most of my family and a few others were gathered around a shiny black lacquer table. Every face was turned toward me and at least two faces seemed to be holding back a snicker.

Instead of paying attention to the weekly case report, recited in a manner as monotone and boring as possible by Senior Associate Garrett Kincaid, I'd been gazing at the view of city from the 20th floor.

"I hope we're not disturbing you by having a meeting during your daydreaming session."

I shifted in the leather seat, away from the scenery and dropped my eyes to the thick report sitting in front of me. "Not at all." I picked up the stack and flipped through it like I was interested in the charts and graphs on every page. "You're easy to ignore."

"If you were pulling cases that made any kind of impact on these numbers, you'd be more interested in this report."

"I doubt it, actually."

"So, how long are you going to coast on our backs, Gibson? Taking penny ante cases, billing next to nothing while the rest of us do real work, practice real law—"

"Real law?" I bit out a sharp bark of laughter. "I don't practice real law because I don't bill four hundred an hour like you?"

"Enough!" Sylvia, matriarch of the family and founder of Kincaid Law, snapped from her seat at the head of the table, her eyes darting from me to Garrett and back. "This is unproductive. Let's get back on track. Garrett, finish up so we can move on."

Garrett's victorious smirk made him look like our father, but of the four Kincaid brothers, he was the most like Mother. The Silver Shark, as she was known about town, was a force in Atlanta family law. Her reputation cut a wide swath across the city. Men and their attorneys trembled when they learned that their soon to be ex-wives had retained Sylvia

Kincaid. Garrett was her pup, eager to be molded into her cold, calculating image.

I was more like our father, Judge. His name was Garrison, but everyone, family included, called him Judge. He presided from a cushy seat on Georgia's Superior Court and the running joke was that he liked it there because it was the only place he had any power. Mother ran the show everywhere else.

My eyes roamed the room as I tuned Garrett out again. Gabriel and Greggory were seated across from me. Born 11 months apart, they were so close, they practically *looked* like twins. They both wore square, dark rimmed glasses that framed the light brown eyes they got from Mother. They even dressed alike—light colored slacks, crisp white shirt and moderately expensive but casual looking jacket.

Garrett and were similar in looks: smooth cocoa skin, espresso brown eyes, tall but not lanky, muscular build and broad across the shoulders— which was where any similarity between Garrett and I ended. There were six years between us and we could not be more polar opposite, from our taste in clothing to our taste in women to how we did our jobs.

How we all came to be Associates at Kincaid Family Law was an easy story to tell. When your mother is a powerful city attorney and your father is a sitting judge, the family business is what you learn from birth. Starting off at Kincaid made the most sense, so we clerked for her when we were old enough. When we graduated, and passed the bar, we were given positions at Kincaid— positions we were expected to be grateful to receive.

I wasn't *ungrateful*. And it wasn't that I didn't enjoy the work. I got a great deal of personal satisfaction from every case I handled. What made me the black sheep was wanting to do more than vacuum money from deep pockets. I wanted to help people. You'd think I was speaking in a dead language when I tried to explain that to Mother.

The weekly report made its usual *thunk* into the garbage can as I entered my office. I settled into the chair behind my desk, flipped open the lid of my laptop and powered it on. As it booted, my eye caught the iconic Atlanta skyline and I was daydreaming again.

My own building. My own office, designed and decorated by me, not Garrett's wife, whom Mother hired to turn Kincaid into a boring and uninspired grey, black and white canvas. My clients. My practice. *My way*.

I had a plan, an escape hatch of sorts that I negotiated before I would step a foot inside Kincaid, before I would agree to work for Mother. It was almost time to make my move and lately, I'd been thinking about taking the leap early.

Though it was closed, my office door swung open without so much as a knock. Mother marched through the doorway, her pink suit a nice contrast to the grey wall behind her.

"I've had enough of this bickering between you and Garrett. It must stop. I'm tired of refereeing petty arguments during staff meetings; I practically need a whistle. What is it with you two lately?"

"Lately?" I chuckled as I signed into the firm's billing and case management software suite. "Have Garrett and I *ever* gotten along?" A rhetorical question, because she and I both knew the answer would be no. I didn't worship him as the oldest in the family. I didn't look up to him, want to be like him. I didn't ask for his advice and, truth be told, his opinion didn't matter. I didn't care what Garrett thought of me.

"It didn't used to be this bad. Throwing barbs at each other during meetings, interrupting business with silly arguments—"

"Maybe you should ask Garrett why he always has something slick to say to me."

"Maybe you should perform in a manner that doesn't give him anything slick to say."

"Okay. Okay." I removed my fingers from the keyboard and wound them together, lifting my eyes to my mother's as she leaned over my desk. She tried to be intimidating but I had towered over her since the sixth grade. "I know what this is about."

"What? What do you think you know?"

"This is about my caseload."

"Gibson, I want—"

"You want me to do things your way and I'm not—"

"It's not *my way*, Gib! There are a thousand lawyers out there hanging a shingle off a shack, taking deadbeat cases. You don't have to be one of them."

I swiveled my chair around to stand, then walked around the desk. I gestured to one of the tufted grey guest chairs but she refused to sit, pulling herself up as tall as a five-foot woman could. Her arms were tightly folded across her chest and, though there was a line across her forehead and her lips were thin and pressed together, she wasn't hopping mad yet. *Yet.*

"The fact that you call my clients deadbeats is disturbing. And insulting. They're all Kincaid clients. They pay their bills—"

"At a grossly reduced rate no one authorized you to offer."

"I'm helping them. Isn't that why we got into this business? To help people?"

A pink hue crept upward from the collar of her silk blouse. She was getting closer. *Just a few more buttons...*

"Gibson, we're off topic. I want this bickering with Garrett to stop. Immediately. Have I made myself clear?"

"I assume you're giving the same order to Garrett?"

She huffed, then stomped toward the door. "Garrett is not the problem!"

"I guess it's time to issue my daily apology that I'm not more like your first-born."

With a toss of her iconic silver head, she left my office. I laughed, loud enough for her to hear me, stop and turn around to glare at me, then continue to her office.

I got her *pretty close* to hopping mad.

Before I could get back to my desk, Gabe walked in, his eyes fixed on Mother speeding down the hall, mumbling to herself. "If you're trying to kill her, you should make sure you're in the will, first."

I resumed my seat behind my desk. Gabe took the guest chair across from me. "You can't kill that old woman. Besides, she doesn't bother me half as much as I let her think she does. And I don't think I've made it into the will yet."

"At this rate, I'm not sure you're going to."

"We do have another parent."

"Like Judge has any say about that."

We both laughed at the prospect of Judge offering a dissenting opinion. Though it had happened, it was a rare occurrence. Judge believed in keeping Mother happy— what she wanted, she got and if he didn't have to argue, he didn't.

"Well, I guess I'd better not count on it, then."

"What crawled up Garrett's ass this morning?"

I shrugged, tapping away at the keyboard, quickly scanning and filing email and documents, building my schedule for the day. "The usual. He and mother aren't fond of my clients. They call them deadbeats, even though they pay their bills."

Gabe visibly cringed and I knew what he's about to say. I lifted a hand to stop the defense of the prevailing attitude at Kincaid that I under billed and over delivered.

"Mother and I have had this conversation over and over again, for the last three years. She isn't going to turn me into a Garrett. Or a Gabe or a Gregg. No offense," I added. Gabe waved me off. "I told her I would give her four years and then I was moving on. She thinks I won't go, thinks she can still mold me. But she's wrong. I'm not a Kincaid attorney. I never set out to be one."

"Garrett does have a point. You could bill a reduced rate but take on more clients to make up the difference but as it stands, you don't have enough clients to bridge the gap."

"I'm not trying to *collect* clients. I'm trying to help people. How can I help people with six hundred case files on my desk?"

"It would only be three hundred if you'd bill more."

I shook my head and dropped the argument, refusing to get caught in the endless merry-go-round. In a few months— maybe sooner— the arguments would be moot.

"Where are ya'll going for lunch today?" He and Gregg went to lunch together nearly every day.

"Thinking about Twin Peaks."

"Twin Peaks." I paused to muse over his choice of lunchtime establishments, a sports bar and grille serving up as much tanned skin and deep cleavage as burgers, wings and fries. "Isn't that place like an upscale Hooters?"

Gabe nodded and smiled, showing off a mouthful of pearly white teeth. "We haven't been in a while, but the last time we went, we saw some pretty honeys up there."

My left eyebrow twitched as it rose. "Honeys."

"Honeys." He repeated. "You know, women. *Attractive* women. Nice figures in short skirts. Long legs in those heels that make their calves look like—"

"Attractive women who serve food to you in revealing clothing and high heels, who put up with men like you and Gregg for less than minimum wage. And shitty tips."

"Well, yeah. But we tip well. We're worth the pain."

I laughed, moving back to my email and case files. "But are you worth the exploitation? I think I'll pass on the *honeys*.

That waste of a meeting put me a few hours behind and I have some motions I need to file. Bring me back a burger with everything on it, though. And onion rings. And uh…"

I flicked my eyes up to Gabe as he rose from his seat. "It's lunch, not a strip club, alright?"

"You take the fun out of everything, Gibson," he calls over his shoulder as he leaves my office.

"Honeys," I mumbled. "*Probably* why they're still single."

CHAPTER TWO

ibson

I avoided Mother and Garrett for most of the day, ducking out in the early afternoon to visit a few clients. My favorite part of the job was being out of the office, out in the community, getting to know the people I work for.

After making a few stops, I headed to a part of town I'd been frequenting quite a bit lately and parked my car. I grabbed my satchel from the back seat of my Jeep and stepped inside Gladwell Books, a family owned downtown Decatur bookstore. As she'd been for the past few weeks, a client was posted up at a table at the cafe. A pair of head-phones sat atop her head, she was sucking down an odd colored smoothie and she was lost in a paperback book.

"Diya," I called to her, softly, tapping her on the shoulder. Her head popped up, her eyes wide until she saw it was me.

She pulled the headphones back, hooking them around her neck and moved a few long braids out of her face.

"Hey, Mr. K— I mean Gib."

Diya looked young, but she'd lived a lifetime in the past year. After she and her ex-boyfriend were picked up for trafficking cocaine with their infant son in the car, her mother contacted me from her hospital bed, begging for my help. Since she was a first-time offender, I struck a compromise with the judge, but the deal had strict stipulations.

I pulled out a chair, setting my satchel next to me. "Sorry to keep you waiting. I had a long list of people to see today. How are you?"

She shrugged. Her eyes dipped to the table and the facade of cheer she always tried to present fell away. "I'm okay. I was hoping you heard something about Daniel."

I shook my head, but tried to keep my expression even. "Not yet. She can take up two weeks to decide."

Diya nodded as her bottom lip disappeared between her teeth. "I know. But I worked so hard. I did everything the judge asked— the drug treatment, the GED program, I got a good job, a place to stay, food in the cabinets, gas in the car. My mom is better— she's been out of the hospital for a while. She can watch him when I'm at work. I'm doing real good, Gib. Better than ever. But...what if..."

"Let's not think about what-ifs right now. Those are imaginary and there's nothing we can do about imaginary things. Concentrate on Daniel, on staying above the line so you can keep him when you get him. Alright?"

Diya's head bobbed a nod in agreement. "What about the other—"

"I was about to bring that up." I pulled a manila folder from my satchel and handed it to her. "Open it."

She shrugged and glanced at it, but didn't reach for it. "It's my case file. I've seen it. I've lived all the stuff in there. I don't need to open it."

"There's something new in it, Diya. *Open it*."

She took it from me and flipped open the front cover. Her eyes skipped down the page I had inserted right on top.

"Dismissed!" She screeched, standing so fast, her chair crashed to the floor. Paying no attention to the chair, she paced the small cafe area of the bookstore and continued reading. "Having shown no further cause or aptitude for repeat offense, the above filed charges are hereby dismissed without prejudice pending judicial approval."

She lowered the folder and glared in my direction. "What's that mean? Judicial approval?"

"Means a judge has to sign it. Check out page two."

She flipped the page and her smile widened. "It's signed! They dismissed the charges!"

"Like the judge said she would if you did everything she asked. You did well. This last bump with getting Daniel back is just that— a bump."

She heaved a long, loud, but happy sigh as she reached for the chair and set it upright again.

"Sounds like good news," I heard from the stacks behind me. I turned to find Renee, the owner of the bookstore, rounding a corner, wearing her green *Gladwell Books* apron and a huge smile. I'd only spoken to her a few times but we had a few connections in common.

"The judge dismissed the charges!" Diya gushed. "I did everything she asked, and she dismissed them, like she promised!"

"That's great news! So, you have a better chance at getting Daniel back, right?"

"We hope," I said, jumping in. "Waiting to hear back from the Judge. Oh, and please thank Debra. If it wasn't for the GED program she runs at the Community Center—"

"Believe me, she was happy to help. She'll be over the moon when I tell—" Someone at the front of the store called her name. She gave us an apologetic smile. "I've gotta run, I'm supposed to helping out front and I'm over here running my mouth." Renee bounced away, leaving Diya and I alone.

I pulled back the sleeve of my jacket to check the time. My eyebrows shot up at the hour. "I've gotta run too. I'll check with the judge early next week and see if I can press for a decision about Daniel. Keep your nose clean, in the meantime."

Diya frowned, rolling her eyes. "Very funny. I told you, I didn't *do* coke. I was just in the car with Armando—"

"Okay, okay," I said, laughing. I stood, dropping an arm around her shoulder to give her a squeeze. "We'll talk next week."

VANESSA

The girls thought it was fun to ride home in Uncle's Cadillac. It was spacious and glided along the streets like a dream. The black leather seats were pristine, since Auntie had the interior redone for their 40th wedding anniversary a few years back. The windshield was wide and so was the steering wheel. I felt like an eighty-year-old woman in the driver's seat, my head barely clearing the dash.

Our condo was a few blocks from Sam and Marilyn, so it wasn't long before I pulled into the parking garage under Haynes Street Lofts. The girls refused to get out of the car until I pulled the top up, so I pressed the button and they giggled while the white canvas slowly arched over them, shrouding them in darkness.

"Are we ready to go now?" I twisted so I could see them, cuddled together in the backseat. Two peas in a pod, they nodded in sync.

"Can we have ice cream?" Jaclyn asked. She loved ice cream. She would eat ice cream for every meal, even in the dead of winter. Strawberry— with real bits of fruit— was her favorite.

"You had stew and cornbread *and* cake at Auntie's. Now you want ice cream?" Jaclyn nodded, grinning a dotted smile of missing teeth, not understanding my point about all the food she'd already eaten. "I guess I can find a small bowl for you and your sister. But then it's straight to the bath and then to bed. I don't want to hear any whining about how you're not tired."

"Okay," they agreed.

We piled out of the car and into the elevator, which dropped us right at our floor. I keyed the two deadbolts and punched in the security code once the door was open. My landlord was a partner in a security firm, so he was extra diligent about locks and alarms.

The girls rushed in and went about their normal routine: backpacks and jackets on their individual hooks, shoes in their baskets at the front door. Socked feet pounded across the dark wood floors to the kitchen, where they climbed up on the bar stools to wait.

I spooned out two scoops of strawberry ice cream and slid their bowls across the counter.

Then I watched them eat, the scoops slowly disappearing as they savored each bite, dragging out the time between dessert and bath and bedtime.

Normally, it grated on my nerves when they purposely moved slowly, but I didn't mind so much tonight. I scooped a small bowl for myself and listened to them talk to each other about this and that; the books they're reading, the kids in their classes, the boy who got into trouble for pulling ponytails. I laughed at their insinuation that life as seven and eight year olds is hard.

I was mostly thankful that our *adventures* of the last year hadn't scarred them.

It wasn't supposed to end up this way. Not so far in the past, I met a ruggedly handsome, wide-shouldered, tall drink of dark liquor in the kind of place where a young woman meets a man of means.

Warren Jackson was everything I was looking for. And *nothing* I needed.

The first few times we talked, he was sweet but aggressive. He was a man who knew what he wanted and wasn't shy about making it plain. He made it plain that he wanted me. He knew what to say, how to say it. He called me "Ms. Jackson", bought me drinks, kept me occupied by buying dances and tipping heavily. He had a smooth tongue and he was persuasive. *Very* persuasive.

Warren was a regular at Red Heels, the club where I danced. Well... stripped. It was dark and seedy and fed the rebellious nature of a girl playing grownup, trying to escape her strict upbringing. I was young and firm with a nice body and I could find the rhythm, which meant I already had a leg up on most of the other dancers.

"You be careful with that one," said Sonja one night, eyeing my stack of tens and twenties, mostly from him. "People talk around here and I hear he likes the younger, less experienced girls. Then he gets rough when she wises up and he don't get what he wants."

I ignored her, tucking away my wad of cash. I'd never made so much before meeting him and I wasn't looking a gift horse in the mouth. "He won't have a problem with me. He keeps the cash flowing like this, he'll get what he wants."

"So you're going to whore yourself out 'cause a fine brother looked your way?"

I eyed Sonja, a hint of a smile on my lips. "You sound like you're jealous a fine brother looked my way and not yours.

Maybe he likes these smooth supple legs and not those dimpled tubes of cellulite you got."

I kicked up my Zanotti heels and rested them on top of the vanity table, putting my long dancer's legs on display.

Sonja rolled her eyes and chuckled, deep in her throat. "Don't act like you're the only one here that has the attention of a handsome, rich brother. I'm trying to tell you what I hear about that *particular* handsome, rich brother."

She paused while inserting a long, sparkly earring into her ear to give me her full gaze. "Now you go on thinkin' you the shit and whatnot. Let a man sweet talk all the good good from you, flashin' money and a black card in your face. He'll use you up, then dump you on the side of the road when he's done with you. Don't say I didn't warn you."

"Yeah, well..." I exhaled with a smile and gathered my clutch and my jacket. I was knocking off early and meeting Warren in a few minutes. "Something tells me Warren Jackson might be the answer to all of my problems."

I bent over her shoulder and looked her in the eye, in the mirror. Sonja was an older, pretty face. Okay body but her face sold her. She claimed to dance because she wanted to, but I had it on good authority that Sonja's day job didn't pay much and neither did the fathers of her three children. She teetered between addiction and sobriety and these days, addiction was winning. I didn't see her lasting much longer at Red Heels.

"You have a good night, Sonja."

"You too, baby." She pointed at my reflection, the tip of a long red nail tapping the mirror. "And be careful. I'm serious."

"Mhmm, I hear you. Old jealous ass." I snickered as I teetered out of the club, met Warren at the back door and slid into the passenger seat of his Mercedes.

We broke up a dozen times over the next year. The last time, I was *through* with him and his need to control where I went and who I spent time with, the guilt trip every time I left the house for any reason other than to do something for him.

And I *hated* that he still went to Red Heels, even after he talked me into leaving. I couldn't dance there, but he could still pay someone to shake her titties in his face? I had it in my head that I was done with him and I was leaving.

Then the pregnancy test came up positive.

Warren did a complete turnaround when he saw the positive test. He promised to finally stop going to Red Heels. He asked me to marry him. "Let's really work at it, Nessa. Let's make this work." *Hmph.*

I gave Sonja the widest grin as I walked down the aisle, bursting with baby in my maternity Vera Wang, smug and giddy in my happiness. She rolled her eyes at first, then smiled back.

See? She was wrong.

Wasn't she?

A year after Olivia was born, Jaclyn came. Warren was moving up in the company, he said. Becoming indispensable, he said. His boss needed him to start going on the road, selling their software in person. Warren was ambitious; he wanted sit on top of the food chain at the company, more than their highest selling salesman of all time. Vice President, Senior Management— Warren wanted that.

I cringed at my naiveté. I was proud to be Vanessa Jackson, former exotic dancer, now mother of two, living in an elegant home in an affluent neighborhood. I thought nothing of his long trips. His irregular check -ins and difficulty staying in touch, to even talk to his children at night was a constant source of arguments, but I never imagined what was really going on.

Warren was quick to remind me of how lucky I was to be chosen, to be "delivered" from the lifestyle I'd been living.

"Do you want to end up like Sonja?" He'd bellow over the phone, if I dared mention that he'd missed talking to the girls before their bedtime. "Dancing in your thirties, hooked on who-knows-what, looking old about the face and fat about the thighs? You better be grateful I took you up out of that and show some respect."

Then one day I checked the mail and the bottom dropped out. Everything Warren had been doing fell out into the open. It was a slap in the face.

"Do we see Daddy this weekend?" Olivia asked, ice cream smeared around her mouth.

I dabbed at her cheeks with a napkin. "I haven't heard from him. He might be on another trip. Let's plan a backup activity just in case, hmm?"

She nodded, easily distracted at her age. But she was also at the age where she longed for her father and it hurt my heart that I couldn't give him to her. His....*whatever she was*, wasn't comfortable being around his children. He could only have them at their house when she wasn't there. The weather hadn't been good for park meet ups and outside play dates, so he avoided my calls and texts until it was too late for him to get them. And then it was my fault for not arranging something sooner.

I pushed away from the counter and dug into my bag for my mobile phone, which had been dead since early evening. I waited for it to make its usual sounds as it charged and came to life. Email, voicemail and texts rolled in. I glanced at the notifications and saw Jackson, Warren pop up on-screen.

Can't take the girls tomorrow. Maybe Sunday. You know I got a lot going on, I don't want to hear it. Be in touch. W.

I deleted the text. If I responded, I'd start a fight. Warren never lost a fight. He would pull all sorts of things out of the air, just to be right, to wear me down until I gave up. His ass made me so *tired*.

I perked up the tone of my voice and put on my 'nothing's wrong' face. "Yep, looks like Daddy has an appointment tomorrow. But it's Free Museum Weekend, so... how about a trip to the Museum of Natural History instead?"

After the girls had bathed, brushed their teeth and were tucked into bed, I stood under a long, hot shower, slathered myself in Jergen's cocoa butter lotion and crawled into my own bed. I was more than tired. I was utterly *exhausted*.

The day had begun with a text fight with Warren, when I asked if he would be seeing the girls over the weekend and if he planned to file for divorce or live with *whatever she was,* avoiding me and our children for the foreseeable future. We went back and forth for the better part of an hour before I gave up, because an argument with Warren is a waste of time.

I hosted an Open House, attended a few meetings, drew up a few sales contracts. And then the car died on the way to pick up the girls. By all accounts, I should have passed out as soon as my head hit the pillow.

But I couldn't sleep. I tossed and turned as the usual machinations of my mind ran, rifling through its virtual file of the last five, ten, twenty years. I spent this time fruitlessly trying to pinpoint the exact moment I veered off a path that would have been so much easier, so much less drama and heartache, so much less frustration with me from my Aunt and Uncle.

And not so much hard work to put myself back in a good place, a place where I was proud to be an example to my children, a great salesperson, a valued friend and family member.

It was cliché to blame it on a specific day, but I felt, to my bones, everything change that day.

Cruisers with flashing lights parked haphazardly in front of the two bedroom house my mother and I shared.

Policemen everywhere, trampling over our things. Yellow tape blocking off the front door. A lump encased in a black bag being loaded onto a stretcher.

Auntie and Uncle turning me away from the chaos and urging me toward the big, burgundy Cadillac.

I was only nine years old, but I felt it. That moment when everything changed.

CHAPTER THREE

ibson

THE ATMOSPHERE AT MINK'S MATCHED MY MOOD. QUIET, dark, mellow.

The high-end steakhouse and cigar lounge was "the spot", a favorite simply because it was elite enough to not be overrun by your average businessman in search of a pretty face to take home. But laid back enough to be able to relax and enjoy all the comforts money could buy: the exclusive circular bar, stocked with aged scotch, brandy, bourbon— whatever the palate desired; premium cuts of prime beef and seafood and locally grown and harvested vegetables; the soft leather seats grouped around tables at the rooftop bar that offered the best view of the city falling under the shadow of the setting sun.

To my left sat a glass of my preferred drink— Knob Creek Single Barrel Bourbon. To my right, a smoking Padron cigar.

The evening would have been perfect were I not looking into the faces of my brothers, but they were gathered around the table, smoking and sipping as well.

"I'm surprised to see Gibson out tonight," Garrett drolled, lighting a cigar and puffing smoke into the air. It lingered before dissipating. He propped an elbow on the arm of the chair and shifted so he could cross one leg over the other. "I would have thought you'd be at home, doing... whatever it is you do out there."

"If you ever came out to the house, you could see what I do out there. It's not like I live in another state." I sipped a mouthful of bourbon and let it slide down my throat. I was halfway through a few splashes and feeling a little loose, which was the only way I could handle being so close to Garrett.

"May as well live in another state," said Gregg. "There's nothing like this out in the suburbs."

"Gib doesn't live in the suburbs," said Gabe. "He lives in the country. There's a difference. And there's definitely nothing like this in the country."

I took the good-natured ribbing the same way I always did— with a grain of salt. Garrett and his wife, an interior designer, owned a gaudy, overly decorated home just outside city limits. Gregg and Gabe had condos in the same complex — the same building— practically around the corner from the Kincaid family home. When the brothers needed a secluded, lakefront country place to have an intimate gathering, I was on speed dial.

"The country, as you call it, has other benefits. I like being able to come to Mink's, have a nice steak, a Stogie, some bourbon. Then I go home and enjoy a sunset from the dock on the lake—"

"And his prize marigolds," Gabe finished.

"I don't grow marigolds. I grow dahlias."

"Dahlias, marigolds, roses, whatever," Garrett scoffed. "Flowers are flowers."

"Flowers are flowers when you buy cheap bouquets at the grocery store. Open your mind. Expose yourself to something more unique and extraordinary. Did you know there are forty-two species of—"

"I'll gain my exposure to unique and extraordinary things from a decidedly more... feminine source." Gabe's eyes tracked the waitress as she moved from table to table, gliding as if on thin air. Her long, bone-straight hair was parted on one side and hung halfway down her back. The deep burgundy of her low-cut backless blouse complemented both her caramel skin tone and the short black mini skirt that didn't hide a single curve.

I returned my attention to my warming drink and the impressive length of ash that my cigar was growing. The Kincaid name opened a lot of doors, called in a lot of favors, generated a lot of interest. My brothers took full advantage and while I didn't begrudge them their fun, I'd lived that life. I wasn't in a hurry to go back to it.

"Heads up," Gregg muttered into his glass. "Pack at three o'clock."

I stifled a groan, filling my mouth with liquor so I didn't start cursing. The name didn't exactly strike fear in my heart, but Kent "Pack" Packard was the last face I wanted to see. I could never see him again and it would be too soon. Shame, since we were as close as brothers at Georgia State and later at Emory School of Law.

"Gentlemen!" He bellowed, making his way over to our table. "Pleasure seeing the Kincaid men, minus Judge, together this evening."

"It's been awhile, Pack. Judge will be by later."

Gabe extended a hand to Pack, after which he made his way around the table but didn't offer to shake my hand. And I didn't offer to shake his. The rest of my bourbon disappeared quickly. I raised my glass to the waitress to indicate that I'd like a fresh pour.

"Gibson, you're looking well."

Pack dragged a chair from another table and squeezed between Gregg and me. He was, as always, impeccable. Pack was a fan of the gentleman's spa even when we were in undergrad. His medium toned skin was smooth and blemish-free. His jet-black hair and accompanying beard was well-maintained by an overpriced stylist. Down to the square cut and buffed shine of his nails, Pack was a well-oiled machine.

He loosened his jacket and the top two buttons on his starched shirt. Great. He's settling in.

"As are you. Melanie must be taking great care of you."

I refused to look his way but out of the corner of my eye I saw his head drop to his chest. He cleared his throat and nervously tugged at his jacket. I'd made him uncomfortable. *Good.*

"You uh... obviously didn't hear. Melanie and I split up. Happened a few months ago."

The waitress dropped by with a fresh glass of Knob Creek, which was great because I needed a swallow or two to coat my suddenly dry mouth. Split up? The devastatingly handsome, *could have any woman he wanted*— including mine— Kent Packard had lost one?

"Hmmm," I mused in an attempt to stop a satisfied chuckle from emerging. "I hadn't heard. That's a shame. Did you lose her like you got her? Taken from you by someone you thought was your friend?"

"Gib, let's not get into it here—" Garrett started, but Pack raised a hand to stop him. Garrett's eyebrows lifted in surprise, but he sat back to watch what I'm sure he thought would be a good show.

"I deserved that," said Pack, directing his speech to me,

though I still hadn't laid eyes on him. "I deserve everything you want to throw at me. I knew I was wrong the whole time we were sneaking around—"

I slammed my glass to the table and sent a glare that could liquefy steel in his direction. "Come on, man. Sneaking around? You mean *fucking my girlfriend*. While I was telling you about the ring I was thinking about buying her, about the house I was going to surprise her with, about the future I'd planned with her. You were wrong for *sneaking around* with her? You were wrong for a hell of a lot more."

"I was wrong. I said I was sorry and I meant that shit. I'll take the heat, but obviously, we both got played. Melanie dumped me six months ago. She hopped over to some big wig Tech CEO in Alabama. He's flying her around in a Cessna. She's all over Instagram and bragging everywhere to anyone who will listen about having lunch in Miami and dinner in New York."

The waitress reached between us and slid a glass of whiskey in front of him. He then took his time choosing a cigar from the selection inside the small humidor she offered to him. From an inside pocket, he pulled a cutter and a lighter and moments later, the air was thick with aromatic smoke from a Cohiba cigar.

"Not saying I know how you feel or anything—"

"Because you don't. What you had with her was a drop in the bucket compared to what she and I had."

"True. Payback is a bitch and I'm going through it right now." He sipped a few swallows from his glass and puffed his cigar. "You can be honest, though you must be pretty happy about the demise of my relationship."

"Happy?" I waved a cloud of smoke from around my head. "You got what was coming to you. So what? What's to be happy about?"

"All my boys, plus one, in the same spot. That's what I'm happy about."

Judge's rich, deep tone broke into the conversation. At 6'4", wide shouldered, broad chested, with a booming voice and commanding presence, it was a natural reaction to stand to greet him. After the customary handshakes and back slaps, I picked up my glass and cigar and offered my seat to Judge.

"I'm about out of here, sir. Take my seat."

"You sure, son? I'm not trying to chase you from the table."

"I'm sure. I'm ready to call it a night. I'll finish my drink at the bar and head out."

I nodded my head around the table to everyone but Pack and stepped to the bar as Judge settled into his seat. As the waitress returned to take his order, I saw Pack slide his chair back and follow me to the bar.

"Take the hint, man. I'm not in the mood tonight, alright? I'm sorry about Mel but I don't want to go down memory lane with you."

"Look, Gib, I'm not going to hang around begging for forgiveness. I do have some pride. I've admitted I was wrong. I've apologized. You can accept it or not, I guess. But me and you... we were tight. I let a woman come between us and destroy it. It'd be cool if we could salvage something from this situation. That's up to you, I guess."

I didn't respond, not because I wasn't speaking to him but because I don't know what to say. I wasn't as angry at Pack as I was at myself, at not being able to detect Melanie's penchant for gold digging the entire time we dated. I could have saved myself— and Pack some heartache. He was sufficiently contrite, he'd apologized and he'd expressed a desire to restore our friendship, one that had meant a lot to me until I found out the woman I loved preferred him to me.

I still felt betrayed. Still felt the knife in my back. Still felt humiliated, in front of my family, our friends, my colleagues and clients.

I tossed back the last drop of bourbon, left the glass and a tip at the bar and walked out of Mink's without another word.

VANESSA

Maxine swept into my office and dumped her designer satchel in an empty chair, one hand on a generous hip and the other pointing in the general direction of the parking lot.

"Vanessa, please tell me someone parked in your space today and that big red monster is not your new car."

I looked up from the listings I'd been studying and notes I'd been taking. I needed to find a house for Dre Prescott yesterday. I was surprised to see her. Since she had the baby — Imani, the cutest chocolate dumpling I'd ever seen, she'd been working part time, keeping sparse office hours here and there and trying to build back up to full time. Virgil had been keeping Donovan together quite well, but I liked it when Maxine was in the building. Her energy was inspiring.

I giggled loudly and laid down my pen, folding my arms and leaning forward onto the desktop. "Yeah, I bought a car the size of my apartment, Maxine. I plan to meet lots of clients in it, take them to lunch and dinner. Show them houses. You don't mind, do you?"

"That's not funny," she said, but she was laughing. The idea that I would buy a behemoth like the Cadillac is silly. "Okay maybe it's a little funny. That car is as old as you. Why are you driving it?"

"It's older than I am," I corrected her. "My car died on me last week. The Cadillac is my Uncle's car. My cousin was poking at it, but I went ahead and had it towed to Audi for repair. To the tune of a few thousand dollars, I'm sure."

"Vanessa, you sell million dollar homes for a living. Buy a new car."

"I can't. My credit is shit and I have so many other priorities begging for my money."

"Then make that deadbeat husband of yours get you something. He's making enough to keep another bitch in a house and clothes and you're driving his babies around in a jalopy? Or a tank?"

"Warren..." I moaned, sucking my teeth. "Warren hasn't paid anything toward anything. He says his job has changed, he's not making as much money as before and with the IRS and all of our creditors after him, he's about to declare bankruptcy."

"Why hasn't he paid anything toward anything? Isn't it the law?"

"He doesn't want to pay for it. He also doesn't want to pay spousal or child support. The longer he drags things out, the longer he goes without a court order to pay support. We don't have the makings of a quickie divorce. I don't even know where he's living— I couldn't serve him with divorce papers if I wanted to."

I tossed up my hands in a helpless gesture. "If I want a divorce any time this decade, I have to file and I need an attorney."

I wanted Maxine to not look at me the way she was looking at me, like she felt sorry for me, like I needed help. Or charity. All I needed was a stroke of good luck. We weren't down and out. I wasn't depressed. We were making it. Barely, but we were making it.

"I can at least help you with a lawyer. I'll be right back."

Max grabbed the handles of her satchel and rushed out of my office, returning a few minutes later. She plunked a thick grey card down on the dark wood. "Sylvia Kincaid. I sold her a house when I worked at Caldwell Realty. Damn near a mansion; I swear the thing takes up a city block and she only paid a little over a million for it. Total steal. She owes me."

She tapped the card with the tip of a fingernail, then pointed at me. "Tell her I sent you. She'll give you a deal."

"Sylvia... wait. Sylvia Kincaid? Like, the famous attorney? The Silver Shark?" I slid the card back across the desk. "Listen, thank you for trying to help me, but even with a super sweet deal, I can't afford her. I'm about to hock my wedding ring to fix my car."

Impatient, she slid the card back over to me. "At least talk to her, see what she says. A consultation is a good place to start. See what you've got, what you need and how you get this thing put to bed. Be sure to tell her I sent you. It'll help smooth things along."

I took the card, but grudgingly so, slipping it into a pocket in my jacket. I didn't know if I'd call her, but I wanted Maxine off my back about it.

"Now." She pulled at the hem of her peplum blouse. "Are you any closer to showing Dre Prescott something he'll want to put an offer on?"

"Today's goal." I picked up the listings I'd been reviewing when she walked in. "I've got him for three hours while his mother and his girlfriend are... unavailable."

Maxine was aware, and as frustrated as I was about the constant presence of Dre's mother and girlfriend. They rejected everything I'd shown him so far, saying they expected more like what you'd see in LA. Whatever that meant. The Hollywood of the South had its own flavor.

"And how did you manage that?"

"I sent them to some out of the way places, in case Dre wants to live a bit outside of town."

She snickered. "Sneaky. I like it. Now look, don't take no for an answer. He's a grown man. No more of this I need to ask my mom business. I want to see an offer on a house from him today."

"Believe me, Maxine... so do I."

She turned to leave again, but stopped. "You're not driving him around in the tank, are you?"

I couldn't help my loud burst of laughter. "No. He's picking me up and we're looking at houses in between meetings with his attorney and his manager."

Maxine heaved a hugely dramatic sigh of relief, which made me laugh even harder. I hadn't had a good, hard laugh in a long time.

"THEY WANT *HOW MUCH* TO FIX THE CAR?"

Auntie's eyes were the biggest, roundest I'd ever seen them. They weren't even that big when I told her I was pregnant with Olivia. With a man I met at a strip club.

"Almost two grand. Something about the fuel pump... and a manifold...thing. Whatever it is, it has to be replaced."

My head pounded with a stress headache. A basket of Sam's golden fried chicken strips sat untouched in front of me. Uncle, who had no problems eating, listened while making his way through a serving of his popular lemon pepper chicken wings.

South DeKalb Audi had called the day before, asking what I wanted to do with the car. It had been sitting behind the shop for more than a week while I'd been trying to decide what to do— sink money into this car, or buy a new one?

I thought I might actually buy a new car, but when I ran my credit, my hopes and dreams of a late model, dependable vehicle were crushed. I cursed Warren Jackson's name all over again. If anyone needed to declare bankruptcy, it was me, but that could ruin me for years.

"That sounds like something Roscoe should be able to fix," Uncle suggested pushing his empty plate to the edge of the table. "Did you have him look at it again?"

I shook my head. "I asked him, but with these foreign cars, it really doesn't take much to mess things up beyond repair. I don't want him touching it unless he knows what he's doing."

"I wish you would let us help you," said Auntie. "If all it would take is a few thousand dollars..."

"I already told you, Auntie. That money is for your retirement. I'll let you know if I get desperate enough to take your hard earned savings." I wrapped an arm around her and gave her a hard squeeze. "I appreciate the offer, but if you're not planning to use that money for anything fun, save it for the girls. I'm not going to be able to send them anywhere but Gwinnett Community College, if things keep going the way they have."

"Well, Lil' Girl," Uncle rumbled, chewing the heck out of a toothpick, elbows propped on the table. "I don't understand turning down money but I do understand pride and wanting to do for yourself. But you need a car or you need your car fixed, and I need my Cherry back."

He smiled at the mention of the classic Caddy that I'd been very carefully driving for over a week. "Now what if what we do is front you the money—" He stopped to glare at me, knowing I would open my mouth to protest. "Shut your face for a second. Nobody is talking about a gift. Talking 'bout a loan. You can work it off."

"I'm barely making ends meet as it is. I don't have money to pay off a loan."

"You can work here. My waitress quit and I need a part-timer. I'll take you over some gal I don't know."

"Here. Work here. At Sam's."

My eyes roamed the homey establishment that had been

showing its age for a long, long time. The tables with names etched into the wood, the rickety chairs, the long walnut bar that probably hadn't seen a shine in years, stacked with cloudy glasses, surrounded by regulars seated on bar stools that had long since lost their cushion. The bookstore next door had painted the brick facade and set out tables and colorful umbrellas, making Sam's look extra drab.

"You want me to work here? For you?"

Uncle folded his arms across his chest and leaned back in his chair. His eyes almost closed... almost. Those beady old browns fixed on me, gauging my reaction.

"When am I supposed to do this work? I have a full-time job and two young children."

"Evenings. Weekends. I'll give you a bump above minimum wage and flexible hours. We'll work out a schedule, week to week, though I'll need more help when the weather starts to turn warmer. Marilyn can watch the girls after school and through the summer."

We both glanced at her. She nodded, her lips rolled inward and her eyebrows raised. In Auntie speak, those gestures meant hell yes.

"But... what about the late hours? The girls go to bed at—"

"Child, I raised you," Auntie protested. "I know what time little girls go to bed. I don't have nothin' more important to do than take care of my grand-nieces. I can pick them up from school, make sure they do their homework, feed them dinner, then take them home and put them to bed. You come on home when your shift is over. We don't live but a few blocks away. In the summer, we can walk."

"Then you don't even have to pay that fancy day care to do what family can do. Saving you money right there. You can pay off your debt working for me. The more you work, the faster you pay it off. Keep your tips to yourself."

The toothpick rolled from one corner of Uncle's mouth to the other. This was not an option I even wanted to contemplate, but it made sense and I didn't see any other way to get my car fixed. Or get divorced. And on a good night, I could make a lot of money in tips. Those tips would buy a week of lunches for the girls. Maybe some shoes or pants, the way the girls were growing.

"Maybe I should go back to Red Heels," I teased, reaching for a chicken strip. Uncle choked on his laughter. Auntie grunted her disapproval, slurping the last of her Diet Coke. "In my dancing days, I would have had this problem solved in about four hours. But... after two babies and eight years, I probably don't have the kind of body they're looking for."

"Naw," Auntie said, with a sad shake of her head and a light sigh. "Probably not."

Uncle was still watching me, chewing on that toothpick. I couldn't bring myself to say the words, so I bobbed my head in agreement.

"Can you start Monday?"

"Yeah. After my appointment with the divorce attorney Max wants me to go see."

CHAPTER FOUR

anessa

THE OFFICES OF KINCAID LAW TOOK UP THE ENTIRE 20TH floor of one of Atlanta's most prestigious Peachtree Road high-rises. I stepped off the elevator, immediately overwhelmed by the quiet. At Donovan, there were six agents always talking, either with clients or on the phone, or with Virgil, wheeling and dealing and sharing information and having conversations. The silence was deafening.

My heels sank into the deep plush of the charcoal grey carpet as I made my way across the empty waiting room to the massive front desk. Two young women sat at opposite ends, each wearing a headset, fingers flying across tiny keyboards and eyes fixated on the thinnest flat screen monitors I'd ever seen.

"May I help you?" The other receptionist offered a bland smile, her pale pink lipstick standing out against her deep complexion.

"I have a two o'clock appointment with Sylvia Kincaid. My name is—"

"Vanessa Jackson," she finished for me, clicking through a few screens on the computer.

"Yes. I'm early—"

"Have a seat. Ms. Kincaid's assistant will be out shortly."

The girl's eyes never left the screen and her fingers never stopped clicking or typing. I turned away from the desk to the waiting room and lowered myself onto a sturdy couch. The room was a study in austere design disguised as class.

Beneath my feet, a sea of grey carpet, accented occasionally by threads of cream. The furniture was light in color, the art on the walls— black and white shots of the city of Atlanta— framed in silver. A shiny chrome coffee urn with accompanying cream and sugar service sat in a corner of the room. Next to the urn were stacks of demitasse white pearl coffee cups. The setup was meant to imply an air of success. It felt cold and impersonal.

A side door silently swung open and a tall, thin woman emerged from the hallway beyond it. Everything about her screamed severe, from her high and tight bun to her dark brows to the thin slash of red that made up her lips.

"Ms. Jackson?" She called, clasping her hands in front of her.

I rose and, out of nervousness or fear, or both, rushed toward her, smiled and offered my hand to shake. "Yes. That's me."

She glanced at my outstretched hand and made no movement to touch me. Instead, she turned toward the door again. "Ms. Kincaid will see you now."

Sylvia Kincaid was a legend in Atlanta. Her nickname, the Silver Shark, was reminiscent of her take-no-prisoners attitude and her pixie cut of brilliant grey hair. She was the attorney everyone wanted on their side if they were being sued— or wanted to sue. This put her and her firm in high demand and their fees in a bracket entirely out of my reach, even with a discount.

I made the appointment and kept the meeting to appease Maxine, but I suffered from no delusions that Sylvia could help me. At the least, I'd get a chance to tell my story and determine how to proceed. And maybe she could recommend an attorney I could afford.

I followed the assistant through the hallways of the suite. More deep carpeting, stark white walls, generic photos framed in silver and closed door after closed door. I noticed names outside each door— Garrett, Gabriel, Greggory Kincaid; her sons, also attorneys in the firm.

My guide led me to a set of double doors at the back of the suite. She rapped her knuckles on the wood twice before opening them. She ushered me in and directed me to take a seat in one of the chairs in front of the most massive desk I'd ever seen. The walnut was stained a dark, shiny lacquer with matching credenza and computer stand.

If was being honest, I was shaking in my boots, tongue twisted intimidated, not only by the office and the quiet and the setting and the upholstered chair I was sitting in that cost more than my car, but by the woman behind the desk, who continued her phone conversation as if I hadn't entered the room.

"Can I get you anything?" Her assistant whispered. "Coffee? Tea? Juice? Water?"

I shook my head, then watched her fiddle with some stacks of strategically placed papers and folders until Sylvia swatted her away with a flick of her wrist.

She set the phone into its cradle and scowled. "Go on, Janet. Messing with things. I have everything the way I want it. Bring me a coconut water. You want one, honey?" Sylvia's eyes settled on my face for the first time. I declined with a terse shake of my head and tried to smile.

When Janet quietly slipped from the room, pulling the door shut behind her, Sylvia folded her arms and rested them on the surface of her desk. She was a lovely woman— light caramel skin tone, lively light brown eyes, full lips and a wide smile.

"So you work for Maxine Donovan? One of her agents, huh?" The tone of her voice hit more on the husky register, as if she'd been a smoker at some point in her life. "Isn't she a dynamo? I loved working with her."

I nodded, pressing my lips together. Sylvia chuckled, then leaned back in her high back leather chair. "Relax, darlin'. My reputation is overblown. I'm only a shark to my opponents." The door opened again and Janet slipped in, setting a bottle of coconut water onto a coaster.

"You sure you don't want one?" Sylvia offered again. "They're refreshing." She twisted the top off and gulped down a few swallows before she sighed and recapped the bottle.

"I'm fine, thank you," I answered, finally finding my voice. "Yes, I work with Maxine. She mentioned that she sold you your home when she was with her old firm."

Sylvia dabbed her lips with a handkerchief before settling back in her chair. "Yes, one of the last deals she struck before she went out on her own. I wish we could have waited. I would have loved to be her first customer. Anyway, helluva deal. We still love the place, even though the boys have moved out."

She shrugged. "The house is large and it's just my husband and I— Judge Garrison Kincaid?" She paused, waiting for me to acknowledge that I knew him. Or *of* him. When I did, she rambled on. "We'll see. I'm sure I'll be calling Maxine in a few years. Now..."

She reached for a file on her desk and flipped it open. I

saw my name on the flap, neatly written in block letters. "You're here for a consultation regarding divorcing your husband of... eight years?"

I stopped telling people how I met Warren years ago. The surprised eyebrows, the tilt of the head, the *look-me-up-and-down- and-pass-judgement* gaze, the whispers behind my back... I didn't invite them anymore. We lived in an affluent suburb of Atlanta, full of women with their talons out, ready to cut down the next person who didn't measure up. I quickly learned to keep my mouth shut and stay coy about my past. The only people that knew about my dancing days were my family and close friends. Not even Maxine knew how I'd come to be with Warren and I wanted to keep it that way. I was a different woman back then— young, naive, rebellious. Hard headed too. I wouldn't look twice at Warren Jackson, if I met him today.

"I met Warren through work," I started, giving the usual rehearsed story. "I was young and he knew exactly what to say and how to say it to get me to do what he wanted me to do. And how to keep me from doing things he didn't want me doing." I dove deeper during my conversation with Sylvia, leaving out any hint of Red Heels. I spoke in generalities about how it started and how I found out I'd been a fool for the past five years.

The foreclosure notice. The IRS notices. The secret Facebook account, the secret *woman* he'd been in a relationship with at the same time he'd been married to me. The times when he said he'd been on a business trip but he was with *her* at some fancy restaurant. The vacations he'd promised we'd take, but he never seemed to have the time, only to see photos of him taking her on those very vacations, relaxing on a white sand beach with a drink in his hand.

Meanwhile, I was shuttling the girls to school and checking homework every night and managing the house.

At the same time, I was trying to build my budding real estate career. I had been replaced, and as soon as his new life was ready for him to step into it, he disappeared from ours.

Sylvia listened, asked questions, made notes, her eyebrows knit together in concentration. "So he says now that he's about to file for bankruptcy? And this is supposed to keep you from filing for divorce or something?"

"Yep," I answer with a nod. "Aside from all the credit card companies after him, he's being investigated by the IRS for tax evasion. We lost the house in foreclosure and there's everything that comes with that situation as well."

"Where's he living? Do you know?"

I shake my head, offering Sylvia a wry smile. "He ran to the woman he'd been cheating on me with. Well... living a whole another life with. I don't know where she lives, he won't tell me. Probably so I can't serve him."

"It's not like we can't find the bastard. Good riddance," Sylvia spit, dropping her notepad to the desktop. "What you're saying is that this man has no assets or net worth, nothing to go after?"

"Well... yes that's correct. But I wasn't really thinking in terms of going after anything. I want to be divorced from him and I want him to provide for his children. I'm not even seeking alimony—"

"Oh honey, don't say that. You spent ten years with this man. Look at the mess he left you in. Then he runs to some other woman, living in her house rent free and not even taking care of his children? The law says he must provide for you and those children. I don't want to hear about what you're not looking for."

"I understand what the law says, but I don't think— "

"Do you know what I do here, what this firm is about? I bring men like Warren Jackson to their knees. We take men who are trying to get around their responsibilities to task. We *make them pay*."

The last three words were enunciated clearly, spoken at a decibel above her regular tone and punctuated by the tap of a fiery red fingertip. "The average divorce will run you fifteen to thirty thousand. If the case is difficult, it could cost more. I want to know if he has any assets, savings, cash money. An IRA, a 401(k), an offshore account. Because we can stipulate that he pay court costs if *he* left *you*. There's a reason you need a firm like Kincaid, not a random firm from the internet, or downloading generic paperwork from the internet and filing on your own. I'm worth every penny and I stand behind my work."

"I see." I cleared my throat, wishing I could sink to the floor and slide out of the room. "I... I'm not sure...well, Maxine wanted me to call you. I don't have much money and I don't believe Warren does, either. I'm not looking to...Look, Sylvia. I don't want anything from Warren but a divorce decree and child support. That's it."

"You know..." Sylvia reached for the bottle of coconut water, slowly unscrewing the cap and sipping a few swallows. "I see a lot of young ladies — mothers, such as yourself— come through these doors with their heart on their sleeves, still halfway in love with the bastard that screwed them over, talking about how they *don't want anything*. Then it turns out the motherfucker has been hiding money, or he's living in the lap of luxury while they're in squalor. Or he had children behind her back or he gave her some kind of disease. And you know what happens? Attitudes change. All of a sudden they want everything due them and more."

"I understand that. And if I had the money to be vindictive, the story would be different. But the simple truth is that I can't afford to go after Warren for everything. I just want a divorce."

Sylvia's full lips pursed. Her eyes slowly closed, thick lashes brushing chiseled cheekbones. "Well. Even with the discount that I know Maxine told you I would give you, I don't think Kincaid could do much for you. I don't do cheap divorces."

"I understand. But…" I hesitated to even ask, but I've already been rejected. What would it hurt? "I hoped that you could possibly refer me to another firm? Another…" I cleared my throat and swallowed. "A more affordable firm?"

Sylvia's demeanor had run the gamut from warm and friendly to combative and now she looked like she wanted to toss me out of her office on my ass. She pushed herself up from the chair and leaned onto the desk.

"I am not in the habit of sending clients to my competitors, Ms. Jackson. I suggest you consult the Yellow Pages. If there's nothing else, Janet will show you to the front desk. The receptionists will validate your parking."

She pressed a button on the phone and chirped brusquely. "We're done, here. Tell Gibson to come to my office, please."

"Of course, ma'am," came the crystal clear response from the speaker.

I stood and slid the handle of my bag onto my shoulder. I was even more eager to get out of that office, out of that suite, *out of that building*. This was a bad idea.

"I'll see myself out," I mumbled, almost stopping to offer a handshake to Sylvia, but she was preoccupied by the stacks on her desk. I'd been dismissed. I pulled open the double doors and hurried down the hall toward the front desk, head down, on a mission. I rounded a corner and walked right into a wide, solid chest.

"Oh!" I leapt backward a few steps and tried to get my bearings. My bag, which slid from my arm mid-collision, was splayed on the carpet between us, half of its contents spread across the hallway.

"Ma'am, I am so sorry. Let me help you clean that up."

A well- built man in a dark, tailored suit squatted to gather my belongings and handed them to me so that I could stuff them inside my bag. I was thankful that I hadn't been dragging around any personal items— tampons, lip gloss... mini vibrators. My datebook, pens and business card case were embarrassing enough.

"Did we get everything?"

His eyes swept the area, then lifted to mine, accompanied by the most handsome smile I'd seen since I first met Warren Jackson. Smiles were my kryptonite and his... *mmmph*. Thick lips, two rows of straight white teeth, deep skin tone and dark, soulful brown eyes, the kind that made you want to pour a glass of brown liquor and get lost in them.

My mouth suddenly felt like it was full of sawdust and my breathing was slightly labored. "I... I think we got everything. Thank you. And sorry for running you over."

"No need to apologize. I was looking at my phone, not watching where I was going." He extended a hand, palm up. Without even thinking, I slid my palm across his. "Gibson Kincaid. Are you a client?"

His question made me laugh, which wasn't a reaction I expected to have at not being accepted as a client. "No. In fact, I met with your mother and we decided that Kincaid isn't the firm I'm looking for."

"Oh?" His eyebrows shot up, nearly to his hairline, which I noticed was lush with dark-as-night curls. "Did she give you the *bring them to their knees, we make them pay* speech? She loves that line."

His smile was devilish. The twinkle in his eye was way too tempting. The lilting, teasing tone of his voice had my thoughts meandering in a direction they had no business going in. I was in this stuffy grey office trying to divorce my husband, not pick up a new man.

"Uh, yep," I answered with a deep nod. "I did get that speech. Unfortunately, as much as I want to uhm... make him pay... Kincaid isn't the firm for me."

"Well, that's too bad, if you really feel that way. But not all of us practice law like my mother does. Some of us are little more sensible."

He smiled again, sending sparks skipping down my spine. "Tell you what," he said, reaching into an inner pocket to pull out a business card holder. He plucked a card from the silver case and flicked it out at me between two fingers. Two long, thick, manicured fingers. "Give me a call. We can talk. If I can work something out, I'd—"

"Gibson!"

We both turned at the sound of Sylvia screeching down the hall, disturbing the quiet. I felt bad that I'd kept him from his mother's beck and call, so I took the card and stepped around him.

"Thanks. Sorry to keep you."

"My pleasure," he said, still standing in the middle of the hallway, clearly in no hurry to answer to Sylvia. "I didn't catch your name, Miss...."

"Vanessa. Vanessa Jackson."

"Ms. Jackson," he responded, extending his hand again. Again, I slid my palm across his and reveled in the gentle strength as it closed around mine. "It was a pleasure running into you. Please do give me a call, before you call another firm."

Before I was ready for him to do so, he released my hand and slipped his hands into the pockets of his slacks.

"I will definitely give you a call, Gibson." I began to back away, feeling like if I didn't start moving, I was never going to get out of the building. And, despite having met Gibson, I wanted to get out of that building. "Have a nice day."

Just then, Sylvia rounded the corner, barreling down the hallway with fists clenched.

"Gib! I've been calling you. When I summon you, I mean right away! I don't have all day." Her eye caught my form lingering near the door the lobby. "Ms. Jackson, I thought you had left. Is there something else I can do for you?"

"No ma'am." I pushed through the door and stumbled back out to the visitor area. There was nothing Sylvia could do for me.

Gibson, though...if I was a different kind of woman, Gibson Kincaid could do a lot for me.

But I wasn't, I remembered, coming down from my high. I was a woman in a mess of a marriage, trying to get out of it. An attraction to a man that wanted to be my divorce lawyer wouldn't turn out well at all.

GIBSON

"So, you turned down her case. Why?"

"Not that it's any of your business," Mother snapped, sliding the small Bluetooth keyboard she used with her tablet toward her. As soon as I'd made it into her office and settled in a chair— and gave Janet the glare that said *go away*— I'd pounced, grilling mother about Vanessa. She seemed like the perfect Kincaid client to me. "It was a dog. I don't even know how she planned to pay legal fees with no money and no money to go after. Her ex is on the verge of bankruptcy and she's no better."

Mother flapped a hand in the air to wave off any further questions about the woman that had just left our offices. I believe Gabe would describe her as a "Honey". Taller than most women I encountered, deep cinnamon skin tone, a mass of curls surrounding her face, light brown eyes, slender nose, full lips. A generous hourglass shape, the kind a woman developed after having children. Bright, pretty smile and a rich sexy tone, like silk over chocolate. It took a lot to catch my attention.

Vanessa Jackson had my attention.

"I don't want to hear another word about her. She's not a client."

"Not *your* client."

"And not yours either. I'm serious about this, Gibson. We don't do pro bono work."

"You always assume people aren't going to pay. There aren't many attorneys out there working for free."

"Pennies on the dollar is not worth your time. And it's not worth mine, either." She punched a few keys on the keyboard and poked at the touch-screen display. "Judge said Kent was at Minks the other night."

An impatient puff of air escaped before I could stop it. Mother's eyes flicked up from the screen of the tablet to meet mine. I dropped my gaze, slowly shaking my head back and forth.

"He couldn't wait to run home and give you the report, huh? I saw him. What of it?"

She shrugged, pretending not to care, but I knew she did. She loved Melanie like the daughter she never had. Then hated her when she left me for Pack. And hated Pack too which broke her heart.

When we were in college, he was the 5th Kincaid. His family lived on the other side of the country and he didn't get the chance to go home very often. I brought him out to the house on the weekends, to family events, out with the brothers. We stayed close throughout law school and the early years of our careers. But when he went behind my back with Melanie, that was it for Mother.

"I was wondering if you spoke to him. And if so, what you said to him. I hope you gave him a piece of your mind."

"You heard Melanie left him, right?" She nodded. I saw a hint of the smug smirk that wanted to plant itself on her face, but she wouldn't let it. "Some rich asshole in Alabama. I'm surprised she hasn't called to gloat."

"That girl. She fooled us all. I should have seen that she was nothing but trouble."

"I should have too. She wasn't like that when we were together though, you know? She was all about us building something together. Something changed... I never even thought..."

I shook my head, trying to loosen the memories that wanted to embed themselves in my mind again. Reminiscing wouldn't bring her back. And I didn't want her back.

"Pack wants to... what's the word? Reconcile. You know, be friends again."

Her fingers stopped moving across the keyboard and her eyebrows lifted. "He does, does he? And?"

"And... I don't know."

"You don't know."

"I don't know. I mean... the way I see it, we're in the same boat. She might end up with this CEO dude, marry him, spend up all his money. Maybe that's what she was looking for all along and she was playing with us until he showed up. Pack and I were the rungs on that ladder."

"This is the exact thing I'm talking about, Gibson. Every person you meet, you try to figure out how you and they are the same, try to put yourself in their shoes. And this is how you end up being everybody's lawyer and not making any money."

"Mother, I told—"

"Yes, you told me." She rolled her eyes toward the ceiling. "It's not about money. But when you leave Kincaid, how do you think rent for office space gets paid? Lights and water and machines and furniture? How are you going to pay for that big fancy country house you have? You undercut and undervalue yourself."

She pushed the tablet and keyboard to the side and folded her hands together on the desk. "I called you in here to talk about extending your contract with Kincaid. We'll maintain your current salary and any benefits you've come to enjoy as an Associate. But I want to see some development in the cases you bring to this firm, or I'll start assigning them to you.

"And at the end of your extension, I hope you'll be the kind of attorney that I've trained you to be. No more of this community do gooder nonsense. I need you working real cases— there's plenty of business to be had and your brothers are doing the lion's share of it."

"Here we go with *real cases* again. Excuse my language, Mother, but this is bullshit. You told me I could pick my own cases and I'm doing that."

"The cases you bring to this firm are not Kincaid material! I just saw the case summary for the girl you got out of cocaine possession with intent to sell."

"Diya wasn't selling; her boyfriend was. She testified against him and got a plea bargain if she stayed on the straight and narrow. Her mother pays the legal bill and Diya is doing fine."

"That's all well and good but drug activity makes it *criminal* law. She should have hired a criminal attorney. There was a child in the car, if I remember correctly?"

"The custody case is what makes it family law. I couldn't separate the two, work one without the other. Daniel is in foster care. Temporarily. Diya is set to get him back any day now."

"Mmmhmm. And what about the man that called you from prison?"

I chuckle. "It was lockup, Mother. It was a drunk and

disorderly charge. He was upset about his cousin being held up at the airport for no reason. He lashed out at the wrong person at the wrong time. He paid a fine. All cleared up."

"Nevertheless, these aren't cases that I want the Kincaid name to be tied to, Gibson. I have a reputation. So do you, and you have a responsibility to its upkeep."

"So..." I laughed, which irritated her. "I have to sit in boring meetings with rich folks... rich *white* folks who fight over who gets the mountain house and who get the Swiss chalet and the city townhouse? Months of arbitration and phone conferences because Molly and Biff—"

"Really, Gibson—"

"— can't agree on how to split their $7.5 million in assets?" I groaned, dropping my face into an open palm. "That's my worst nightmare."

"Well, maybe it'll grow on you. Because I'm not releasing you from Kincaid until you're working on cases that will benefit you and give you the experience I want you to have."

I lifted my head slowly as what she was saying began to sink in. "What do you mean, not releasing me... what does that mean? We agreed—"

"You need my blessing and my money to leave this firm. You're not ready to fly this coop and I won't let you leave until you are."

"You can't be serious. Your kind of law practice is not real-world experience, Mother."

Her eyes landed on the stacks piled neatly at the edge of her desk. "These cases are real. The bills are real, and the checks are real."

"And if I refuse to work on a bullshit divorce or some custody arrangement based on who gets paid to keep the kids?"

Her eyes narrowed and her lips curled inward. "You'll do

what I tell you to do. Or your existence here will be miserable."

I pushed myself up from the chair and headed toward the door. If I didn't leave her office in the next few seconds, I would say something I couldn't easily take back.

But then I couldn't help myself. "It's already miserable. Bring it on."

CHAPTER FIVE

ibson

ON A SMALL PATCH OF LAND OUTSIDE A SPRAWLING country house, a few paces across a deep green, perfectly manicured lawn, I dug my steel shovel into Georgia clay. I turned it, reveling in the sound of the moving dirt, working up the roots from the weeds that had taken hold over the mild winter.

A breeze blew in from the lake that shimmered in the setting sun. The day had been cool but not cold. It was beginning to warm up, which was good for my garden. And for me. It wasn't time to plant yet, but I liked to work the soil and get it ready for the bulbs and seeds that I'd be laying in it soon.

Aside from the prize-winning dahlias that I had been cultivating for the past few years, my spring and summer garden was usually bursting with color and variety— from lilies to thistle, sage, mountain fleece and geraniums as well as a few types of roses.

Beyond the flowers, trees and shrubs was the raised bed vegetable garden, bordered by landscaping wood and concrete blocks, covered with a dome of plastic tubing and vinyl to protect the plants from blazing summers and heavy rain. As a habit, I spent a few hours a week in the garden, planning and organizing, maximizing the space for the vegetables I wanted to plant this year.

It was as much therapy as it was gardening. Working with my hands or my tools gave me something to do while I mulled a course of action, a trial argument, the wording of a motion, or worked out some frustration. I hadn't planned to be in the dirt tonight, but my blood was boiling and I wasn't one for hitting the gym. I'd come home, changed into my gardening clothes and headed right outside to catch the last hours of sunshine.

I stabbed the shovel into the dirt, rotating my wrists to turn it and reveal the dark, moist earth underneath, reaching in to grab weeds and toss them aside. My mind wasn't on fresh, crisp vegetables or bright flowers, though. As I drove the shovel into the clay, my thoughts were consumed by my conversation— well, argument with my mother.

The plan had been to give her the first few years of my career. Get my feet wet. Learn about being an attorney by *being* an attorney. No law school student graduates with any practical knowledge of what it means to be a lawyer. We knew case law, could recite it by heart. Billing? Case management? Client management? All concepts learned with experience, which is why Mother and I agreed that it would be great to gain initial experience at Kincaid.

But then I was supposed to move on. She'd give me seed money to open my own firm and spread word around town about her son's law practice. That was the promise, almost four years ago.

I thought I understood why Garrett, Gabriel and Gregory never left Kincaid— they were too comfortable too accustomed to the way Mother does business and practices law. And they made too much money to go elsewhere.

Now I saw that maybe Mother made it too hard to pull away.

Maybe she's right. Maybe I'd get out there and fall on my face. Maybe it'd be a mistake.

At the end of the row, I turned around to inspect my work. *But it'd be my mistake to make.*

I stepped back from the bed and stood the shovel up, leaning on it while I wiped sweat from my forehead. I counted out the rows I'd dug in preparation for planting warm season vegetables— snap peas, cucumber, okra, squash and tomatoes and soon after that, onions and potatoes. I could also get some herbs in—

My plans were interrupted by the ring of the phone, sitting across the yard where I'd left it. I laid the shovel down next to the garden bed and strolled across the lawn, grabbing the phone up before it rolled to voicemail.

"Gibson Kincaid," I answered, dropping into one of the chairs placed around a glass topped patio table.

"Hello." I recognized her voice right away, even over the phone line. Most of my body came to attention at the sound. "This is Vanessa Jackson. We met earlier today, at Kincaid?"

"I remember. I hope you're calling to discuss your case."

Deadbeat and low paying as the cases were, I had plenty to keep me busy, so why I was fixated on offering her representation was beyond me. Maybe it was her eyes, or the cloud of disappointment and dejection that surrounded her as she came out of Mother's office, but *something* compelled me to reach out to her.

Background noise, which sounded like a bar, almost over-powered her voice as she answered. "I was, actually. And I'm sure you spoke to Sylvia after we met, so you know all the details and I want you to know that I'm not looking for a handout. I'm in a situation and I need legal help to get out of it."

"I wasn't expecting you to ask for a handout. And I didn't speak to my mother about your details." Which wasn't a lie. We quickly moved on to her usual grievances during our meeting. "So, why don't you tell me about your situation and how I can help."

"Well," she began with a sigh. The noise behind her quieted, then disappeared as I heard the soft thunk of a door closing. "I've been separated for a year. Not legally. My husband... left. He's moved on but we've made almost no progress with dissolving our marriage. Things are getting ugly so I need to move as quickly as I can without compro-mising support for my daughters. Sylvia seemed hell bent on going after money and assets and..."

She sighed a soft breath into the phone. "That's not really what I was looking for."

My eyebrows rose at the mention of her daughters. "You have children? And he's not providing for them?"

"Yes, two. He sees them when he feels like seeing them, which isn't often. The bigger issue is that there's no support order because either he won't agree to anything or he threatens to file for bankruptcy so there won't be any money to pay a support order —"

"Vanessa," I gently interrupted. "Hang on a second. First, it's not up to him. If he's telling you that he controls the amount he pays or even *if* he pays support, he's talking out of his... well, you know. We file for support and the judge awards it to you and it comes out of his paycheck, whatever that is. If he's not earning, it piles up in arrears until he is working.

"Now, if he's left the family home, he's living with someone else, has begun another relationship, we have a case for abandonment and the divorce may go faster. But child support is separate from a divorce action."

"Oh... I..." The line was quiet except for the barely detectable hum that told me she was still there. "I didn't know that. He said..." She huffed. "So, I could have filed for support a long time ago?"

"Let's not worry about what you could have done. The past is lived and we can't go back. Let's talk about the future and what I can do for you."

By the time I finished talking to Vanessa, she sounded more hopeful, less terrified and desperate. Her almost ex-husband was a piece of work— the lies he fed her kept her right where he wanted her, just below the surface, scrambling for air, poor and scared to make a move. She barely knew which way was up.

The sun was a crimson, glowing line along the horizon. The evening was getting cooler and the breeze coming off the lake was chilly. I pulled myself up from the patio chair and ambled toward the doors, sliding them open and stepping into the house. I worked my gardening boots off my feet and left them at the mat that I kept near the door.

"I'd like to you to review some documents and fill out some paperwork so we can get started. We can also discuss my fee."

"Does this mean you want to take my case?"

"It's more a question of if you want to retain me. This isn't a quickie divorce but it's not complicated, either. I promise you, though, that you'll be a free woman soon."

"Wow," she replied, practically breathless. "With everything that's been going on, I thought— I can't even believe it's possible right now. Thank you."

"Don't thank me yet. You haven't seen my fee schedule."

I laughed and was happy to hear the return of a low, sexy giggle in my ear. I moved to the kitchen, where I pulled a container of leftover steak tips and rice from the refrigerator, placed it in the microwave and set the timer for a few minutes. I leaned my hip against the counter and listened to the fan as the machine warmed my dinner.

"I can't imagine that you want to come back to the law office to go over paperwork. I'm usually out in the community a few days a week. Is there a place I can meet you?"

"Uh..." A deep, heavy breath sounded over the line. "I'm a real estate agent, so I could be anywhere at any time during the day. But... actually, I had to pick up a second job at my Uncle's restaurant. I'll probably be here most nights. Sam's Bar & Grille, on Broad in Decatur. You probably don't know the place—"

"Home of Sam's famous lemon pepper chicken wings? I sure do know the place."

She sucked in a breath, which I read as surprise. "How do you know about Sam's?"

"I take some meetings at Gladwell Books next door. It's nice in there, but after a while, a man needs something more substantial than a cinnamon raisin scone and fancy coffee. It's an old fashioned place for sure but your uncle knows how to... how do they say it? Put a hurtin' on some chicken?"

"Yeah, they say that, but I'd better not tell him that someone called his lemon pepper wings *famous*. We'll never hear the end of it."

Her lightened mood was palpable over the line, now. She was laughing freely, which was a nice sound. "So... I'm here from six to nine most nights. Stop in for dinner when you can and we can talk."

"It's a date," is what I said, before I could stop myself. "I mean... I'll stop in."

"Sounds great, Gibson. I'll...I'll see you soon."

The line disconnected and I tucked the phone away, then opened the microwave door to quiet its incessant beeping.

"Just another case, Gib," I mumbled to myself. I dumped the container of beef and rice onto a plate, then headed to the living room and settled into my favorite leather recliner. The widescreen mammoth TV popped on at the press of a button, mid-broadcast of a basketball game.

Just another case. Yeah. Right.

I PULLED OPEN THE HEAVY WOOD DOOR AT SAM'S BAR & Grille, pausing to wipe my feet on the mat at the entry way. It was raining, so the mat was already soaked and wasn't doing much to rid my shoes of leaves and mud.

"Pull that door shut tight!" Called a raspy male voice from behind the bar. I reached back and pulled the handle as the door caught a gust of wind. I wrestled with it, then overpowered it and pulled it shut with a slam. "Thank ya," called the voice again. "If you don't shut it real good, it'll bust open and be like a tornado in here."

I moved toward the bar, hand outstretched. A new addition, a flat screen TV, had been hung above the bar and the few restaurant patrons in the place had their eyes glued to it.

"Good to see you, Sam. How are you this evening?"

He gripped my hand with a tight, strong grasp and gave it two polite pumps. "Rather be sittin' next to my lady on an island somewhere but this here ain't half bad I guess." He chuckled, then leaned onto the bar. "You want some o' them wings you order every time you come in here?"

I couldn't help the grin that spread across my face. "And a side of fries, if you don't mind."

"You the one payin' for it; I don't mind at all." He turned to bark my order to the cook in the kitchen. The cook confirmed and he turned to me again. "I 'spose it's after business hours at whatever fancy job you got that makes you wear them shoes that ain't for walkin' in the rain. What can I getcha? Brown or browner?"

"Not quite after business hours for me, Sam. Actually..." I leaned in and lowered my voice. "I'm looking for your niece, Vanessa. Is she around?"

Sam's expression morphed from a friendly disinterest to a suspicious scowl. A large wooden bat appeared from somewhere behind the bar. He gripped it in one large hand.

"What you want with Vanessa? You been in here spyin' for her triflin' asshole of an ex-husband? I ought to throw you outta here right on your—"

"Uncle!" I tried not to let my relief at being rescued show on my face, but I'd never been so happy to hear a woman's voice. "Stop it! Put that down. This is Gibson Kincaid. I *hope* he's still interested in being my divorce lawyer."

Sam's face slowly relaxed, still suspicious but less angry. "Alright," he growled. "Good thing Vanessa was here. You almost got it, son. Never know who might be comin' through and what they want. My policy is to beat that ass and ask questions later."

"Oh please. You haven't hit anything outside of a baseball with that bat, and it's been thirty years since *that* happened."

I was happy to see the bat lower and disappear behind the bar again. "You ain't got to tell the whole place my business, girl."

Vanessa laughed, then hooked a hand into my elbow and pulled me toward the back of the restaurant. "I'm taking a break, Uncle. We'll be in the back."

"You just got here, talkin' about taking a break. And 'sposin you want me to deliver his order to your table?"

"That'd be great," she said over her shoulder. To me, she winked and said, "Don't worry about him. He's all bark."

"All the same, I'll stay in his good graces."

At a booth in a corner of the restaurant, the surface of the table showed that she'd been there a while— stacks of folders, envelopes and papers covered half of the table. "I brought everything I could think of that might help. I thought you'd want to look at it all. And I wrote up a summary of my... situation."

"These will probably be helpful, though not immediately. If we have to go to court, I may need it."

I slid into one side of the booth and set my satchel at my feet. I rested my elbows on the table and clasped my hands together. She mimicked my pose but I noticed her hands trembling. "You seem tense. How are you doing?"

"Up and down since our conversation last night. I spent a lot of time on the internet, researching things." Her eyes lifted to meet mine. "Not that I didn't believe you. I wanted to see for myself. I've been so..."

She exhaled a deep sigh and brought her hands to her cheeks. "I feel so stupid. When it comes to Warren, he has a way of saying things that you don't question. When he said I couldn't make him pay because we weren't divorced... and that I couldn't divorce him because he'd never sign the papers—"

"I've heard it all. The rantings of a man trying to maintain control. Hardly ever lawful or enforceable. That's why you need a good attorney, an attorney who's interested in more than your wallet."

She started to laugh, but covered her mouth with her fist, hiding a small but smug grin. "What's your mother going to say when she finds out you picked up my case? She said Kincaid couldn't help me."

"*Sylvia* Kincaid can't help you." I grabbed the handle of my satchel and set it next to me, flipping open the top and pulling out a thin file. I opened it to the first page, a contract that stated a client was retaining my services. "*Gibson* Kincaid is going to do everything he can to make sure that you get your divorce."

"I like the sound of that," she said, her eyes roving the first, and then the second page. "So... there are a lot of blanks on this fee schedule."

"Because we need to talk about that. It doesn't do any good for me to bill an insane amount that you can't pay. Why be in hock to your lawyer, right? What works better is for us to figure out how long we think we'll work together and agree on an amount per hour that you can afford. If we need to work with a cap, I'll work until that's satisfied and then we can negotiate a higher cap."

"Oh. Okay. That's... different." She smiled, digging a pen out of the pocket of her apron. "I've never heard of an attorney working it that way."

"Sometimes you have to think outside the box. I'm not free, of course. But I'd like to help you. If you'd like me to."

I could have slapped my own self for how deep and seductive my voice sounded. I wasn't trying to get her into bed, just to sign the contract. I talked to hundreds of clients, many of them young, attractive women. I had no problem talking to them, being professional, business-like, straightforward. That I couldn't talk to Vanessa without putting on *that tone* was working my own nerves.

"I know I should read this first, but I feel like I can trust you. You're telling me everything I want to hear and I don't even care if it's lies. I'm so desperate to get away from my husband..." She signed and dated the blanks on the contract with a flourish, then slid them across the table to me. "I'm willing to take the leap."

"You won't regret it." I signed the line above my typed name on the contract. "And there are no lies. Take this home and read it, top to bottom. It's very straightforward, but if there's something you don't like, we can strike it. Cool?"

Vanessa had visibly relaxed. Her shoulders weren't hunched around her ears, her jaw wasn't square with tension, and her hands didn't shake anymore. She nodded, her eyelids at half-mast. Her lips were bent, very slightly, in a dreamy smile.

"Cool. Everything sounds cool."

"So you work here, part time?"

She nodded. "Temporarily. My Uncle's way of helping me out." She reached for a glass of water that she'd set to the side and closed her lips around the straw. My mind went into overdrive imagining those lips doing the same thing, somewhere else.

She licked her lips and slid the glass away. I must have been staring, because she tilted her head and stared back, her brows raised.

"So... lay this out for me, Mr. Kincaid. How will this work?"

"Gibson. First, you can call me Gibson."

So I was attracted to her.

So it affected how I handled her case.

So I was offering her the lowest rate I'd ever *ever* offered a client.

So my mother was going to have a screaming fit, right after we'd had that argument about my fees and the cases I brought to Kincaid. Right after she'd told me not to take this case.

The woman that sat across from me had hope. She saw light at the end of the tunnel and the thought that she might soon be free gave her face the sexiest expression.

And I put it there.

CHAPTER SIX

anessa

"I LOVE A SPRING AFTERNOON, DON'T YOU? IT'S NOT HOT yet, and the flowers have started to bloom and the birds are chirping—"

"Okay, who spiked Sonja's orange juice?"

Sonja was louder, her voice grittier than usual. She'd probably had a very late night and, despite it being early afternoon, quite possibly hadn't slept yet.

"Nobody gotta spike my drinks. I never leave home without my flask. Besides, maybe I'm still drunk from last night, loud mouth heifer."

Our table burst into loud, raucous laughter. It *was* a beautiful day, nice enough to sit outside on the new patio at Ruby's Soul Food. The place had been around forever, but the general manager, Ruby's oldest son, had been making steady improvements over the last year, making it even more popular than it was before.

The parking lot had been paved and striped, he'd had new concrete poured around the restaurant and added tables so guests could sit outside. The back patio was an extended wood deck that had been built over the winter. We'd snagged a reservation the first weekend it would be open.

Every so often, a few of the ladies I used to dance with got together to catch up. Sonja, who I'd known since my first day at Red Heels; Karen, aka Moxie, who had started at the club a few months before I stopped dancing; and Tania and Evin, who were new to "the life". Sonja did her best to take new dancers under her wing and show them the ropes. She hadn't danced in years, since she managed to work herself into a job as Talent Director at Red Heels.

"Besides, I don't have to be drunk to be in a good mood. Chill, damn." Sonja reached for one of the biscuits that the waiter had set on the table, so fresh they were still steaming. She split one open and spread a pat of butter on one half.

"We're chill," said Tania, reaching for a biscuit as well. "But you're cheerful. Almost like you recently stabbed someone with a stiletto or something."

I giggled, nursing a piping hot mug of coffee. "Ya'll got Sonja all wrong. She's not violent. Her mouth is her weapon."

"She's mean," quipped Evin.

"She's not mean, either," said Karen. "Do what she says and get on her good side and she'll be your best friend. She'll look out for you and everything. Am I right, Nessa?"

"She *is* mean. But she means well. If I had listened to Sonja back in the day—"

"You wouldn't be mommy to those beautiful girls," she interrupted, around a bite of biscuit. "At least they look like you and not their father."

That earned another round of laughter, even from me. These were the moments that I loved and looked forward to, with people that mattered to me. My aunt and uncle were great— they had taken the girls to a production at the Children's Theater of Atlanta so I could have brunch with my friends. But these ladies not only knew me, they knew my life.

They knew what it was like to be a PTA mom by day, by night a seductive vixen writhing to the rhythm of a heavy R&B beat. They knew all about nice homes, nice cars, expensive shoes and shiny gems, but also stares and nasty looks. Or worse, propositions from men who thought dancers were prostitutes in their spare time. They knew what it was like to balance motherhood, relationships and a career in a profession that was seen as exploitative.

Some of us danced to rebel. Some of us danced to make money. Some of us danced because it was a way out. *All* of us danced because we chose to.

"What's the latest with him, anyway?" Asked Evin. "I feel like I haven't heard his name in a while."

"Mmm," I hummed, setting down my coffee cup. I'd been keeping an eye out for the waiter with our orders. I was ravenous and ready for chicken and waffles. "He's been quiet. Quiet means he's plotting. But whatever he's doing doesn't really matter anymore."

I paused and inhaled a long, cleansing breath. I hadn't even said it out loud yet, so it didn't feel real yet. At any moment, things could fall through and I'd be right where I'd been for over a year.

"I finally hired an attorney. And I'm filing for divorce."

After a round of quiet applause, Karen lifted her mimosa to the table. "Well, amen and hallelujah! I don't know why brunch didn't *start* with that piece of good news! Cheers to you, girl."

Sonja brushed biscuit crumbs from the front of her blouse and shook out her napkin before laying it across her lap again. Then she reached for her glass and tapped it against Karen's.

"I told her Warren was full of shit. He can't say what she can't do. Do it and see what happens." To me, she asked, "Does he know yet? I'm guessing not, since your phone isn't blowing up right now."

I shook my head. "We haven't filed yet. The easiest is to have a process server deliver the papers. But I don't know where he lives..."

I shrugged, then perked when I saw the waiter approaching, his arms laden with plates and bowls of Ruby's brunch special, Chicken and waffles with sides of cheese grits all around. I rubbed my palms together in anticipation.

While the waiter set down our plates and bowls, I continued. "So we're going to file by putting an ad in the paper. He has a certain amount of time to respond. If he doesn't see it and the time limit expires, the divorce goes through."

"Except Warren is the type to run a Google search on himself," Sonja grumbled. "Ain't no way he won't respond. You can bet on that."

"You can't serve him at work?" Tania asked, already digging her spoon into creamy, southern cheese grits.

I sucked my teeth. "Girl, what work? Warren lost his job, I guess, but signed back on as a contract salesman. He works from home, wherever that is, Of course, I can't get his home address from Service Software. All they have listed is a PO Box. So, we either hire a private investigator to find him, or place an ad in the paper. I barely have money for an attorney, let alone an investigator."

"He's not worth that money or the time spent thinking about it," said Sonja. "Too bad you can't dance it off."

"Don't think I haven't thought of that. I suggested it but Auntie and Uncle weren't amused."

Sonja chuckled. "They weren't amused the first time, either. As if I would let your old ass come back to Red Heels. You probably can't even do a decent backbend, let alone pole work."

"Just because I haven't danced for money in eight years doesn't mean I don't still have moves. Don't make me get up in this respectable establishment and demonstrate, Sonja."

"Mmmmm, I hear you talking."

"Yeah, you hear me. I danced rings around you back in the day, lady. Don't you forget it."

"Sure did," Sonja agreed, proudly nodding. "But only because I was on my way out. You couldn't out-dance me when I first started. Let you tell, it I was old and jealous but I knew what I was doing and what I was talking about. You thought you was the shit. Then you let your naive self get mixed up with Warren when I *told* you about his ass—"

"How many times do I have to say you were right about him?"

"Until I'm satisfied that you learned your lesson."

"Who did you hire to do your divorce, Vanessa? Sylvia Kincaid stripped Dennis to. the. bone." Karen made slicing motions with her hands, then laughed maniacally. "He probably can't buy toilet paper right now."

I wanted to roll my eyes, both at the mention of Sylvia and at Karen's ex-husband Dennis. Karen was the "dancing to put herself through school" dancer. She was there for the paycheck and resisted advances from a handsome silver fox for years. When her financial aid fell through one semester, it was nothing for the well-to-do real estate mogul to write a check.

He swore he wasn't trying to change her, wasn't trying to rescue her. But, like Warren, he eventually expected her to be a Stepford Wife. Stay home, have babies, join the PTA, volunteer. Entertain his corporate buddies and be the pretty, sexy, chocolate thing on his arm.

The divorce was bitter and brutal and dragged on and on, due in part to Sylvia going for the jugular at every turn. I knew exactly how she worked and how much it cost to retain her because of Karen.

"I had a consultation with Sylvia, but... well, she rejected me." I mumbled the last part under my breath.

"Rejected you. As a client? How does an attorney do that?"

"She found out I don't have any money, and neither does Warren and basically kicked me out of her office. If you don't look like a million bucks and aren't swimming in diamonds, she's not interested."

"Uhm... okay...." Karen paled, as much as a caramel toned woman could pale. She pawed at the rocks in her ears, then the pendant dangling from her neck. The diamond encrusted watch she wore was blinding when it caught a ray of sun just right. "Is that a dig at me? You think I was wrong for going after everything I could?"

"Don't put words in my mouth. I didn't say that."

"You may as well have. If you have something to say, Nessa, come on with it."

"Karen." Sonja glared until Karen huffed, rolled her eyes and tossed her napkin on the table, then pushed her chair back and got up. We all watched her shapely hips sway side to side, her extra high Louboutin's striking a rhythm so strong that the entire deck vibrated with each step.

"Did I sound like I was coming at her?"

Evin rolled her eyes and propped an elbow on the table, resting her fingers on her temple. "Ever since the divorce hit the paper, her phone's blowing up with bloggers trying to get interviews, her Facebook page is a mess and Twitter has named her *Karrine Steffens, Jr.* She's about to have a nervous breakdown."

"Karen will be alright. She just needs to a minute. You

were saying?" Sonja gestured me to continue with her fork before spearing a syrup soaked slice of waffle. "Your attorney."

"Well, I did end up hiring a Kincaid. One of her sons. I ran into him while I was trying to get out of that office. He asked if I was a client. I said no. We chatted for a minute, he gave me his card and told me to call him." I lifted and lowered my shoulders in a *that's that* shrug.

Karen stomped back to the table and resumed her seat. She was obviously still fuming, but didn't say a word. She picked up her knife and fork and proceeded to eat chicken and waffles as furiously as I'd ever seen a person eat.

"Which of her sons is doing your divorce?" Tania was on her mobile phone, her long fingers clicking through screens. "There's Garrett, Greggory, Gabriel and Gibson."

"Gibson," I answered. Karen snorted, almost choking on her food. "What did I say, now?"

"Nothing," she answered. "Gibson is cheap, is all."

"Okay, I don't care how cheap he is. Bruh is *foooiiinnneee.*"

Evin swooned, grabbing Tania's phone from her hands and enlarging the photo. She handed it around to everyone but Karen, who obviously knew what Gibson looked like. "All that pretty brown skin, looking like a Hershey bar. Wanna lick him *up!*"

"Sop him up with a biscuit, my mama used to say," said Tania, taking the phone back. "How many of them are single? That one on the end looks like he has a steel rod up his ass."

"That's Garrett," said Karen. "He's married and not even worth tempting away. He's so bland and boring. The other three are single but the two in the middle are so close they might be fucking each other."

"Karen, what do you mean, Gibson is cheap? How much money does it take to file some papers?"

Karen shrugged, obviously still bristling and not in the

mood to talk to me. "He takes a lot of...smaller, less costly cases." She paused, making gestures with her hands before going back to her meal. "I don't know. He's like... a community lawyer. Nothing like everyone else at the firm."

"That's why I like him. He's charging me based on what I can afford. He's not spending a ton of money on things I can't pay for, like private investigators and looking for money that isn't there. I don't care if Warren has a Swiss bank account. I want to be his *ex*-wife sometime this decade."

"Well, let's not be hasty, honey," said Sonja. "If he has money somewhere, you need some of that."

"He's talking about bankruptcy. He barely has a pot to piss in and the IRS is about strip him to. the. bone." Despite being mad at me, Karen sent me a wry, sideways smile. And winked in my direction.

"I might get married, so I can get a divorce and hire Mr. Gibson Kincaid," said Tania, before closing the browser and tucking her phone away. "He's nice to look at, at least."

"He is more than *nice to look at*," I admitted. "The day I met him he was wearing this amazing dark blue tailored suit. He was all broad shoulders and pretty smile and *nice to meet you miss* and manicured fingernails and good smelling cologne. The other night he brought my contract and paperwork to me at Sam's and at one point he gave me this... look. It was probably innocent— I mean, I'm a client and he's a professional, but...it was all I could do to not climb over that table and into his lap. I almost wish he wasn't my divorce lawyer."

"Why?" Evin, her eyes growing wider when we all laughed at her question. "What?"

"Unh-*unmh*," Karen grunted. "Never sleep with the divorce attorney. It's the oldest cliché in the book."

"But..." Evian scratched her temple, her forehead creased in confusion. "...why?"

"Think about it, Ev," said Karen. "A divorce isn't exactly a celebration. Every process, every court date, every argument is a reminder that you sucked at keeping your marriage together. You're completely vulnerable, and on top of that, who knows how long it's been since someone worthy has been close to the kitty. Somebody shows up, ready to make all your problems go away? And makes you feel like a winner? And don't let him be even a little bit good looking."

She shook her head, her lips in a downturn. "You're trying to get your rocks off and he's ready to don his Superman cape."

"Besides, I fell for that good lookin', smooth talkin', *I'm here to rescue you* mission ten years ago and look where I am now. Trying to divorce this shady motherfucker."

I gulped down a swallow of ice water, my gaze landing on the flowering Magnolias behind the cafe stirring in the light breeze. "No more men with an "S" on his chest for me."

"And that's why we don't date men from the club," Sonja announced, and pushed her decimated plate away. "No matter how handsome they are, how rich they are, how much they talk about how they're different and you can still dance even if you're with them and how many credit cards they add your name to. Let these two—" Sonja directed a finger at me and Karen. "Teach y'all a lesson. Do what I say and stay out of that mess."

"Unless he's stupid rich and you can marry him, then divorce him and take him for all he's worth," added Karen, fingering her diamond pendant. I couldn't tell if she was joking, but I'd place a wager that she wasn't.

After brunch, we gathered near the front of the restaurant, giving hugs and promising to get together again soon. I was the first to step away, heading toward my car which was finally fixed and running well.

"Vanessa."

Even if I didn't recognize her voice, I knew it was Karen

by her heavy, staccato footfalls. I had almost reached my car, but stopped and turned around. "Before you start, I wasn't starting anything with you, Karen."

"The hell you weren't. Maybe you didn't mean to, but you looked right at me when you made that crack about swimming in diamonds. I earned everything I have, alright?"

I chuckled and turned away again. "Sure you did."

"I just wanted you to know that your mouth isn't as slick as you think it is and I didn't appreciate your commentary."

"You didn't *appreciate*— "

I whipped around and walked the few steps back to her, close enough to see the crow's feet around her eyes and the age lines around her lips. The divorce may have hit Dennis hard, but it hit Karen harder.

"How about next time we get together, don't wear your entire jewelry trunk to brunch. You could signal Delta planes with all that bling, bitch. We're not all living off of alimony payments from stupid rich, lovestruck, pussy drunk assholes. Some of us are working two jobs to make ends meet. Some of us had to hire the *cheap* lawyer at Kincaid. And while your biggest problem right now is where to spend all of Dennis' money and being nicknamed after a gold digger who wrote a tell-all book, I have real life issues to deal with, like how to get out of this marriage before I drown and my children are ruined. I'm not at all concerned with what you don't *appreciate*, Karen."

When I finished, I stepped back, waiting for a response. As I figured, she didn't have one. I turned around and walked to my car. Just as I reached for the driver's side door, I heard her walking away. I smiled at myself, in the window reflection and popped open the door.

I sat in the car, one foot inside, the other still on pavement, driver side door wide open. I watched Karen walk, head down, toward her Jaguar, another parting gift from

Dennis. I could only hope, when I was on the other side of this misery, that I could walk with my head held high.

I inserted the key into the ignition and sighed a thankful breath that the car started right up, purring like the fine piece of German engineering that she was designed to be.

CHAPTER SEVEN

ibson

I HAD NEVER BEEN SO EXCITED TO GET A CALL FROM A Judge's clerk, but this call had me on my feet, scrambling for my keys.

"Yes, of course," I muttered into the phone. "Regular welfare checks, I'll tell her. Absolutely. Thank you. And thank Judge Perry for me. She won't regret taking this chance on Diya."

I ended the call with my thumb and swung the door closed with my index finger. I knew where I could find Diya on a Tuesday at 2PM and I was excited to give her the news about Daniel in person. The judge had granted her custody and she'd be holding him again in 48 hours.

"Gibson Charles Kincaid!"

Mother was screeching at the top of her lungs and racing down the hallway. That meant she'd seen the petition to file

Vanessa's divorce. I knew she'd be angry. I wasn't expecting dramatics, but in hindsight, I should have.

I turned halfway so I could watch her light complexion turn purple. "I'm on my way out to see a client. Can you yell at me later?"

"Don't get smart with me, boy. I told you, explicitly, that Vanessa Jackson would not be a client at this firm. You went right behind my back and offered representation."

"Because she needed help. And not your kind of help."

"And the fee you're charging her won't cover the pens you use. What about this business do you not understand, young man?"

"I get it, Mother. I'm not doing it the way you want me to do it."

"Well, that's for damn sure. I want you to dissolve your contract with Ms. Jackson. Today. The fee is simply not substantial enough and there's nothing we can do for—"

"Mother. Stop and listen to yourself. Seriously. We are attorneys at a family law firm. We can file her damn divorce is what we can do for her. It's what I'm going to do for her." I moved to step around her, leaving her sputtering in the hallway.

"Don't let your manhood dictate the clients you choose, Gib!"

I stopped and turned, my mouth hanging open.

Her lips parted in a sardonic smile that I recognized. It was the smile she wore when she'd caught opposing counsel or client in a lie or misdeed. She loved other people's mistakes.

"Mmmhmmm. Don't think I didn't see you watching her tail sashay out of here, all smiles and hair and *please take my case, cheap ass lawyer*. Maybe you're hoping she'll give you a little something to offset the fee—"

"Mother!"

"Oh come on, Gib! You don't see it? She might be enticed by that low fee, that nice suit, that head of hair you got from your daddy, but what she wants is what's sitting in your back pocket, son. Your *wallet*."

"You're unbelievable," I muttered, heading back down the hall. "You're not going to talk me out of representing her. If you don't want her to be a Kincaid client, release me. I'm used to working out of a coffee shop. I'll take her case with me."

Knowing she'd never take me up on it, I kept walking right out of the suite.

I strolled into Gladwell Books and headed straight for the cafe, where I knew Diya would be— either at one of the bistro tables or curled up on one of the overstuffed couches that Renee had added to the shop. Along with vintage wood side tables and lamps, they gave the bookstore a "living room" feel, which made people want to sit down, unpack, and stay awhile.

But Diya wasn't at a table in the cafe, nor was she smashed into the corner of a couch, her nose in a book and headphones over her ears.

"Are you looking for our favorite bookworm?" Renee had snuck up behind me, obviously amused by how high I'd jumped when she spoke. She giggled while looping her apron over her head. She reached behind her back to tie the strings around her waist.

"Yeah. Diya is usually here, but I don't see her. Have you talked to her lately? I guess I should have called..." I pulled my phone from my bag and scrolled to the D's in my contact list.

"You probably won't find her here as much, though she

promised she would still come in now and then. Debra gave her a job at the community center. Since they started the day care, Diya figured that if she got Daniel back, she could have him there and not have to leave him with her mother all day."

Renee paused, tilting her head with a small smile. "I hope you have good news, Mr. Lawyer Man. And that's why you're rushing in here, all out of breath, looking for her."

I laughed, tucking the phone away. "I do, actually. That's great to hear about her new job. I'm surprised she didn't call me."

"I think she wanted to make sure it worked out first. She was doing fine at Spit Spot Cleaning, but it was night shift, and a lot of strenuous activity. She needed a little more money, and... now she can see Daniel during the day. I hope?"

"That's the plan," I said, moving toward the door. "Listen, thanks for the update. I want to give her the news first and let her spread it around. I'll go out to the center and find her, tell her myself."

I found Diya at the East Side Community Center, sitting at the front desk with a wide grin plastered across her face. She stood when I walked in the door, nervously wringing her hands.

"Gibson! I didn't expect to see you today! Please tell me you have good news and you're not here in person because you didn't want to let me down over the phone because I've been hoping that you'd hear from the judge soon and I promise if you're here to tell me what I think you're here to tell me I'm about to—"

"Whoa. Whoa, Diya. Take a breath. You're about to turn blue."

I slid my bag from my shoulder and set it on the half circle of glass that made up the check-in counter, where parents signed their children in and out for Before and After school programs, current GED students signed in for sessions or testing, and others came to take various classes and use the available study rooms. The center also offered opportunities for seniors to socialize and counseling appointments for those that needed them, court-ordered or otherwise. Debra Macklin, the Center's Assistant Director, had transformed the place from "a place to dump your kids for the day" to a center that enriched people of all ages.

Diya's position as the Front Office Coordinator was perfect for her. Her youthful exuberance and bright smile was welcoming and it was great to see her as a role model to others. She'd come a long way and I was proud to have a hand in that.

"Well, I do have good news for you."

"You do? What is it, Gib?" Diya panted, hardly breathing. I wanted to tease her a little longer but I really was concerned she would pass out.

"You think you're ready to for your son to come home?"

The scream that she let out could probably be heard throughout the building. And maybe beyond. Diya scrambled around the counter and jumped into my arms, squeezing my shoulders tightly and squealing *thank you thank you thank you* in my ear over and over again.

When she pulled back, she was openly crying— tears streaming, sniffling and beet-red nose crying. I heard a door open down the hall and heels clicking toward us.

"What is going on out here? Who's screaming?"

Debra rounded the corner, her face full of concern. As soon as she saw me, then Diya's tears, her face fell. "Diya, honey... Oh, Gibson, you couldn't have waited until later to give her the news?"

"Ms. Debra, you don't understand. I get Daniel back! I get my son back!" Diya was sobbing by this point, gripping the counter like she was about to sink to her knees.

Debra sprang into action, grabbing her by the arm and

guiding her around the counter to her chair. "Okay, come on. Sit down. Grab some Kleenex. Wipe your face. No, don't rub like that. Dab, dab, dab. Get yourself together."

Debra straightened to beam a huge, grateful smile while she stood next to Diya, rubbing her back. "This means a lot to her, as you can tell. Especially since we opened the child care center. Now she'll be with Daniel all the time." She squeezed Diya's shoulder, jostling her a bit.

Diya laughed, still dabbing at errant tears. "I can't believe it. It's been the longest year of my life. So, when do I get him?"

"The Judge's order said 48 hours, but I'm going to contact the social worker and see if we can get things moving today. I'd expect to see him any time between now and... well, a couple of days from now. How are you, for having things ready for him? I can get you some cash—"

"Oh, no, no, no," Diya responded, violently shaking her head. "My mama wouldn't hear of you giving me money. You've helped us out so much, way more than any lawyer ever would. Between this job and a little money I've been saving, we're set real good. Besides, Mama's been praying so hard about her grandson coming home that his room is decked out. She lost her mind at the toy store."

"That's good. This means regular welfare checks. They'll come see you at work, see him at daycare, see him at home. It's important that you stay above board, alright? And if you run into any trouble with anything, *especially* with Daniel's father, I'm your first call. Don't worry about the fee. Just call. Agreed?"

The tears were gone but the wide smile stuck around as she nodded her agreement. I gave her hands a parting squeeze. "I'll leave you with your good news and I'll be in touch with details about picking up Daniel."

I walked out to the chatter of Debra and Diya making

plans for a Welcome Home party, both of their voices pitching high with excitement. I climbed into my Jeep and dumped my bag on the passenger seat, then dug my phone out of the front pocket. I'd missed a few calls from Mother, but I was in no hurry to call her back. I could predict what that conversation was going to sound like and I wanted to put it off as long as possible.

Seeing no other pressing appointments or issues, I started up the Jeep and pulled out of the parking lot, headed back toward downtown Decatur. I knew exactly which client I was going to see next.

"Lemon pepper wings and a side o' fries, if I don't mind," Sam called out, as soon as I stepped into the bar. I grinned and waved, heading toward the table that, by habit, Vanessa and I had claimed as our meeting space.

I knew she wouldn't come in for a while, but I liked to sit at our table and work for a few hours. The low rumble of the TV, Sam's joking and cackling with his staff and customers and general sounds of business were easy to tune out. When Vanessa was on shift, she stopped by often to make sure I was taken care of. Most nights, when she took her long break, she'd bring whatever she'd ordered for dinner and eat with me.

I settled in at our table, unpacking my bag as I went. A tablet, Bluetooth keyboard and mouse, portable Wi-Fi device, a few notepads, folders, my cell phone and a couple of pens easily covered the table in a few minutes. I started up my Spotify *Daytime Jams* playlist, covered my ears with headphones and got to work. My first order of business was to email the social worker that handled Daniel Conway's case and find out when Diya could pick him up.

When my wings and fries appeared at my elbow, I made room for the plate, scooting things down the table. I looked up, expecting to thank Sam, but it was Vanessa that brought the plate to me. I smiled, wider than I probably should have, pulling the headphones from my ears.

"I wasn't expecting to see you until later," I said, rolling my wrist to glance at my watch.

She was fresh faced, wearing no makeup except for a pop of deep red color on her lips and had her hair slicked back, bundled in a low ponytail at the base of her neck. She looked... young. Though she probably *was* young.

"I had an Open House and no reason to go back to the office, so I decided to come in. This way I get off earlier and I can put my girls to bed. You're staring at my face. Why?"

I blinked a few times, then tore my eyes from her shapely, thick lips, made even sexier by the crimson lipstick. "I... I just... I don't think I've seen you so... I mean..."

She laughed, swatting at me with a bleached white towel from the pocket of her apron. "The air in here is so heavy with grease. I'm trying to talk Uncle into some healthier options— you know, baked or broiled. He says that's not bar food."

She rolled her eyes toward the front of the bar at Sam leaning against a wall, his eyes fixed on the TV. "Anyway, I usually wash my face before I come in here now. It's gross getting all this grease caught in my makeup. But I can't not wear lipstick, so..." She shrugged, and if I wasn't mistaken, blushed a little.

"I guess... that's good to know. You uh... you look nice. With the... uh..."

"Thank you. Not that I asked what you thought."

"Not... not that you did. I was offering a compliment. Not that you needed one."

"Not that I did." She tipped her chin toward my piles at the other end of the table. "What are you working on tonight?"

"Uh... privileged, first of all. I can't tell you all my

clients' business. But I'm working on some good news for one of them. And for you. I'm drafting your divorce, actually."

Her eyes lit up then, and she slid into the booth opposite me. "Really? Is it... could we file soon?"

I plucked a crispy, fried wing from the plate next to me took a bite and almost moaned at the juicy, lemony, peppery taste. Whatever Sam used to season his wings, he could sell in a grocery store. "I could have a draft to review tonight if you wanted to see it."

"I want to see it. I need to know that something's happening, you know?"

"I'm working, I promise. I'm not just here for the wings." I wiped my fingers on the napkin she handed me from a stash in the pocket of an apron. "You haven't heard from him, have you?"

She shook her head, her lips scrunched into a scowl. "Nah. We don't talk unless it's about the girls and he never wants to talk about the girls."

Vanessa's ex made me twitch with anger like no other ex-husband ever had. I couldn't imagine having someone like Vanessa in my life, let alone two lives we'd created together, and then leaving them for someone... *better*. Did better even exist?

You don't know her, man. She could be evil incarnate, I told myself.

I'm a pretty good judge of character, I argued back. *I think I'd know if she was evil.*

You didn't know about Melanie...

That thought slammed me into my current day, present situation. Vanessa was a client. Having a visceral reaction to hearing about her soon-to-be-ex-husband wasn't... well, it wasn't great. But I could use that anger to work harder and faster.

To get her free of him. So that I could stop feeling creepy about being attracted to her.

"How you workin' and you over here chummin' it up with your lawyer?" Sam had swung past our table and stopped to harass his niece. "Every time I look back here, you over here talkin' to him. If I didn't know better..."

Vanessa's eyes were wide. I'd never seen her get up from her seat so fast. "Uncle, stop it. I brought his order and stopped to talk about the divorce. You want me to get divorced, right?"

"Like I want my hair back." He smoothed a palm over his shiny, bald dome. "Make sure you're working and not socializing, Lil' Girl. Feelin' like you back in high school and wondering why you and your girlfriends are giggling so much if you supposed to be studying." He turned away, mumbling and shuffling back toward the front of the bar.

"I'd better get to work," she said, watching him walk away. "He's harmless but annoying. Holler if you need anything."

VANESSA

My plan to get off early and surprise Olivia and Jaclyn went off without a hitch. Lately, I'd only seen them in the morning when I dropped them off at school. On occasion, I could see them after school, between my days at Donovan and my nights at Sam's but those visits were fleeting. By the time I got home, they'd long since been in bed and Auntie was half asleep on the couch. I craved real time with my babies and, gauging from the reaction I got when I unlocked the door of the condo while the sun was still shining, so did they.

"Mommy!" Both girls came pounding down the hall in stocking feet, nearly knocking me over with long arms wound tightly around my waist. I laughed, letting my bag slide from my shoulder onto the floor and trying to kick off my shoes.

"You're home so early!"

"The sun is still out!"

"Alright, alright, girls. Hi, hello, I love you too! Can I get situated for a second, here?"

They released me long enough for me to hang my bag on its hook in the hallway and kick my shoes to the corner so they weren't in the way in the morning. Cradling one of my daughters under each arm, I walked them back into the living space where they'd been comfortably sprawled out, having just finished dinner and watching TV.

Auntie was in the kitchen, loading the dishwasher, the ever-present smile on her face. "Nice to see you so early this evening, Vanessa. I'm sure the girls will love the extra time with you."

"And I'll love the extra time with them. I've missed these little rug rats." I rubbed the tops of their heads. "Have you girls done your homework? Reviewed your reading and math assignments? Anything I need to sign?"

"Auntie makes us do our homework as soon as we get home from school," Olivia grumbled.

"And we have to do our reading and practice spelling words too," added Jaclyn.

"You know what, girls?" I looked from one to the other and started laughing. "Auntie did the same thing to me. I couldn't play until my homework and chores were done. But now you're all done and you can relax until bath time, which is in..." I leaned over to check the clock. "An hour. Go on and sit down, watch your TV show. I'm going to talk to Auntie for a minute."

They plopped back into their usual spots on the couch, right next to each other, and proceeded to chatter through whatever show they were watching.

I climbed up onto a barstool at the kitchen counter. Auntie wiped her hands on a dish towel before folding it and leaving it next to the sink. "At least I know the rules haven't changed since I was little," I said, glancing at the girls over my shoulder, then back to her.

"Consistency is key," she responded. "That, a little luck and a lot of prayer. They're good, good girls. Sweet. Positive attitudes. You've done an amazing job with them."

"I couldn't do this without you and Uncle. From the money, to watching them when I have to work—"

"Oh hush, girl. Family does for family. How are things down at Sam's?"

"Good. Better than I thought it would be. I actually look forward to going in. Uncle is pretty laid back and he has so many regulars, they already know me and I know their orders. Makes it easy."

"Mmmhmmm. I heard there's a new regular." Auntie eyed me, leaning against the counter. "And that ya'll spend a good amount of time talking."

I rolled my eyes at that. I hadn't realized Gibson frequenting the bar was a topic of conversation when I wasn't around. "He likes to work there, I guess. And since he's working on my divorce, I don't mind him coming in. I get my updates first hand."

"How's that coming? When is he going to file? And when does Warren find out? You know you need to remind the school that he's not allowed to pick the girls up or—"

"I know Auntie. I'll remind them in the morning."

I slid down from the stool and walked back toward the door to the bag I'd hung near it, retrieving the pages that Gibson had emailed me and I printed in Uncle's office. Once I was back in the kitchen, I laid the pages out on the counter. "This is the draft of my divorce petition. I'm going to look it over later, and if everything looks good, we'll file tomorrow."

My stomach lurched at those words. *We'll file tomorrow.* "I'm so nervous. I don't know what Warren is going to do or say. I know it'll be bad. I'm afraid this is all a dream and that he'll find some way to stop this."

"You know what bravery is, Vanessa?" Auntie asked, making her way around the counter to wrap a healthy arm around my waist and lean her head on my shoulder. "Bravery is being scared out of your wits, shaking in your boots, doubting what you're doing the whole way, but doing what you need to do anyway. You've *got* to. For you. For those girls. For your sanity, and your future. My goodness, Lil' Girl. You are so brave."

I patted her arm with one hand and curled the other around her face as I laid my head on top of hers. "I'm scared. But it's going to get done."

After bath time and reading time and messing around, *wasting time before bedtime*, when the girls were finally tucked into their beds and lightly snoring, I slipped into a hot shower and plugged a new pod into the aromatherapy diffuser that Sonja had given me for Christmas the previous year.

Tonight I used a scent combination called *Unwind*, since I was so on-edge. I soaped up, inhaling the essential oils and massaging them into my skin, allowing them to do their job of relaxing me and calming my thoughts.

I stepped out of the shower, toweled off, slathered myself neck to toes with Jergens lotion and slipped a long tee-shirt over my head. I poked my head into the room down the hall, smiling at the sounds of deep slumber coming from the twin beds I'd squeezed into the room. Then, I padded into the living room, intending to pick up a little and turn out lights so I could head to bed. I saw the pages of the draft on the counter and grabbed them on my way back to my bedroom.

I pulled the covers back and slid between cool sheets before slipping on my reading glasses and turning on the lamp to give the draft a good read.

The petition was straight forward. Everything had to be

spelled out to be included. "Nuances are unenforceable," Gibson had said. "If you want it, we need to include it in the petition. You're not likely to get everything you're asking for, but you'll get nothing that you don't ask for."

To that end, everything I'd asked for had been covered: in exchange for spousal support (which he was likely to contest anyway because Warren believed that independent women didn't need help from men), I'd asked for a nominal amount of support for Olivia and Jaclyn, in increasing amounts as they aged and their expenses grew. I'd also asked for a percentage of court costs and repayment of money I'd paid on credit cards that he had maxed out. I wasn't likely to be awarded much of anything except child support and a divorce decree, but even that would be great.

I leaned over and grabbed my phone from its charging dock. It was past 9 o'clock, but I knew Gibson would be awake and I didn't want to wait until morning to tell him to move forward.

Petition looks great. Everything I wanted. I know we won't get it all, but it's worth asking, right?

I hadn't expected a response, but three dots appeared on my screen as soon as I sent the text.

Gibson Kincaid: Always worth asking. I'll file in the morning. And place the ad in the AJC.

My heart galloped double time at the thought. I knew Warren would see the notice in the paper and that would start World War 3.

Could we do the ad kind of sneaky? Maybe the Sunday edition? I'd at least get the weekend to be happy.

Gibson Kincaid: Whatever you like. I can aim for Sunday. That'll be a thick one and he might not even see it.

Oh, he'll see it. I smirked, knowing Warren. He was an

online and print subscriber, and Sonja was right— he was the type to google himself. *I just want to delay it, if I can.*

Gibson Kincaid: Agreed, then. Sunday. You nervous?

Terrified. I hope I can sleep. I did some aromatherapy, though. I feel more relaxed than I did earlier.

Gibson Kincaid: I thought you left early to see your girls? You worked in a spa appointment? :)

Oh, no. Home-made spa. You hook this thing up to your shower...

I chuckled, stopping myself from over-explaining a girly shower thing to a man. *What am I talking about? You don't care.*

Gibson Kincaid: Maybe I do. You hook it up to your shower....

Gibson Kincaid: ... And...

And... it mixes essential oils with the steam and the water. It energizes or relaxes or de-stresses. You care about this?

Gibson Kincaid: If I'm honest, I have no idea what you're talking about, but you had me at shower. If it helps, I'm happy you're able to relax.

It helps. Matter of fact, I feel pretty relaxed right now.

Gibson Kincaid: So that's from the aroma thing. Or me?

I smiled, knowing this conversation was very slowly moving into an inappropriate exchange between client and attorney. But also not caring.

Probably a little of both. Though you're pretty soothing. You have a way about you...

Gibson Kincaid: A way? Is that like... feeling a way about something? Is feeling a way a bad thing?

laughing Not bad. You're good at reassuring, Keeping your promises. I guess you're good at the rescue thing.

Gibson Kincaid: Rescue? Is that what you think I'm doing? Rescuing you?

Whether you intend to or not, I feel like you're hauling me out of a burning building. I'm grateful.

Gibson Kincaid: When you're paying for my work, gratitude is not necessary. Cashier's check or credit card will do fine.

Has your mother found out about your newest client yet?

Gibson Kincaid: Uh... yeah.

And?

Gibson Kincaid: She's not happy. Let's say that.

I cringed, hoping I wouldn't see Sylvia Kincaid soon. Or ever. *Damn. I hope it's nothing irreparable...*

Gibson Kincaid: My issues with my mother didn't start with you or your case and won't end there. Don't feel bad.

Gibson Kincaid: I do things differently than she would. But I can look myself in the mirror and I can sleep at night. Makes it worth dealing with her.

Ever thought of not working for her?

Gibson Kincaid: Every day.

Gibson Kincaid: That's the goal. I'm working on it.

Gibson Kincaid: Listen, I'm still at Sam's and he's running the sweeper and mumbling about people still sitting here. Guessing he means me.

Gibson Kincaid: I'm going to pack up and head home. It's a drive out to my house and I shouldn't have sat here this late.

I'm sorry to keep you... it's late. I could have texted in the morning, I guess.

Gibson Kincaid: Don't be sorry Vanessa. You were the highlight of my night.

My face burned hot at the perceived compliment from Gibson. Did he mean it to sound that way? Probably not. But I was reading it as one. And enjoying being complimented.

Ok. Talk soon...pls let me know when you file.

Gibson Kincaid: Of course. Talk soon.

I pressed the lock button on the phone and plugged it

back into the charger, snapped off the lamp and settled back against the pile of pillows under my head. Sleep was coming for me, fast and furious.

But first, thoughts of Gibson Kincaid danced through my head. His deep, sexy voice and wide, sexy smile and muscular, sexy arms and smooth, sexy, chocolate skin and... *sex*.

Sex. Sex.Sex.Sex.Sex.

I wanted to have sex with Gibson Kincaid. Loud, filthy, delicious, liberating, satisfying sex.

The kind of sex that reminds you why people *have* sex. The kind of sex where you can't walk right afterward. And you don't give a shit.

I wanted that kind of sex. With Gibson Kincaid.

My heartbeat galloped in my chest and I could barely breathe. My imagination ran overtime with images of our bodies tangled together, glistening, panting, gasping for air, clinging to one another. I heaved a frustrated sigh and rolled over, fighting the urge to kick up a fantasy starring my divorce attorney and stroke myself to a sweaty orgasm.

I was, thankfully, exhausted, every breath bringing me closer to deep slumber, where I hoped I could at least dream about sex, because that might be the closest I got to *actual* sex with him.

Besides... he's a man with an S on his chest.

CHAPTER EIGHT

anessa

"Here you go, gentlemen. There's ketchup and hot sauce on the table."

I set the large pan of wings and giant bowl of seasoned fries that a group of college-aged guys had ordered in the center of the table and handed the serving tray off to the busboy as he passed. "I'll get refills all around too. Can I get ya'll anything else?"

"Your number, if you're handing things out, pretty." A much too young but very handsome man was trying his best to flirt with me. His skin tone was deep but his eyes were golden brown. His face bore the start of what might eventually grow into a goatee, someday.

I laughed, gathering empties and discarded straw wrappers from the table. "Zero. As in the number of chances you have with me." A tenor chorus of *"ooooohhh"* and *"cuuuur-rrrvvveee"* sounded around the table.

"You could have let me down gently, Miss," he said, his grin showing that he wasn't the least bit hurt or deterred by my deflection.

"You can't even grow hair on your face and you're trying to push up on a woman probably ten years older than you? I admire your hustle, but there was no way to gently let you know that you don't have anything I'm looking for."

My internal radar went off, and I looked up toward the front door as the table burst into claps and laughter. Gibson stepped into the bar, wiping his leather Clarks on the welcome mat and staring at his phone. He was *oh- so-casually* handsome in a dark blue polo shirt that seemed molded to his chest, his arms, his torso. Dark rinse boot cut jeans fit him like they'd been styled specifically for him. I stifled a long exhale as I realized I'd been waiting all morning for him to come in.

He glanced up as I turned to see him walk in and smiled, giving me a brief wave with the phone in his hand. He motioned that he was heading to his usual table, which I'd been keeping clear in case he happened to stop by.

"Oh, I see..."

One of the other young men at the table started, having watched my brief interaction with Gibson. "See, that's what's wrong with women today. They're not willing to work with a young brother, be in the trenches with him, build something with him. They want that money, that swagger, some of what's already been established with some corny square that walks around with a satchel over his shoulder and wears boat shoes rather than a young buck tryna make a difference in the world. See, black women today are counterfeit, in that—"

"Man, shut yo' ignorant, hotep ass up!"

I couldn't help joining his friends in clowning the young man as I left the table and made my way to the handsome man with swagger, a satchel and boat shoes. Which weren't boat shoes— young men didn't know what nice loafers looked like.

"Hey, you." I slid a thick paper coaster onto the table, as well as a napkin and a set of silverware. "Can I get anything for you?"

"Hey," he greeted me back, unpacking his bag and getting himself situated. "Some water would be great. I've been on a two-hour marathon conference call this morning and my mouth feels like cotton."

"On a Saturday? No days off, huh?"

"Very few," he responded, but with a smile. "I like it that way. Keeps me out of trouble. Speaking of... any word?"

It had been quiet. *Too* quiet. Gibson filed the divorce on Wednesday. It was Saturday, and I hadn't heard from Warren. Though he wouldn't be notified by process server, because I couldn't pin down where he lived or worked, I was still sure that someone somewhere would let him know that official documents had been filed with the courts to end our marriage.

The notice was scheduled to run Sunday in the classified ads in the Atlanta Journal Constitution:

I, VANESSA LYNN JACKSON, am serving notice through publication to WARREN KEITH JACKSON for divorce in Fulton County. WARREN KEITH JACKSON, you are hereby notified to plead to said Complaint within thirty (30) days from the publication hereof. If you fail to plead to the Complaint or file a counter Affidavit within thirty (30) days of publication, the court can enter a final decree in divorce.

The ad ended with contact information for Gibson at Kincaid Family Law Firm.

Would Warren respond? Absolutely. It was *how* he would respond that had my nerves shot. Would he show up at

Donovan? Would he come to Sam's? He knew where my Aunt and Uncle lived, what my usual haunts were. Would he wait until I thought I was safe, and then pounce?

Or would he actually let it go? Let *me* go, let our marriage end and let me move on?

"Not a peep." I leaned against the seat across from him, weary from worrying and waiting, on edge from anticipating his response... whenever it came. "He for sure doesn't know yet, because I would have heard from him. He's not the type to not respond."

Gibson seemed satisfied. "At least you've had some peace. You're working day shift today. Because of the game?"

"Yeah. Uncle figured the place would be busy." I waved my hand around the nearly full interior of the bar, most of them watching the Atlanta Braves Season Opener. "My aunt will drop the girls off later and we'll walk home. We just live a few blocks away."

"Sounds like a great day. And it'll be nice to spend some time with—"

"Order up!" Uncle bellowed, loud enough for me to hear at the back of the bar. "Let's get a move on, Vanessa!"

I inched away, giving Gibson a withering look. "I'm being rudely summoned. I'll come check on you in a min—"

"Order up, Vanessa! I'm not gon' call you again!"

"I'm coming, Uncle!" I yelled back. "If you don't stop showing out, I'ma tell Auntie on you!"

THE CROWD HAD BEGUN TO THIN OUT. THE BRAVES WON the home opener and everyone was jubilant, ordering more drinks and more food, but by late afternoon, the bar was down to its usual Saturday regulars and the familiar humdrum of activity.

I took advantage of the lull in business to wipe down tables, sweep around the bar and move chairs back to their respective areas. Gibson was still in his spot, headphones on, head bobbing to whatever music was pouring out of them, fingers flying over the Bluetooth keyboard. He made sure to keep his food and drink orders coming and tipped very, very well. Otherwise Uncle would have a lot to say about him sitting in the bar all day.

I didn't mind him coming in at all.

The thoughts I'd had about him a few nights ago hadn't exactly died down, but I wasn't panting like a Labrador in heat for him, either. He was a good looking man, about my age or a few years older, sexy, and single. He was doing a lot for me, at great personal sacrifice. *Of course* I was attracted to him. I hadn't had anything resembling sex in a year and a half, by my calculations, and I was about to be divorced. I should be attracted to *a whole lot* of men.

I thought about the young man that had hit on me earlier in the day, and wondered— if he was older, with a career... and facial hair... would I have paid him any attention? I'd *never* been attracted to *a whole lot* of men. Despite all the options that walked through the doors at Red Heels, only Warren caught my eye. And only he could hold my attention. For a while, at least.

The door to Sam's swung open so violently that it slammed against the brick front of the building, causing the entire room to shake. In the doorway, with the sun behind him, was a silhouette. A tall, wide-shouldered, foreboding silhouette.

"Warren, wha—"

He came straight for me, clutching a page from the newspaper in one hand. Once he was within a few steps, he grabbed me by the arm and yanked me toward him. He shoved the newspaper in my face and snarled, "What the fuck is this shit? Huh?"

I managed to twist out of his grip but not for long. As soon as I got a couple of steps away, he grabbed me by the shoulder and pulled me back, wrapping a thick hand around the back of my neck.

"You think you slick, don't you, bitch?" He growled in my face, inches away from me. His eyes were bloodshot, like he hadn't slept in a long while and his breath was putrid, like he'd been drinking for days on end. "I told you, I wasn't signing no fuckin' divorce papers. How you gonna put an ad in the goddamn paper talking about you divorcing me? Huh?"

"Need to let her go right now, 'less you want this wood upside your head." Distracted, Warren turned to find Uncle standing behind him, the big wooden bat he kept behind the bar in both hands and poised to strike. "Don't think I won't bust that big head wide open, Warren."

Warren chuckled, but his grip loosened. "You ain't gonna hit nobody with that bat, old man. You forget, I know you. You ain't been able to say shit to me for ten years and you ain't gon' start saying shit to me now."

Uncle lifted the bat higher and cocked it back like he was about to hit a home run. A loud, resounding "Sam, no!" stopped him.

Gibson rushed from the back of the bar and grabbed the bat. "All he has to do is file a complaint and you have a world of trouble. You don't want that." To Warren, he said, "You need to let her go. Right now, before things get worse."

Warren chuckled, the sound deep in his throat. "Worse? Who is this? Somebody's knight in shining armor?"

Gibson moved with lightning speed, landing a punch in Warren's neck, right in the windpipe. It was enough to get him to release his grip, after which Gibson grabbed me and moved me behind him.

"Vanessa, go! Sam, get her to the back, behind the bar somewhere." Sam did as he was told, wrapping his arms around me and ushering me behind the bar and into the kitchen.

Warren had recovered quickly, glaring at Gibson with narrowed eyes. "I don't know who the fuck you think you are, lil' punk, but this is between me and my wife. Need to get the fuck back and mind your own business."

"If I have to hit you again, you're either going to jail or the hospital. You need to make your way out of here while you still can."

I thought Warren was going to give up and walk out. He lowered his hands and shuffled a few steps to the door. But at the last second, he lurched forward, shoving his shoulder into Gibson, pushing him back into the bar. I heard Gibson gasp for air, but he was still standing.

And then all hell broke loose. After ordering me to stay in the kitchen, Sam and about three other men landed on Warren, trying to pull him off Gibson, who was pinned against the bar. Warren was furious, yelling and cursing at the top of his lungs. He reminded me of a rabid dog.

"You can't divorce me, whore!" He yelled, getting an arm free enough to point at me in my hiding place in the kitchen. "So you can move on to some other nigga? You so goddamn independent, I don't need to give you no fuckin' money! I told I wasn't paying you shit and I meant that. I'll see your ass in court. Let *go*!"

The small crowd fought with Warren until he'd been forced out of the door. Then the door to the bar was shut and locked while they watched him get into his Mercedes and speed away, his tires burning thick, black lines into the pavement.

The place was quiet. Eerily so, the only sound being the low murmur of the TV in the background. I poked my head around the kitchen doorway and watched activity slowly resume. A few customers righted the bar stools and tables that had been knocked over in the melee. Uncle bent over to pick up the bat that he'd threatened Warren with.

I left the kitchen and headed straight for Gibson, who was trying to catch his breath and wiping sweat from his forehead.

"Gibson, are you okay?"

"Me?" He shrugged, offering me a lopsided grin. "Oh, yeah. I'm fine. He didn't hurt me."

"Are you sure?" I reached for him, feeling around the area where Warren's shoulder had slammed into him. I was surprised to feel a firm wall of muscle under his polo shirt. "Do you need to go to the hospital? You could have internal bleeding."

Gibson grabbed my hands and squeezed them, then tipped my chin up with his index finger so he could see my face. "I'm fine. How are you? Do *you* need to go to the hospital?"

"No, no." I shook my head. "I'm okay. I'm sorry—"

"No, *I'm* sorry. I'm going to speak to my paralegal. I don't know how that notice got published today instead of tomorrow, but believe me, someone is going to pay for that mistake."

"Gibson, no. It's not worth someone losing their job."

"But tomorrow the bar would have been closed and he wouldn't have been able to find you."

We'd plotted the placing of the ad with every consideration and contingency... except that the ad would run early. Had it run the next day, it would have given him some time to cool off before I saw him. He would, for sure, call or text, but Warren didn't know where I lived, so a scene like today wouldn't have happened.

"He's a suspicious person. He was going to find it eventually. If not him, one of his friends. He was going to come find me eventually."

"I don't know where you learned that throat chop move, young man," said Uncle, back behind the bar. He pulled a beer from the cooler and offered one to Gibson. "But it was good. Almost as good as a hit with my bat would have been."

"I'm the youngest of four brothers," said Gibson, twisting the cap off his beer. He took a few long swallows before continuing. "A kid has to learn how to defend himself pretty quickly."

"Vanessa, I think you ought to go on home." Uncle said, one eye on the door. I eyed it too, like Warren might come busting through it again. "I can handle the rest of the evening; it should be quiet."

"But... Auntie was bringing the girls. And we were going to walk home."

"I'll take her home." Gibson set his beer on the bar, already headed back to his table.

"I'll call Marilyn, tell her to keep the girls with her for a while. I don't want him waitin' around, trying to follow anybody."

"Uncle, I'm fine. I don't—"

"Lil' Girl, I don't put my foot down too often, and I know you're almost thirty, but get your bag and let this young man get you home and safe. This ain't no request and I'm not gon' tell you again!"

I popped my mouth closed and moved to grab my belongings from his office and back out to the front of the bar. Gibson was waiting, satchel over his shoulder, keys in hand.

"You make sure she gets inside, doors locked, alarm on. You hear me?"

Gibson nodded and waved, then took me by the elbow and guided me to a grey Jeep Grand Cherokee parked at the curb. He opened the passenger side door and made sure I got inside, closing the door behind me.

When he got in on the driver's side, he inserted the key and turned it in the ignition. The engine purred to life, as did the navigational system and the stereo.

"Seat belt," he said, pulling his over his torso and snapping it in.

"We're going three blocks, Gibson."

"I didn't just defend your honor back there for you to die in a slow moving traffic accident. Seat belt."

I rolled my eyes but grabbed the belt and pulled it across my body, snapping it into place. "Defended my honor?"

"Something like that." He put the SUV in gear and pulled away from the curb. "Which way are we going?"

I pointed to the right and gave him directions to my condo. While he drove, I was nosy, looking around the interior of his vehicle. "This is a very nice ride. Not what I expected a lawyer to drive, though."

"Really? What do lawyers drive?"

I shrugged. "I don't know. Benz. BMW. Something not a Jeep."

He laughed. "My brothers drive Range Rovers. Is that a lawyer's ride?"

"Yeah. That's a lawyer's ride. Leather interior, wheels that spin, probably."

"Not quite that bad, but yeah. Built in TV's and stupid shit like that. Waste of money. I like this car. It suits me."

I relaxed for the few minutes it would take to get to my building. "It does, actually. It's nice. Luxury, but understated. Not flashy. Like your shoes."

"My shoes aren't flashy? Are they supposed to be?"

"Clarks aren't your average shoe. But your footwear isn't ballin' out of control or anything. Believe me, I've seen some dumb footwear. A client showed up for a house tour in some

$1300 shoes once. She had to take them off halfway through — walking around some folk's house in stocking feet."

"Thirteen— damn, I forgot you sell houses to rich people with too much money. Where do I turn in?"

I directed him to a parking spot near the resident entrance. Before he could turn the car off, I laid a hand on his arm. "You don't have to see me in. I'm fine from here."

"Did you see that bat your uncle has?" Gibson's right eyebrow lifted. "I'm not going to let him use it on *me* for the first time. He said to make sure you get inside. I'm going to make sure you get inside." He turned the key in the ignition and the engine whined to a stop. "Let's move."

I grabbed my bag and he grabbed his, and he followed... more like *escorted* me to the elevator, up to the fourth floor, to my front door. I unlocked the two deadbolts and the knob lock and as soon as the door was open, disarmed the alarm system.

"See? I'm in. Safe."

With the tips of his fingers, Gibson pushed me further inside, then walked in behind me and closed the door behind us. "You mind re-arming that?"

I punched in the code as he stepped past me, towards the living room. "Uhm, hey. First, please come right in. Second, drop those understated but expensive shoes at the door. The guy that owns this place had these floors re-done before I moved in here. I'm trying to keep them looking nice."

Gibson smirked, but kicked off his shoes and lined them up neatly next to mine. Then he slipped his bag off his shoulder and set it on the couch, a microfiber L-shaped piece that took up most of the living room.

"This is a cool place. I like the exposed brick look. You have a nice view of downtown."

He walked to the window and bent to peer out of it. I

hung my bag on its hook and dropped my keys in the bowl I kept them in on the kitchen counter.

"We like it. Took a while to get us into it and even then, we had to call in a favor, but... at least it's ours. You've seen how my Uncle is. I love him and my Aunt Marilyn, but I couldn't live with them anymore."

Gibson turned away from the window and walked toward the couch, settling into a corner and motioning for me to join him. I hesitated, but only for a second, sliding onto the couch but keeping a few inches of space between us. I tucked one leg under the other and turned so I faced him.

"He seemed a little scared for you, back there."

"Yeah. He did. But that's not the first time he's been scared for me so...." I shrugged and averted my gaze, knowing more questions were coming but not wanting to answer them.

"Has Warren ever been physical, before? Like that?"

"Not... like that."

"But he's put his hands on you before?"

My non-answer probably answered his question. I saw him tip his head toward me and my attention snapped back to him.

"You have some bruises forming, where he grabbed you," he murmured. "Not too bad so far. But it's definitely going to leave a mark."

I blew out a breath, a long one, and turned away, resting my elbows on my knees and my face in my hands. "This was my life, for years. He liked to threaten me. Grab at me, pull me around. He never touched the girls, but I was sure it was only a matter of time..."

I paused, gulping back a sob, wrestling with my emotions.

"Everything was fine until I started working. The girls were in school and I was sitting around, playing socialite all day. That definitely wasn't me. I decided to take some courses and get my real estate license. He thought it was stupid. He said I was too dumb for college, that I should depend on my looks until they run out. I finished my course, landed a job. He didn't like that. Didn't want me to have my own resources but it was... spending money. I'd use it for me or the girls. Then I got a job at Donovan Realty."

I glanced at Gibson, who was sitting next to me, listening. Watching.

"Big houses, fancy houses, million dollar homes to very important clientele. It was definitely a come up. My boss sold your mother that monstrosity of a house your parents live in. I started making serious money at Donovan, learning from my female boss, feeling smart and empowered, like I could do anything I set my mind to. Warren... wasn't into that feminist shit, he called it.

"I started to see how he treated me, how he talked to me — he had no respect for me. I was something to do, somebody to manage his house. He took longer trips, started withdrawing from us. Not only attention, but money. I wasn't paying attention. I woke up one day and he was gone and the house was being taken and my credit cards were cut off. I had no gas in my car a few thousand in the bank. Thank God I had the good sense to open my own account, or he'd have cleaned that out, too."

I felt Gibson closing the space between us, then laying a hand on my back. The adrenaline rush and the subsequent shock was wearing off. In its place was fear. And exhaustion. I felt my body begin to tremble, a sensation I couldn't control, no matter how hard I clenched my fists and squared my shoulders.

"I knew something would happen. I thought I was ready, but... Gibson, I was terrified."

"It's okay," I heard, a whisper in my ear. His arm slid

across my shoulder and cradled me close to his body. "He didn't hurt you. You're safe. It's okay."

"I knew... I knew..." I tried to say, through sobs that wracked my body. "I knew I couldn't get away from him. He'll never let me go."

I collapsed against him, out of energy. Out of words. Out of stoic strength and positivity.

GIBSON

Never let her go? I twitched and clenched my jaw. First in anger, then in the effort to not to show my anger to Vanessa.

"Let me make something clear to you. I know what I'm doing, and I'm good at it. I've got something for everything he thinks he can throw at us. I will not stop until you're away from him for good."

But Vanessa was shaking her head, wagging side to side. "He's just going to keep coming and coming. He'll keep at it until I'm out of money and I can't fight anymore."

I tipped her chin up, so she could see me. So I could see her. "I don't think you heard me, Vanessa. It's not a matter of money. I made a promise to you and I'm going to keep it."

"Bu—"

I blocked her lips with my thumb, so she couldn't say what I knew she was trying to say, what she said all the time. She wanted to make sure I knew she couldn't afford an expensive divorce. And I did know that.

But it had no bearing on the service I wanted to provide to her. I wanted Vanessa to be divorced. For her. And for me.

Admitting that to myself was more difficult than it should have been. It meant, a little bit, that my mother had been right. From the moment I met her at Kincaid, my *manhood* had been dictating how hard I would work on Vanessa's divorce.

She hiccuped, which seemed to bring her to some level of stability. She glanced around at the room that was darkening in the approaching sunset, then got up from the couch and headed down the hall. I heard a door close and the faucet run, heard her blow her nose and then... nothing. For a few... *long* moments, I heard nothing.

"Vanessa? Are you okay, back there?"

Vanessa appeared around the corner, stopping to lean against the wall. She was still in her clothes from working at Sam's— a white button up blouse and black pants.

"I'm fine. Just embarrassed."

"About?" I sat forward, resting my elbows on my knees, clasping my hands together.

"Where do I start? About my life blowing up in front you. About Warren's behavior. About not knowing enough, when I met him, that this would be my life, ten years later. You must think I belong on one of those dramatic ass shows they have about women who have nothing going on but drama."

I laughed. "One of my brothers is addicted to *Love and Hip Hop*. I have to hear the update every week. I don't think you belong on any of those shows. Besides..."

I loosened my fingers and spread my hands wide. "I'm an attorney. In a family of attorneys. And my father is a judge. I could tell you some stories that would make today seem like a day at the park."

She laughed, halfway covering her face with a hand. "Really? Like... like what? I need to be consoled."

"Come sit," I said, patting the sofa cushion next to me. "And I'll tell you some. You'll feel normal in no time."

"Uhm... okay..." She backed up a few steps, angling her thumb back down the hallway. "I want to change really quick. I smell like Sam's, and..."

"Take your time." I started to sit back against the couch, but thought I would ask. "Unless you'd like for me to go?"

"No," she answered, quickly. "Please don't leave me alone. Not yet. I'm... I'll be right back."

She whirled around and rushed back down the hall. When I heard the shower come on, I relaxed, sinking into the couch, then reached for one of the remotes on the coffee table in front of me. I pointed it at the small TV on a stand across the room and scrolled through a few channels, most of them snow.

A purple remote sat next to where the original remote had been placed. I grabbed it, switching to the HDMI menu. It didn't seem hard to navigate the screens and programs. She was logged into Netflix and the kid's channels popped right up.

"Oh, we don't have cable. Enough to watch the news. I'm sure you figured that out."

I hadn't heard Vanessa come back down the hall. She had put her hair up in a high ponytail, scrubbed her face and donned a long Falcons t-shirt and black leggings. She sat down next to me on the couch. I caught a hint of vanilla as she scooted back and got comfortable.

"Somebody at work told me about that Roku thing, though. I got it for the girls. If they want to watch something on cable, we go to Auntie and Uncle's."

"I have a thousand cable channels," I admitted, sliding the remotes back onto the table. "And nothing good is ever on. I only watch baseball, the occasional home improvement show here and there. I don't know why I have so many."

"We were the same way. It was crazy, what we were paying to watch a couple of channels. Not only that but satellite radio, random subscriptions. I had to let it all go, but this little thing and Netflix helps me make sure the girls don't feel deprived."

"I'm sure they don't feel deprived."

She shrugged. "I do my best, but kids can be cruel and I

just don't want them singled out because they look... you know. Like they don't have much. It's been a long time since I could buy them a name brand they recognize."

"Is that them?" A silver frame on the end table held a photo of two medium toned little girls with ponytails, big smiles and their arms around each other. They both wore t-shirts, jeans and sneakers.

"Yeah." Vanessa beamed. "Those are my girls."

"They look happy. Looks like they have a lot, actually. You're doing a good job, from over here."

Her eyelids lowered a little. She fidgeted with a loose thread at the hem of her t-shirt. "Thanks. I'm hard on myself. About everything."

"Who isn't?"

She tipped her head up, her eyes wide and questioning, unbelieving. "What do you have to be hard on yourself about?"

"Did I mention I come from a family of lawyers? Over-achieving, one-upping lawyers? Sharks, if you will?" I laughed when she laughed. "Some days I question everything I do, everything I want to do. I keep hoping I'm doing the right thing, and that my family will see that. I especially hope that my clients see it, otherwise I'm wasting my time. Got my mother mad at me for nothing."

"As the only one of your clients in the room, I assure you that I see it."

"Yeah?"

"And I'm sure your other clients see it too. Sylvia wouldn't have punched Warren in the throat."

"Actually..." I laughed, loudly at the mental image of my mother doing just that. "If you get Sylvia Kincaid mad enough, she'll do a lot of things you wouldn't imagine she would."

"Sounds like more stories I need to hear. But, for the record, it was pretty sexy that you did that."

I turned my head toward her, hyper aware of how close our bodies were. I felt her body heat, smelled her shower gel — or her aromatherapy oil— and saw a spark of something in her dark eyes when I looked into them. Something I thought I had seen before, but I'd written it off.

Tonight... it was definitely there.

CHAPTER NINE

*G*ibson

SHE MUMBLED SOMETHING BUT IT WAS LOST IN THE CRUSH of our mouths together as I leaned into her. I pressed my lips to hers, firmly so she knew I definitely wanted this... but gently so she didn't think I was forcing myself on her. She responded, pressing back, then tilting her head and opening her mouth.

The first brush of her tongue against mine took my breath away. I braced myself to stay under control, but the longer we kissed, the more effort it took to stop myself from throwing her back onto the couch and pouncing on top of her.

The kiss deepened, with her tongue doing as much swirling and sucking as mine was. Vanessa groaned a sound that sent my body a *strong* message. I was straining against my jeans, a sensation that wasn't painful but it wasn't comfortable, either.

But I had no plans to stop. I'd been fighting my attraction to Vanessa for weeks, hiding it under professionalism and integrity. Whatever was happening between us wasn't giving into an off-hand, sudden desire. It had been smoldering, smoking just under the surface since we'd met.

Vanessa lifted a hand to my face and cupped my chin, her thumb stroking my cheek as the kiss slowed, then ended. When our lips parted, she didn't move away, but she kept her eyes closed. Her shoulders dropped and she let out a soft sigh.

And then she opened her eyes. I didn't know what I expected to see in them, but I searched them anyway for any hint of how I was supposed to react. She was a client— was *currently* a client. Her angry almost ex-husband had, a few hours ago, tried to attack her. I was supposed to be making sure she got home safe, but was somehow on her couch, kissing her.

"Gibson. I don't know what to say..."

"What's there to say? Haven't you ever kissed your divorce lawyer in your living room?" She laughed, which I took as a good sign. "Seriously, before you start apologizing and ruining the moment... don't. I enjoyed it."

"I don't want you to think that—"

I moved quickly to place a finger over her lips. "What did I say? I don't think anything. Except that you're really good at that."

"You too." She chewed on the corner of her bottom lip as she smiled. "I uh... enjoyed it too."

"Good. So we're two consenting adults enjoying something."

"Why do I get the feeling you're trying to convince yourself of that?"

"Because I am. I—"

"Nuh uh." She pressed a finger against my lips, then. "You don't get to ruin it, either."

"You're right. So—"

I was interrupted by a shrill ring. I started to tell her to ignore it, because we were on the edge of something, but I remembered what had happened earlier in the day and that her children weren't home yet. So while Vanessa went in search of the phone, I reigned myself in. Something could happen... but I needed to be okay with nothing happening too.

"Hey, Auntie! How are the girls? Oh, good. Watching what? No, don't let Uncle scare you... I'm fine, a little shaken up is all..." Her voice faded, then disappeared as she took the phone down the hall.

I needed to stretch my legs and return some circulation to other parts of my body, so I stood and returned to the window I'd stood at earlier. I leaned onto the windowsill and gazed out at the scene. It was a bustling Saturday night in downtown Decatur. People were on the street, walking from store to store, building to building, talking and laughing. The sun was almost gone, dipping below the horizon, coating everything with a pinkish rosy glow. It wasn't anything like the sunsets I saw out at the lake from the dock, but the picture was postcard beautiful.

"My Aunt and Uncle are going to keep the girls until the morning," Vanessa said, walking past the living room to the kitchen. She slid the phone into a charging stand and made sure it was powered up. "They've eaten and they're watching a movie and Auntie is tired and..."

She exhaled, hands on her hips, then moved around the room to snap on a few lamps, dousing the room in light. "Uncle is afraid that Warren will wait to see if I show up to pick them up. Or if Auntie will leave to bring them home. They want me to stay put for a while."

"So you're stuck with me, then."

"More like you're stuck with me. If you don't mind, that is. I totally understand if you have to go—"

"I don't have to go anywhere, Vanessa. I'm staying right here. How about some dinner?"

"So this hotel sued their insurance company for not paying damage claims after a storm. The attorneys didn't get along— had *never* gotten along, and couldn't agree on the simplest of things, like where to meet for a witness deposition. So they wanted the court to intervene to decide for them."

Vanessa's jaw dropped in disbelief. A forkful of the chicken, black bean and rice bowl she was eating was frozen halfway between the plastic container and her mouth. "They wanted to use the legal system to decide that?"

I nodded, shoveling a Korean chicken taco into my mouth. My manners went out the door long ago, before it had taken a half hour to decide what kind of food we were going to order, and then what restaurant we were going to order from. And another ten minutes to work out the delivery details. Vanessa was wary about giving out her address, so she never ordered in. I didn't want to leave her to pick it up, so I'd met the delivery driver on the street when he arrived with our food— forty-five minutes later.

"As you can imagine, Judge wasn't amused. He issued a ruling that they either decide on their own, or meet on the courthouse steps in five days for a game of... wait for it..." I chuckled, before revealing the rest. "Rock, paper, scissors."

"Shut up, Gibson."

"I'm not joking. And neither was he. But neither attorney wanted to show up at the courthouse steps so Judge Kincaid could administer a kid's game, so they got their shit together. The funniest part was that Judge issued a legal ruling. Neither wanted to be in contempt of court, so had to file a motion to call the game off."

"Oh, I hope he made them sweat."

"He took a full day to grant the motion. They both thought they had to show up and play rock, paper, scissors while Judge mediated."

She laughed, tossing her head back and cackling into the air. "Okay, I'll admit that's funny. And petty."

"Yeah, Judge likes telling that one. He's got a hundred of them, from his days working up the ranks of circuit court. If you start messing with people's money, they get petty."

"Mmm," she mused, chewing a mouthful before swallowing. "A woman I used to work with just got a divorce. They fought over the stupidest things. Bath mats? Candlesticks?"

"Those are the kinds of divorces I don't like working on. I feel like an overpaid referee. Mother loves them. The longer they argue, the more she bills. The more money there is to fight over, the larger her fee."

"Seems like...." Vanessa paused, pressing her lips together in thought before continuing. "I don't want to shade your family's business and your job or whatever..."

I chuckled while working a piece of chicken from between my teeth. "Go right ahead. I do it all the time."

"It seems like they're in it for the money. Yeah, you can make a lot of money as an attorney. I can make a lot of money as a realtor. But shouldn't the basic desire be to help people? To like..."

"Guide them through our convoluted justice system? Find a couple or a family that perfect house?" I nodded. "Yeah. It *should* be."

I fished out the last morsel of spicy chicken and slid the empty container on the coffee table, then washed that last bite of dinner down with a swig of cola. I stifled a belch and gave my full, round belly a pat.

"That was a first for me, Asian-Mexican fusion. It was good."

"Mmmhmm," Vanessa agreed, scraping the last grains of rice from the bottom of the bowl and setting her empty container inside mine. "Though, I think you were really hungry. You inhaled four tacos in no time."

"That too."

"The owner is a friend of Maxine's. He opened up a few months ago and we can't get enough."

"You think he'll let me occupy a table at TaKorea every night?"

"Probably not. And I'm not saying that because I want that tip you leave every night. Which, I meant to tell you, is way too generous."

"No, it's not."

"Gibson," she chided, but quietly so, rolling her eyes up to mine. "Thanks. For... the tips. And for today. And for making sure I got home okay. And for staying here with me."

"You feeling safe is thanks enough for me. Do you feel safe?"

It took her awhile to answer, but when she did, with her eyes rolled up to mine, with her sitting so close, almost right up against me, with her tone so low it was almost a whisper, I knew we were talking about more than seeing her home.

"I feel... more than safe."

VANESSA

I could already hear Sonja's hoarse, brash voice in my ear about not listening to her. Again. About not giving in to being vulnerable and lonely. And horny. About not falling for a man with an "S" on his chest. About not sleeping with my divorce attorney.

It was that... well, I couldn't help it. For all the pep talks I'd given myself to ignore those feelings, that magnetism, that longing— yes *longing* for Gibson, I didn't care. All the reasons I *shouldn't* ran down the drain when I slipped into the shower, then changed into something I knew I looked casually sexy in. All the reasons I *couldn't* flew out of my head when I insisted he stay, even though I felt fine.

And when he was more than eager to play hero and appease me.

One of the skills I learned on the stage was how to read cues. It was one of those things that wasn't taught— you had it or you didn't. You could cultivate it, but it was nearly impossible to instruct someone in picking up body language. It was how I knew a client was ready to sign an offer on a house, or was ready to agree on a price and put their house up for sale.

It was also how I knew I had a man in my clutches and I could get almost anything I asked for— drinks even though I was underage, money, gifts... at least while he was under my spell.

Gibson was under my spell. And I wasn't even *trying*.

It was in the heavily lidded, glossy eyes when he looked at me. It was the hunger in those eyes, the Adam's apple bobbing as he swallowed over and over, the slightly quickened breathing. It was the depths to which his tone dipped when conversation meandered into anything intimate and personal I called it his Quiet Storm voice.

And the growing lump in his jeans.

I heaved a long sigh and leaned into the couch cushions, hooking one leg over his. His thigh muscles tightened; I clenched at the sensation of a rock hard muscle under my leg. I gripped his forearm and laughed when he flexed.

"Stop showing off. I get it, you work out."

He smiled and stopped flexing. "I don't... well, I don't traditionally work out. Not at a gym. I find things I like to do and call that exercise."

"So what do you like to do that gives you arms like..." I worked my fingertips against the taut muscle of his arm. "...these? And legs like those?"

"I'll tell you but you have to promise not to laugh."

"What would be funny about how you exercise?"

"You never know what people find funny. Promise you won't laugh."

"Fine. I promise not to laugh. Share with me, Gibson."

"Well... I live pretty far north of town, on a few acres of land, on a lake. I do a lot of swimming, kayaking, stand up paddling. You know... water sports."

"Okay. I'm not tempted to laugh yet."

"And uh..." He moved so he could pull his phone from his pocket. "Well, I'll show you."

He unlocked his phone and scrolled to an app, then clicked on the latest photo and handed me the phone. The photo was of a gorgeous, vibrant, colorful garden full of different kinds of flowers. "This is the bulk of my exercise. Planting, weeding, playing around in the dirt, getting it ready for the next season. I grow flowers. Dahlias, actually. A few other varieties but the dahlias are the prize winners. And then..."

He scrolled quite a few photos backward to another of him, standing inside a canopy covered garden bed. He wore a floppy straw hat, a sleeveless tee-shirt that was covered in dirt but showed off a whole arm of muscles, and cut off sweats that were...well, they fit him. Behind him were rows and rows of vegetables.

"You grow all of this?"

He grinned. "Summers are poppin' at my house. Fresh flowers and vegetables from April to about October. I'm thinking I might do strawberries this year. I haven't grown them before."

"Fresh strawberries from the garden," I swooned, scrolling through his Instagram feed, feeling myself being drawn in deeper and deeper with this man. Not only was he a distractingly handsome, incredibly sexy goody two shoes lawyer, but apparently, he also had the green thumb to end all green thumbs.

"Well, it's no wonder you had to learn how to punch a guy in the neck," I joked, looking through more pictures of fresh cucumber, greens, tomatoes, peppers, not to mention the roses and lilac.

"I do take a lot of shit, especially from my brothers. But it's worth it when I'm out on the patio and I smell a breeze wafting over from the garden. Although most of the time it's overpowered by whatever I have on the grill."

"Wow, Gibson. I want to say I would have never imagined, but... it fits you. It's very... Zen. It must be nice to have Zen."

"You should come out sometime, get your Zen on. You'd love it. The girls would have a lot of room to run around and play."

"I'm going to put that invite in my pocket. Don't be surprised if I take you up on it."

"I won't," he said quietly. "I'd love to have you. Out to the house, I mean."

I'd love you to have me. And I'm not talking about the house.

I handed his phone back to him. He set it on the coffee table next to the couch. "I kind of... feel like we're dancing around something that we should talk about. I'm not trying to ruin the moment. I'm actually going for the opposite."

Gibson shifted on the couch so that he was facing me. He seemed relaxed, and more than that, relieved that I was bringing the discussion back to our first real intimate moment together. "I was trying to follow your lead on that, but I'm all the way open to talking about it."

"Good. Me too. I mean, we're adults, right? We should be able to talk about these things."

"Right. And not just about the kiss from earlier. We should talk about how I've wanted you since I met you that day at Kincaid. How I decided that I wanted to know you and I hoped you would call. But that even if you didn't, I was going to take your file from my mother's office and look up your phone number."

I laughed, dipping my head in mock shyness. "That's not ethical, counselor."

Gibson laid his arm across the back of the couch, his fingers pulling gently at the tendrils of hair that hung from my pony tail. It brought thoughts and a longing for him to bury both of those big hands in my hair.

"I didn't care. Still don't. I hang out in a bar every night so I can see you. I'm pretty sure your Uncle thinks I distract you while you're working. And he's right. I mean... could it be more obvious that I want you?"

"My Aunt mentioned something the other night about that. But you hadn't made a move, so..."

"What would it look like for me to sign you up and then ask you out? If nothing, it's given me a reason to make sure I get this case closed for you."

"And I have a violent husband who's very interested in making sure that doesn't happen."

Using his thumb, he tipped my chin up so I was looking straight at him. His eyes were so dark but so emotional. I was comforted and felt more at ease knowing I was more than some proceedings to him. My case mattered to him.

"I'm not worried about Warren. But you are, so I'm taking that seriously. I'm trying to move slowly... the last thing I want is to take advantage of you."

So then...I jumped him.

I couldn't take it anymore. There was only so much good natured, fine upstanding man I could deal with at one time. He was saying very pretty words in a deliciously sensual tone and he was so close I could feel his pulse and smell his cologne and touch his body and imagine it being wrapped around me.

So I jumped him.

I cut off his well-meaning trail of excuses as to why he hadn't made a move with a press of my lips to his. I sat up, rising to my knees and moved so I was straddling his lap. His hands gripped my waist and pulled me close against him while he shifted on the couch to give my legs a little room. I felt him, both the heat and the length, press into me. My natural reaction was to grind my hips into him, but I was quickly frustrated by the layers of fabric between us.

I pulled my lips from his and dismounted, a movement that confused him until he realized what I was doing. I laid back on the couch, pulling him with me. He eased himself down and settled his body between my open legs before dipping back to my mouth for another kiss.

"That day," he muttered between swipes of his tongue across mine. "When you came to Sam's with the red lipstick. I wanted to kiss you. Actually there were a couple of things I wanted you to do with those lips, but mostly I wanted to kiss you."

I giggled, but mostly at the way his lips tickled my skin as they trailed across my cheek and down my neck. "The way you stuttered and stared, I thought you might not have seen a woman in lipstick before."

"Women, yes. You... you're not *women*. You're not some

random person I know." His lips gingerly closed around my earlobe. The sensation sent shocks through me.

Gibson pulled back, searching my face. "You alright?"

I lifted my hands to him, cradling his chin, and pulled his mouth down to mine. "I'm more than alright." While we kissed, my fingers went walking— across his shoulders, down his arms, to the band of his jeans.

He shifted so I could get a hand between us. I gripped him through his jeans, almost moaning out loud at the feel of him in my hands, his girth as my palm wrapped around him. I popped the button fly and unzipped him, rubbing the backs of my fingers against the soft cotton he wore under his jeans. I could tell by the thin fabric that they were boxers, so I felt around until I found the opening.

Gibson let out a grunt as I explored his body inside his boxers, then wrapped my hand around him. His dick was warm and rigid, standing at attention as much as it could while confined to cotton underpants.

I stroked him, using long, languid, rhythmic passes up and down. Gibson's breath was hot on my neck, his teeth taking scintillating little bites of my skin. His hips began to move, matching the rhythm of my movements. I gripped him tighter, letting his hips do the work of pumping his dick into my palm. He sped up, uttering a groan. He was getting harder— and hotter. The view of him thrusting between my legs but not actually inside me was driving me crazy.

As if he could read my mind, Gibson sat up slightly and moved a hand between us, inching it up my thigh and over my mound. When his fingers grazed my clit, it set off a chain reaction— my nipples rose, the hard buds poking through the shirt I was wearing and my pussy gushed. My hips rocked up off the couch, as if my body was seeking contact with his.

"Mmmm," he groaned, watching my body move in

response to his fingers as he swiped across my clit again and again. "You like that."

I could only nod and mumble *unh huh* as he stroked and rubbed and teased me through my leggings. When I felt like I couldn't take the pressure anymore, I moved his hand away and pulled at the waistband, pushing the leggings down my hips until I could kick them off.

Gibson's hands returned, though this time he wasn't obstructed by fabric. I hadn't been wearing panties under my leggings, so my body— the lower half of me, was on display. He glanced down at me, his mouth open, then licked his lips.

I knew the feeling. I still had his dick in my hand, holding on for dear life.

His head lowered to kiss me, his mouth pulling at my lips, sucking my tongue, while his fingers rubbed and stroked me. A long, thick finger slipped inside me while his thumb rubbed my clit in circles. I arched, tossing my head back.

"Shit!" I almost screamed, wrapping my free arm around his shoulder and pulling him close to me. My hips responded, thrusting to try to take him deeper.

"That feels good! Don't stop!"

"Sorry, I have to," he said, as he did just that. I missed the feeling of him inside me almost immediately. "I feel like you might come sooner than I anticipated and I want to be inside you when you do."

"Please say you have a condom, Gib. Please."

He laughed, sitting up and reaching for his back pocket. He pulled out his wallet and slipped two thin packets from a pocket. "I have two. Not... that I thought this was going to happen. I like to be prepared."

"In case this happened," I said, taking one of the packets from him and ripping it open. I tossed the wrapper on the table and waited for him to pull off his jeans and boxers and settle between my legs again before handing him the condom.

He rolled it on as I watched, covering his long, gently curved, thick dick with the almost opaque latex.

Even with the condom on, I couldn't stop looking at him. I reached for him, letting my fingers glide across the surface, then close around him. I positioned myself, legs open wide, hips tilted up, and guided him to me. I felt him push past initial resistance and then sink into me with one stroke. The feeling was.... *oh my God*. I was full of him, my legs wrapped around him, his weight on top of me and I was in lusty, glorious sex heaven. Gibson must have agreed, because I felt him let out a long groan. I rolled my hips, grinding my clit up against his pubic bone, which made my pussy clench and seemed to wake him up.

His hips began to move, working in short strokes, then longer and more forceful strokes until he was mercilessly pounding, pausing every so often to sink deep into me and grind against my clit.

"Goddamn," he panted.

"Mmmph!" I whimpered, rolling my t-shirt up to reveal my bare breasts. I played with them, bouncing them in my palms and flicking my nipples while he pumped into me, hard and fast.

"Are you close? I'm coming with you."

"*Yessss*," I hissed, just as my back arched and my thighs began to shake. Gibson plunged deep, winding a hand between us to stroke my clit while I bucked my hips against his body. My whole body clenched and I wrapped myself— legs and arms— around him as I came, grunting his name into his ear with every jerk of my hips.

When it was over, my legs fell open and my arms around him loosened. Gibson pulled out, then moved down the couch and took my clit into his mouth. I was still so sensitive it was almost painful, but he was gentle with his strokes, teasing me with the tip of his tongue until I grabbed his head and pressed him into me, rocking my hips into his face while flicking a nipple with my thumb.

I grunted so hard it made my throat hurt, so loud I thought my neighbors might come knocking any second. Gibson moaned, rolling his eyes up to mine. He smiled, remnants of me all over his face. "Fuck, right there," I cried out, my body shaking with the beginnings of another orgasm. He took me into his mouth and sucked and licked *and sucked* me until I was spent, then collapsed back onto the couch, weak and lightheaded.

I couldn't move. Not a single limb.

And didn't want to.

Gibson moved up my body again, dropping kisses from my mound to my breasts, taking each nipple into his mouth and flicking his tongue over it before settling gently on top of me. He kissed the dip in my throat, nibbled a little at my neck, then dropped his lips to mine. It was all I could do to open my mouth to receive his tongue and the slow, heady kiss he gave me.

"Holy shit," I sighed, when I could. "It's been a long time for me, but… that was some damn good fucking, Gibson."

He laughed, the sound coming to my ears but the vibration bouncing through his chest to mine. "I have a feeling it was damn good fucking *because* it's been a long time for me too."

"I need about twenty minutes to recover and then I'm down for more."

CHAPTER TEN

anessa

"So you lost both your parents when you were young? That had to hit hard."

"Mmm..." I moved in his arms, making sure we were still skin to skin, plastered together on the couch. "My father died when I was two or three. He was never around much. My mom died when I was nine. Overdose."

"You don't have to talk about it if you don't want to. I was asking questions, getting to know you."

I smiled, reassuring him with a kiss. "It was a long time ago. I've lived my whole life, pretty much, without them. My parents were both heavy into drugs. I mostly stayed with Auntie and Uncle anyway. When she died, it made it official."

"But still, nine is pretty young to lose a parent. You had to know what was going on, even if you didn't understand."

"I knew." I sighed, resting my forehead on his chest. "And I understood. It didn't make it any easier to deal with. It didn't make *me* any easier to deal with. I gave my Aunt and Uncle a hard time. It got worse when I found out Auntie had taken out an insurance policy on my mom."

That was the one secret Auntie and Uncle kept from me. I found the paperwork on accident, while looking through some documents. The policy and the copy of the check that was sent as payout were clipped together and shoved into the back of a drawer.

I threw a fit. We had lived lean for all those years, Auntie and Uncle acting like they didn't have much money and me feeling like it was my fault they were poor, when all the while they'd had this money stashed away. This money that they made off my mother's death.

Little did I know, they'd been saving it for me.

When I turned eighteen, the account was turned over to me. And I lost my fucking mind. It wasn't much, but my fool ass had never had much. I thought I was rich.

Shoes, clothes, makeup, jewelry, everything I ever said I wanted, and Auntie said, "oh, that's so wasteful, Vanessa" or Uncle said, "Ain't no need in buying that", I bought it. I'd lived a whole life without name brands, without being able to take trips with my friends, without having spending money. While I had the money, I was living it up.

Auntie and Uncle were uncomfortable with my spending habits. That money was meant to stretch, to help support me through my college years, they'd said. I informed them that I wasn't *planning* to go to college. It had never been my life's dream and I was never known as a smart girl. They said they wouldn't force me to go, but I had to get a job or move out of the house.

So I got a job. Dancing at Red Heels.

"My aunt and uncle are all I've ever really known, in the way of parents. I treated them like shit when I was a teenager. And beyond. I met Warren pretty young; we dated off and on before I got pregnant with Olivia. We got married and moved to an upper crust area of town and I acted like I was too good for them. Until I needed them."

"If it's any consolation, I'm not a shining example of parental treatment myself."

"You?" I tipped my head up to look at him, brushing my lips against his chin. I expected his goatee to be wiry but it was soft as a down blanket. He could rub that up against my body any old time he wanted.

"That's the second time tonight that you've been incredulous that I'm a human being." He bent his head to meet my lips in a kiss. When he pulled back, he smiled. "I might need to scale back my community lawyer act."

"I think you're too far gone. But tell me your wild stories about growing up with Sylvia Kincaid as a mother."

"She's not as *Mommy Dearest* as you'd imagine. She's definitely the boss and not loving and caring by any means. She's the type to send the nanny to come give you a hug because you look sad. Or have the cook make your favorite dinner when you bring home straight A's. I think my brothers got stuck in the rut of trying to please her. And they're still stuck there."

"But you're... let me guess... *different*."

"I didn't used to be. But I was in high school, a star rugby player while pulling straight A's and she still found things to complain about. I was never going to make her happy. So I stopped trying."

"Which probably drives her crazy. Sylvia seems the type to demand compliance, or else."

He nodded, his head bobbing in agreement. "She tries to control me, to pull me back in. The harder she tries, the more I rebel. It's almost a game now. I try to see how mad I can make her. How many shades of purple she can turn before she gives up."

"So am I a pawn in that game?"

He didn't answer. Not verbally, anyway. A dip of his head to one side gave me the answer I was looking for.

"I took your case to help you. I'd never waste your time or your money to spite my mother."

"But—"

"But... taking your case is part of my overall plan to get her to let me leave the firm with the money and support she promised me. Not just your case, though. There are a lot of cases that are part of that plan. And more that will be."

"Hmmmmm," I mused, quietly. I wasn't sure how I felt about that, about being used as part of an overall plot. But I was getting divorced. For cheap.

"Tonight had nothing to do with your case or my beef with my mother. Tonight had everything to do with me thinking about spending time with you and not being able to get you off my mind. Tonight was all about me. And you."

"I'm so relieved to know that fucking me on my couch had nothing to do with your mother." I giggled when he dug his thumb into my skin, right under my rib cage.

"So... what was tonight about, for you?"

Great question. What *was* it about? Relieving stress after a long and heinous day? Forgetting Warren, leaving him behind? *Replacing* him?

Or getting some dick, having an orgasm and trying not to fall for Superman?

I pushed myself up, almost sad to pull away from muscular arms and warm skin and the way his voice sounded so deliciously deep when I was listening to him talk with my ear against his chest. "For me, tonight was about..."

I twisted around so I faced him, then lifted a leg over his body so I was straddling him. The boxers that he'd put back on were bulging again, his length clearly outlined in the light blue fabric.

"Pure unadulterated fun. And maybe I'm still a little rebellious. I shouldn't have, but I couldn't stop thinking about having sex with you. I got the feeling you felt the same."

Gibson chuckled, digging his fingers into generous hips. "You got that feeling, huh?"

"Mmmhmmm."

I bent to kiss him, but he sat up halfway to meet my lips. When we parted, he said, "Any chance we can not do this on the couch, this time? I need a lot more room to work. And so do you."

He didn't need to say another word. I hopped off his lap and helped to pull him up. I bent to grab the second condom and felt him hardening against my ass as he pressed himself into me. His hands smoothed across my skin until they were full of my breasts. I felt his lips nibbling my earlobe and the sensation drove me wild, sending sparks down my back.

We inched down the hall toward my bedroom, collapsing together onto the queen size bed. He laid next to me, then leaned over me, capturing my mouth in a deep, slow kiss. I whimpered as I felt his thumb on my nipples, then felt his hand move south, parting my legs so he could touch me.

"Damn, you get so wet," he mumbled, his finger massaging my pussy lips and then rubbing my clit in a circular motion with enough pressure to make my hips buck against it.

I writhed under his touch, loving the taste of him in my mouth, the last bits of cologne scent on his skin. He pulled back from another kiss and gazed down at me, all the while his fingers doing their own magic on my clit.

"This okay with you?" He asked.

I pretended to ponder for a quick moment, then shook my head. "Nope. Something I need to do."

"Something you need to— oh...." I sat up, then rolled him

into his back, scooting down the bed until I was eye to... well, dick. I'd been thinking about having him in my mouth for weeks and now I could.

He laid back as I took him in, licking around the head first before sliding him deep into my mouth and bringing him back out, then doing it again. And again. Faster, while gripping the base of his shaft and humming sounds that I hoped he knew meant I was having a good time. His hips moved in time with the bobbing of my head, his hands buried in my hair and short breaths coming from his mouth.

His dick pulsed, a sign that he was close. He sat up, pulling me off of him, then gripped my hips and moved me so I straddled him. He grabbed the condom, ripped it open and rolled it on while I watched, again.

"I could watch that all day, you know."

"That could be arranged. I need a lot more condoms."

As soon as he was sheathed, I rose onto my knees and waited for him to point himself in the right direction. And then I sank onto him, breathing the most pleasured sigh I think I've ever let fall out of my mouth. He felt *so good*. Different than I was used to.

Which was *good*.

I worked myself up and down, grinding my hips against him until he was buried to the hilt. "I think I'm gonna enjoy this."

Gibson smiled, one of those smoldering, sexy smiles to let me know he was thinking the same thing. He gripped me, thrusting up as I rolled my hips.

"*Motherfuhhh*... this feels amazing."

"Good, baby. Take your time."

I hissed, feeling his thumb working my clit. "I'll take my time next time. Right now I want to fuck you until I can't walk tomorrow."

GIBSON

This is the last time I do a favor for Greggory.

I stifled a yawn and doodled in the margins of my notepad. I was sitting in on a mediation session while Gregg was in court. It had been the most boring four hours of my miserable life. I eyed the clock, inhaling deeply and sitting up in my chair so I could try to stay awake for the last fifteen minutes.

"I was afraid he'd never let me see them. So I broke into the house and took them," Gregg's client said, her voice warbling. She sniffled, then dabbed dry eyes with a hand-kerchief.

"Okay, Paul, can you understand that? That's why Roxy took the dogs and hid them away, because she was afraid you'd never let her see them?" The mediator, a middle-aged woman with mousy brown, dull hair that fell past her shoulders had a low, soothing tone that might have been great for the session, but was a little *too* soothing for me.

It didn't help that I hadn't had much sleep lately.

Vanessa and I were seeing quite a bit of each other, though it was piecemeal, whenever we could steal a minute. I was still working out of Sam's, especially since Warren seemed to be filing briefs daily against the petition for divorce. Every motion, no matter how ridiculous, required a response. For a man on the verge of bankruptcy, he was doing a lot.

We tried to act normal, but it was hard. The looks, even the fleeting ones, sent my brain into sexually charged over-drive. The random touches, the whispered comments as she walked by, the phone calls every night— they all had me chasing her for any sliver of free time.

Every few days, Vanessa would make an excuse to her Aunt about keeping the girls at her house. She'd finish up her shift at Sam's and head home. A few minutes later, as normal, I'd pack up and head out.

But instead of going home, I'd go to Vanessa's. We had an hour... two at the most, but we put that time to good, sweaty use.

Tonight, she'd taken the evening off. Sam had turned the bar over to his assistant manager and he, Marilyn and Vanessa took the girls to dinner and one of those kid's movies they'd been begging to see. I'd pulled a promise from her that she would give me a little extra time later in the weekend.

The moment the mediation ended, I shook hands all around and promised Gregg's client that I'd deliver my notes to him. Right after I transferred them to a clean sheet of paper, not one with curlycues and the initials "V.J." in the margins.

I swung open the door to my office, planning to drop the notepad on my desk and grab my bag and keys. I could be home and in my gardening boots in an hour.

"Hey, thanks for sitting in on that session, man. I owe you." Gregg strolled into my office, looking courtroom sharp in a heather gray suit and crisp white shirt. His tie was the standout, a bright yellow with dots of red and blue, with a matching pocket square.

"You do owe me. Those two need a mediator to decide how often each of them gets to see the dogs? And she wasn't getting enough time with them so she *kidnapped the dogs* and hid them from him? Those people are exactly why I don't want to work on the Kincaid book of business."

He laughed, working the buttons loose on his jacket. "I hear you, but they're prize Pekingese. Worth a lot of money. Apple of mommy and daddy's eyes. You should see the fee schedule for their care, from the vet to the groomer to doggy day care."

Gregg clapped his hands, rubbing his palms together.

"You up for a drink and a smoke? Just us. Maybe Gabe, depending on if he got out of court in time to beat traffic."

"No Garrett?"

"Nah. The wife has a design thing she's dragging him to."

I was about to beg off, since I really wanted to go home and get some sleep, but being able to sit at Mink's without Garrett's smirk across from me was tempting. It had been awhile since I'd had a smoke and yeah, Gregg owed me.

"One drink, one cigar," I said, fishing my keys out of the bowl I kept them in on my desk. "It's been a long week and I'm tired."

"That'll get me started," said Gregg, leading the way out of my office. "I think I might see if one of the honeys up there wants to get together. We've been talking a little bit, these last few weeks. I think I made a dent in her armor."

"If you called her a honey to her face, you didn't make a dent in anything but your chances of her taking you seriously."

CHAPTER ELEVEN

*G*ibson

WE CLAIMED OUR USUAL TABLE, THE LAST CLUSTER ON THE right side of the patio with the city skyline in view. Gregg and I settled in and ordered a drink for Gabe, who was on his way from court in another county.

"Have you made up with Mother yet? Or are you two still on the outs?"

I chuckled, sipping a fresh pour of Knob Creek and lighting a cigar. On insistence from the owner of Mink's, I was trying something new. He'd come to our table as soon as we sat down and offered a stogie from his recent shipment, including the toasted, nutty flavored Ashton Cabinet I was smoking.

"You know we don't make up anymore, Gregg. We avoid each other for a couple of weeks. Then she asks me to do something inane and meaningless, I agree for the sake of us getting along, and our argument is forgotten."

"Yeah, so. Where are you with that?"

"Why does it matter to you?"

Gregg grimaced. "You know how grumpy and nit-picky she gets when you two are fighting. She turns on Gabe and me and all of a sudden we're worthless."

"So you're mad that you're getting the treatment I usually get?" I laughed, taking a sip from my glass. "I think you can take it for a few weeks. I've been taking it for a long time."

"Is it even worth it? This case— it's a divorce, right? Why's she so... I don't know. She's seething about it."

I shrugged my shoulders. "I know she has an issue with how much I charge to represent some of my clients, but she seems to have a personal objection to Vanessa Jackson. Something about Vanessa bothers her."

"What do you think it is?"

"No idea." I sipped, deep in thought. "It can't be the money; it's got to be something more than that."

"Well... is this client young? Attractive? You know what I mean?"

I bobbed my head, trying to control my expression. Vanessa was more than merely attractive. And I was more than merely attracted to her. She was beautiful. Sexy. Funny. Human but not fragile. And I'd developed some very meaningful feelings for her. "She's relatively young. Very attractive. What does that have to do with Mother?"

Gregg pulled at his goatee and pushed his thick, black rimmed glasses further up his nose. "I wouldn't say she's jealous, per se. More wary. She definitely doesn't want a repeat of Melanie."

"I thought she was going to have a nervous breakdown the first time I brought Melanie home." They'd eventually gotten close, but my mother's initial reaction to Melanie was stiff and formal and she seemed stressed whenever I brought up my relationship with her. It was odd to see such a cool, calm collected public figure in emotional disarray.

"You have no idea, do you Gib?"

"He has no idea about what?" Gabriel pulled back the chair we'd saved for him and picked up the whiskey we'd ordered. In an unsurprising turn, he wore a dark grey suit with a bright yellow tie and pocket square.

I shook my head, my gaze bouncing from one brother to the other. "Do you two call each other every morning and talk about what to wear? This was funny in high school, amusing in college, but now you're over thirty and it's creepy."

Both laughed. "Sometimes, yeah," said Gabe. "We have similar taste and we shop together. It happens." He made a motion to the waitress to bring the humidor with the selection of cigars. "What is it that Gib doesn't know?"

"About Mother. How he's her favorite."

That made me laugh so hard, I choked on a mouthful of bourbon. "Uh, no. I think you've mistaken me for Garrett, her lapdog."

"No... no." Gregg shook his head, then leaned forward. "I don't think so. Garrett gives her exactly what she wants, when she wants it. He's not a challenge, no trouble at all. Gabe and I are alright, so long as we toe the line. You, though... "He smiled, a long finger unwrapping itself from around his glass to point at me. "You're the favorite."

I glanced at Gabe for consensus. "You think this too?"

"Oh, for sure. You're worried about making the will... we'll get whatever scraps you don't get."

"You're joking, right? I defy her at every turn. She takes issue with every client I have, every case I take, everything I do."

"Secretly, though?" Gabe leaned in. "You're the one that

makes her think. Keeps her on her toes. You make your own path. She never knows what to expect with you. It's like she looks forward to the challenge."

"She'll never admit it," added Gregg. "She'll never say it out loud and you probably won't ever feel it. Just... know that you're the favorite. So maybe this deal with this particular client of yours, Ms. Jackson—"

"Oh, the Jackson case?" Gabe laughed. "She's definitely feeling threatened."

"Threatened? That doesn't make any sense. She's *Sylvia Kincaid*. She could buy and sell Vanessa a hundred times over." I shoved the cigar in my mouth, puffing away.

"I saw the fee you're charging her. You're out of your mind, man! There's cheap, and then there's your fee. It's obvious that Vanessa is more than a client to you."

This gave me pause. How could they already tell? How long had it been *obvious*? And was that what Mother had meant about not letting my manhood choose my clients?

"What do you mean, obvious?"

"Obvious as in every time I call you, you're at that diner where she works. Obvious as in barely charging her to do her divorce, even though you're getting briefs every day and they all have to do with the Jackson case."

"Obvious as in every time I mention Vanessa Jackson, there's a look you get..." Gabe paused, then grinned and jabbed his finger in my face. "There it is."

I swatted his finger away. "What look?"

"That look that says that woman is more than a client to you."

Gregg tipped his glass into his mouth, emptying it and waving to the waitress for more. It was the one he was sweet on, with the long dark hair and the hazel eyes and smooth, tawny skin, visible through the backless blouses she liked to wear. She smiled and nodded, giving him the "just a second" finger. That was a lot of attention from her— she tended to be cold and methodical, like the rest of the wait staff, as if they were mere appliances and not people. Maybe Gregg did make a dent in her armor.

"If we can see it, you know Mother can," Gregg was saying. "And it's Melanie all over again. She's going to lose you to a woman you'd do anything for, when you won't do the most basic shit she asks you to do."

"And when she gets you back, you'll be a broken version of yourself. Like you were when Mel left."

"I guess I never thought of it like that. You know, losing her son. She's not... motherly. But regardless, even if there was something between me and Ms. Jackson, it's got nothing to do with her."

"Gib, we're not the ones you need to talk to about it. We're not jealous of a lady taking your time. But on the brotherly advice tip? Be careful. You never know what you're stepping into when you cross that line. It's not like she's your average woman. She has history, with a man that won't let her go without a fight. Gotta wonder what the rest of that story is."

No kidding. I was thinking about the motions from Warren's attorney that I still needed to answer. He was determined to take this divorce to court— for no reason than to punish Vanessa. He'd lose, but not before she spent a lot of money to defend herself and he spent money that he could be putting away for his children.

"Gentlemen," boomed a familiar voice behind me. My eyes rolled by habit. Pack grabbed a chair from another table and slid in between Gabe and me. "I was across the room and thought I saw the Kincaid brothers over here. Where's Garrett? And Judge?"

"Garrett had a previous engagement," Gregg answered.

"Judge and Mother are at a fundraising dinner with Mayor Reed. $500 a plate. Too rich for my blood."

"Yeah, I got an invitation to that, but passed on it. Good to see you, Gib."

"Same to you," I lied. "I'm surprised your secretary let you out of your office. Isn't this busy season for tax attorneys?"

Pack shrugged. "Yes and no. It picks up some before tax time, but my client list has become a collection of more... interesting cases. Not your typical itemization errors and audit investigations. I'm more specialized. The majority of my clients are in some deep shit with the IRS."

The waitress arrived and presented the humidor to Gabe. He and Pack picked cigars, then Pack clipped the ends and lit both, blowing smoke up and into the atmosphere. Gabe smiled up at her and she smiled back before stepping away.

"At any rate, it's a Friday night and since I know I'll be in the home office all day tomorrow, I don't feel guilty about relaxing tonight. How's business at Kincaid?"

Gabe and Gregg answered, keeping the conversation light and general at the same time. I kept silent, not wanting to talk to Pack any more than necessary. I acknowledged his efforts to make it back to my good graces. I wasn't sure that was going to be possible. Despite the kind of woman Melanie had to be to go after Pack, he still took her, with open arms. That kind of man was no friend to me.

I emptied my glass, regretfully tapped out my cigar and pushed away from the table. I stood, pulled my wallet from my back pocket and dropped a few bills on the table.

"I'm going to head out. I have a full day tomorrow as well."

Pack looked hurt, rearing back. He grabbed my wrist to keep me at the table. "Gib... stay. Every time I come around, you run off."

"I'm not running off. I told Gregg I'd have a drink. I've had my drink."

"So you're not leaving because of me, then?"

"Like I said, I have a long day tomorrow." *And I'm leaving because of you.*

"Yeah, well. Take this money with you," said Gregg, snatching up the bulls and handing them back to me. "Tonight is my treat. Thanks for your help."

"Do me a favor and don't ask for my help again."

"HEY, VANESSA, YOU GOT THAT REFILL FOR ME?" ONE OF the regulars tapped his empty beer bottle on the bar, trying to get her attention. She was mindlessly wiping a white towel over an already clean table.

"Oh. Oh, yeah. Sorry." Vanessa dipped behind the bar and grabbed a bottle and an opener.

"No, no. Light beer. C'mon, I always drink light."

"You're right," she said, swapping the regular for lite, then popping the cap and sliding it over. "Sorry, I'm off my game today."

"Get it together, girl. I've never had such bad service in here. It's a shitty place, anyway. The drinks are overpriced and the wings are salty."

"Maybe you ought to head on up outta this shitty place, Roy." Sam came around the corner from the kitchen, wiping his hands on his apron. "And don't come back for the over-priced drinks or the salty wings."

"You know I didn't mean nothin' by it, Sam. Just talkin'."

"I don't take kindly to that kind of talkin' to my niece. You been around here long enough to know that. And don't nobody call her *girl* but me. Don't get to thinkin' you can say what you want around here. This ain't that kinda place and I ain't that kinda man."

"So she can take all day to serve and then serve the wrong thing and I have to take it?"

"Naw, you can take yo' ass outta here like I said—"

"Uncle! Roy! Enough." Vanessa stepped between them and raised her hands to quiet them both. "I gave him his damned lite beer. He's going to drink it and shut up."

She exhaled a heavy breath, then spun on her heels and turned around. She was headed to the back of the bar. Straight to me. "I'm taking a break."

I hurriedly cleared off half of the table, in time for her to slide into the booth, fold her arms and lay her head down on them.

"Rough day?"

She groaned into the wood of the table, the sound echoing up. I glanced up at Sam, who was watching us from across the bar, so I couldn't reach out to her, hold her hand, stroke her hair, kiss her lips, assure her that everything would be fine.

She sat up, rubbing her eyes. She looked exhausted— not just tired, but worn out. "I have shown Dre Prescott— you know, DJ Fresh Beats? Approximately a million houses. Nice houses. Luxury homes. He'd be living amongst the super rich. *He* finds a house, on his own, mind you. Like, a four bedroom house. He'll probably gut it and rebuild it and turn it into what he wants, but I wish he would have told me to find him a cheap shack in the middle of nowhere."

"That affects your commission, right?"

"Yup. I'll still make a commission, but I was counting on him buying a big, stupid house. He called this morning and told me he wanted to put in an offer right away. So I was working on that, trying to feed the girls breakfast and get ready for my shift here. Then the social worker called..."

She paused to roll her eyes. "Warren was at the meeting place to pick up the girls, demanding that I bring them *right that second*, even though he was a half hour early. Maybe he's afraid that I'm going to file for sole custody, which means more child support for him. It's the only reason to explain his sudden insistence on seeing them."

"They're his children. He should want to see them."

"Should. His past behavior isn't an indicator of what he should want to do. He's motivated by what *I* want. If I want full custody, he's going to make sure I don't get it. If I want a divorce, he's going to make sure I don't get it. If I want to move on with my life... with someone new..."

She tilted her head to the right and let a small smile appear before it disappeared again. "He's going to make sure I don't get to do that."

"Remember what I promised you? That I was going to get this done? That whatever he makes up to throw at you, I have something for him? He's not even coming with anything creative, Vanessa. Stick with me, here."

"I'm here, Gibson." She reached across the table and, in a bold move, grabbed one of my hands, winding her fingers between mine. "I'm really stressed out. I can't wait for this to be over. But I'm here."

"Hey, why don't you bring the—"

The door to Sam's opened and two chirpy, high pitched voices rang out, "Hi, Uncle!"

Sam came around the bar, glancing back at Vanessa and then to the two waist high little girls that ran to give him a hug. They were near identical, one only slightly taller than the other. Both had shoulder length braids, wore jeans, t-shirts and sneakers.

They were *perfect* replicas of Vanessa.

She and I slid out from the booth and rushed to the front

of the bar. "What are you girls doing here? Where's your dad?"

"He dropped us off and told us to come in here," said the older girl. "He said he's not allowed to talk to you, but to tell you he had things to do and he would see us next week."

"How come he can't talk to you, mommy?" The younger one asked.

The best description of Vanessa's expression was bewildered. Warren had dropped her children off and driven away. "Uhm... we... it's something between me and daddy. Have a seat over here while I figure out what we're going to do."

She ushered them to seats at a table in the corner while Sam went back behind the bar. "How about if Uncle Sam makes these little ones something special?"

He reached above his head and pulled a blender from a shelf. "Now, this is an event." Vanessa muttered, under her breath. "The blender doesn't make an appearance very often."

"So, Warren dumped his daughters here? At a bar. On the day he insisted on seeing them, early even, conceivably to appear to be involved in their lives and avoid having to pay more child support?"

"Yeah. Which means his... *woman* probably called." She closed her eyes and inhaled a calming breath, through her nose. After she blew it out, she opened her eyes again. "Have I mentioned that he makes me tired?"

"So... they can't stay here, right?"

"Right. So...uh..." She scratched her temple, then ran a hand over her hair, smoothing back the pony tail. "I'll call my Aunt to come get them, I guess? But by the time she gets them to her house, my shift will be over. I guess I'll cut out early and take them home."

"I have an idea, if you're up for it. And you trust me."

"If I trust you?" One of her eyebrows tilted upward and she gave me a sideways glare. "What do you have in mind?"

"Before the girls came in, I was about to suggest that you all come out to the house. It's a nice day, there's plenty of room for them to play. The lake isn't warm, but the pool is heated. And you won't know what to do with all the Zen I've got out there."

"Oh, Gibson...we... we couldn't impose on such short—"

"You can. I insist." I grabbed her hands, in full view of Sam who was openly eavesdropping, and squeezed them. "You seem stressed today, and that was before Warren dropped the girls off. I know once you get out there, away from the city, in the fresh air, you'll be able to relax. I'll even throw some stuff on the grill. We can eat something besides chicken strips and lemon pepper wings."

"All that sweet talkin' and hand holdin' don't work on me," said Sam, from across the room. "Don't find yourself tossed outta here, son."

I laughed, but I kept my eyes on Vanessa. "What do you say?"

She closed her eyes in a long, slow blink, then opened them again. With a smile, she said, "Sure. Why not? I want to see the garden anyway."

CHAPTER TWELVE

anessa

I PULLED ONTO THE INTERSTATE BEHIND GIBSON'S JEEP AND trailed him heading north. He'd said his house was "a little out of town" but the address he plugged into my GPS showed a fifty minute drive.

"Mommy, who's that man?"

I found Jaclyn's almond shaped eyes in the rearview mirror and smiled. "Who's what man, sugar?"

"That man at Uncle's restaurant. He was holding your hand."

"That's Gibson," I said, giggling, returning my attention to the road. Gibson was weaving through traffic, trying to get through the jam and I didn't want to lose him. "Remember my friend, Mr. G? I introduced you to him a few minutes ago. You forgot already?"

"She means like... *who is he*, mommy," said Olivia the

Translator, smacking her lips in that know-it-all tone that I'd been trying to work out of her.

"He is my friend. He's helping me take care of some stuff with daddy."

"You mean the divorce?"

My eyes popped back up to the mirror. "Where did you hear that word?"

"I heard you talking to Auntie. And Auntie and Uncle talk about it. My friend Kaya's mom is divorced."

"Is she? How's Kaya feel about it?"

Olivia shrugged her shoulders. "Fine, I guess. Her mom and dad don't fight like you and daddy."

"Yeah, I'm sure that's hard, and I'm sorry, honey. It doesn't change the fact that we both love you very much."

It means your father is a selfish narcissistic psychopath.

"And when you're with daddy, don't worry about what's going on with me and him; have fun with him, okay?"

I watched both girls nod their heads in agreement and returned my attention to the road. I was still closely following Gibson as we broke through afternoon traffic and sped up.

My cell phone buzzed in its holder clipped to the dashboard. I smiled at the name that popped up and slid my thumb across the screen to take the call.

"Hey, stranger."

"Hey stranger, yourself," Sonja's smoky tone was scratchy across the line. "This text you sent me must be the reason I ain't seen or heard from you in weeks."

"Hang on. Let me connect my earbuds."

A few moments of acrobatics later, I plugged earbuds into my ears and turned the radio on, directing the sound to the speakers at the back of the car. "Can you hear me?" I asked her. "I don't want the girls to hear what I'm saying."

"Comin' in clear."

"Okay." I put both hands on the wheel and checked the rearview mirror. Olivia and Jaclyn both had their heads buried in books. "So you got my message."

"I don't know what the hell it means, though."

"It means what it says."

"What does it say, Nessa? **Superman leaps panties in a single bound.** What does that mean? Who is Superman?"

I grunted and rolled my eyes, then growled through my teeth, "The man with the S on his chest?"

"The man with the... oh! Superman! Divorce lawyer? Girl, you could have said that."

"I didn't want an incriminating text message laying around. You know how you leave your phone sitting out for hours."

"We're not talking about me today. Don't change the subject. How long has this been going on?"

"Couple weeks."

"Mmmmmm." There it was, the *I'm judging you* reproach that I was expecting. "You're allergic to good advice, ain'tcha girl?"

"Don't start with me."

"What do you mean, don't start with you? I told *you* not to start with *him*. It doesn't even matter, I knew you was gonna do him anyway."

"You did not."

"Did so. Every time I talk to you, it's Gibson this and Gibson that out of one side of your mouth, while you're busy protesting too much about not sleeping with your divorce attorney out of the other side. I knew it was gonna go down."

"Fine, so you know some things. What do you have to say about it?"

"Why does what I have to say about it matter? What do *you* have to say about it? Is this what you want?"

"For now."

"For now. *Unh huh*. And you're happy? Or at least satis-fied? He's hittin' all the right spots?"

My body flushed in response to her question, popping up a memory of Thursday night, when he'd barely made it in the door before he was all over me and we ended up screwing against the wall

And later when he was on his knees with his face between my legs and wouldn't let me move until I promised to find a little extra time to give him because I wouldn't see him on Friday.

"*Mmmph*. Yeah. *All* the spots."

"What you text me for, heifer? To brag that you gettin' some, like I'm not?"

"Who you gettin' it from, Sonja?"

"Somebody you don't know."

"Unh huh. You still an old jealous ass. I don't know why I texted you. To get your perspective, I guess. I mean... I shouldn't be...*with* him. He's my attorney. Right?"

"Girl..." She sucked her teeth and uttered a grunt under her breath. "*Shouldn't* went out the window the second you turned on that Nessa charm. You knew exactly what you were doing."

Sonja insisted I had some kind of magic charm that drew men to me, and that I turned it on and off like a switch. It was how she explained the long line of loyal clientele I kept at Red Heels, ignoring the fact that I was young, with a nice body, dancing for men who frequented a strip club. I never claimed to be the smartest person in the room, but I didn't need a math degree to figure that out.

"So you text me some clues so I can figure out that you're giving up the cocoa, and now you think I'm going to lecture you and tell you that you're wrong, so that you can either rebel against it or you'll have a reason to stop."

"Yes, so if we could get the lecture out of the way..."

"Naw, I don't have a lecture for you, girl," she answered, surprising the hell out of me. "My lecturing days have been over. You're a grown woman. Gon' and do what you gonna do. All I'ma say is good luck and keep your eyes open."

"That's it. Good luck. And keep my eyes open."

"The same advice I gave you when you met Warren. Remember?"

"And look what happened."

"You gonna stop screwin' Superman if I say stop?"

The silence that followed was too long. It answered the question for her. And for me.

The few hours a week I shared with Gibson were fun and exhilarating and gave me a break from everything else going on in my life. The real estate clients and the regulars at the bar and my friends and everyone pulling on me. Gibson was only concerned with me and my pleasure, and wanted to give me that without making demands. I was beginning to feel spoiled by that.

"That's what I thought," said Sonja, with her all-knowing, self-satisfied tone. "Like I said before, and like I tell these girls at the club that ignore my advice: don't get caught up. It is what it is and no more. You hear me?"

"I hear you, but that's about men at the club. He doesn't know about Red Heels. He doesn't know anything about that part of my life."

"Hunh. So how does he think you met Warren?"

"I told him we met through work. And that I was a real estate agent, so... I guess he thinks we met that way. He doesn't need to know how I met Warren to represent me."

"No, I don't guess he does. But we're talking about more than representing you, aren't we? Nessa, if you want this thing with Superman to go anywhere, you're gonna have to belly up to the bar and own up to some things."

"You just told me not to get caught up, that it is what it is. Now we're talking about this going somewhere?"

"That was before I knew you cared enough about what he thinks to not tell him the whole truth. You're about to wade into the deep end, girl. Can't say I didn't warn you."

"Warn me? About what?"

"About when he finds out what you used to do for a living and how you met your husband. I looked up those Kincaid people. They travel in important circles. You think Mama Kincaid wants her son to fall for an ex-stripper? How about *Judge* Kincaid?"

I'd only texted her so I could have someone to talk to about Gibson, but Sonja had my mind reeling. I was so used to hiding my past that I hadn't even thought about what would happen if Gibson found out that I used to twirl and gyrate around a stage, nude from the waist up and not much on from the waist down. And those were just the highlights.

"I've been warned, so thanks. I guess."

"Don't be mad at me, Nessa. I'm saying truthful things."

"I know. And I'm not mad. I didn't think about all that stuff."

"Mmm. Letting wet panties do all the thinking for you, huh?"

"Sonja!"

"I saw the picture, girl! He's a fine lookin' piece of man. None of what I'm saying means you can't have a good time."

"Keep my eyes open." I sighed, nodding though she couldn't see me. "I gotcha."

"So what are ya'll doing today? You sound like you're in the car? Where are ya'll going?"

"Gibson invited us out to his house. He has some lakefront property about an hour outside of town."

"An invite to the lakefront house, hunh? Well, now. Ya'll have a real good time."

"I'm taking note of your *tone,* Ms. Sonja."

"Don't need to be takin' note of nothin'. I said have a good time and I meant it."

"We will. Thanks."

"For what? I ain't done nothin'. But I want to hear *all* of the details when there aren't young ears around. You hear me?"

"Yes ma'am. I'll call you soon." I disconnected the call and pulled the earbuds out.

Sonja gave me a lot to think about.

Nothing between Gibson and I had to change. We could still meet up and scratch the itch that seemed to always need scratching these days, and he never needed to know the whole story because what we were doing might not go past getting that divorce decree.

On the other hand, we just started getting to know each other, and were enjoying each other's company. Who knew what might happen, if we just let things... happen? The one thing I did know was that if Gibson was someone that needed to know the whole truth about who I used to be, I wanted him to find out from me.

Thirty seven long minutes later, Gibson flipped his turn signal and made a move to exit the interstate to an access road. I followed him as the neighborhoods slowly changed from closely clustered homes and tiny lawns to sprawling houses with acres of trees and wild grasses around them.

Olivia and Jaclyn were paying attention now, calling out every animal they saw: cows, chicken, even a few sheep and a lot of horses. To our left, the sun's rays bounced off of a shimmering lake. The whole scene gave me such a peaceful feeling, I understood why Gibson called this piece of nature his home.

The Jeep turned off onto a paved road, and a few minutes later an enormous sky blue house came into view. Flanked by trees, the three story structure was nestled next to the lake. A small boat bobbed in the water that rippled in the light breeze.

Gibson parked in front of a three car garage and got out of the Jeep, pointing at me to pull in next to him. The girls were in such a hurry to get out and explore, I heard their seat belts pop as soon as I turned the engine off. I unbuckled my own seat belt, stepped out of the car and took a good look around.

"See, that wasn't that bad." Gibson stood next to my door, slipping off his shades and hooking them onto the collar of his shirt.

"It *was* that bad, but all of this makes up for it." I inhaled a deep breath. "This air and these trees and that lake and... this *house*." I waved my hands around, grinning like a fool. "This is amazing, Gibson. Beautiful."

"I'm happy you like the place. Let me show you guys around." He pocketed his keys, shoving them into his jeans and led us toward the front of the house, which was situated at an angle so you could see the lake from the front or the back.

"So, how much do you think this place goes for?" Gibson asked me.

"Oh, a pop quiz for the realtor. Okay." I looked around, rubbing my palms together, already calculating in my head. "How many bedrooms? Bathrooms? Square feet? Updated appliances? Wood floors?"

Gibson laughed, waving me off. "Never mind. I was going to test you but I see I shouldn't."

"No, for real!" I called after him. "What does it go for?"

"Never mind, Vanessa."

"Don't make me look it up, Gib."

"Look it up; I don't care. "

"Okay, okay. Without more information, I'd guess

about...." I scrunched up my nose, made a face. "Seven and a half. Give or take fifty."

"Seven and a half? Is that realtor speak?"

"$750 thousand. Thereabouts."

"Good guess, realtor. $699 thousand. I got it for around $575. A friend of a friend built it, was looking to unload it when the economy tanked. Swooped right in."

My eyebrows lifted. I was impressed. "Wow, that's a very good deal, Gibson."

"Thank you. I've been known to broker a good deal now and then."

He paused on the brick porch at the front door that was painted a deep eggplant. He pulled his keys from his pocket and unlocked the door, pushing it open so we could enter. "Come on in."

———

"WHAT DO YOU CALL CHEESE THAT'S NOT YOURS?"

To his credit, Gibson did a good job of pretending to think hard about this question. After a few moments, he looked at Jaclyn and shrugged his shoulders. "I don't know. What do you call it?"

"Nacho cheese!" exclaimed both girls, laughing riotously like it was the funniest joke ever told. Gibson laughed, but mostly at their antics.

"Okay, girls. I have one for you. Where do pencils go for vacation?"

Olivia and Jaclyn glanced at each other, then had a little whispered conversation before turning back to Gibson with questioning expressions. "We don't know," said Olivia. "Where?"

"Uhmmmm... Pencil-*vania*?"

Both girls nearly collapsed in loud giggles at his joke.

Gibson laughed too, which made me laugh. Both girls were huddled together in a single lounge chair, their bodies wrapped in large, colorful towels that Auntie had bought them before our last beach trip. The moment they saw the pool during Gibson's house tour, they begged to change into the swimwear that we'd stopped at home to pick up.

I'd changed into my swim suit as well, a cute black two piece with plunging neckline and a high waist. I grabbed our towels and my cover-up and followed the girls out to the pool, where we were enjoying the cool water and the spacious patio.

Gibson got up from his lounge chair and strolled onto the deck to check the barbecue grill. He lifted the lid, which released a plume of smoke into the air. The breeze blew the smoke past us and I caught the scent of wood chips and sizzling beef. He was grilling burgers for the girls, steaks for us and corn on the cob from the garden, but not from the current year. He'd picked them last year and froze a portion of his harvest so he'd always have vegetables.

I sighed and closed my eyes, slumped in my own lounge chair, stretching my legs out and wiggling my toes in the warm spring air. The girls chatted with each other for a few minutes, then I heard them jump back into the pool and start a game.

"Brought you a treat." I opened my eyes to find Gibson squatting next to me, handing me a glass of amber liquid with a slice of grilled lemon on the rim.

"This looks dangerous." I took the glass and sipped a little off the top. I felt the kick of bourbon but also the sweetness of peach and a little lemon and brown sugar. "But it's *gooood*," I swooned, licking my lips.

He smiled. "My special blend. I made it a little more manageable than usual. I make this when I want to get nice and mellow."

"Oh yeah," I said, taking another, bigger sip. "I feel mellow coming at me, like a locomotive."

"I made a bourbon-less version for the kids. There's a pitcher over there by the pool." He nodded his head to a couple of plastic drinking cups with straws and a bright yellow pitcher sitting on the edge of the pool. He sat down in the chair next to me and kicked his feet up with a satisfied groan. "Food will be ready in a few."

"Olivia and Jaclyn are having a great time. They're going to shrivel up like prunes."

"It's no big deal. I like having ya'll out here. Especially you." He said the last two words in a tone so low I barely heard them. But I did, and they made my heart flutter. I smiled over at him and took another sip of the drink he had made for me. "How's the Zen acquisition going? Smooth?"

"Zen has been acquired. I'm so glad you insisted on us coming out here."

"Mission accomplished. I knew you'd love it."

"How long have you lived out here?"

"Uh...." He scratched his chin, his eyes narrowing in thought. "About five years, I guess? Yeah. It was going to be a surprise—" Gibson cut himself off, mid-sentence, waving away the rest of the words. He took a long sip of his drink and licked his lips.

"It was going to be a surprise..." I looked over at him, almost leaning out of my chair to hear the rest of that sentence.

"I uh... I don't really want to get into it. But it's... I've been here five years, okay?"

"Okay. Sorry." I sat up, rested my head against the back of the chair and watched the girls race from one end of the pool to the other.

"Her name was Melanie. We met at Emory, we hit it off right away. She always talked about wanting a house on a lake and this place seemed perfect when I found it. My plan was to buy it and propose to her. Surprise her with it.

"I closed on this place and I planned to propose a week later. I was going to come out here, set it up with some nice flowers and... romantic ambiance. Had it all set. I told my best friend from college about it, because I was happy, you know?"

I nodded, gesturing with a hand for him to continue his story.

"A couple of days before I'd planned to bring her out here, she and my best friend—we call him Pack, showed up at the house. I was still living with Judge and Mother. They stood together. Holding hands. United front to tell me that they were together. Had *been* together, behind my back. Pack wanted to tell me before I brought her out to propose and made a fool of myself."

"Wow. Like... *wow*..."

"Yeah. Wow is pretty much what I've been saying for five years."

"Are they still... did they stay together? Do you know?"

He laughed, then, taking a few swallows of his drink. "Nah. They broke up six months ago, actually. Pack came into the cigar lounge my brothers and I go to, broke the news and tried hard to sound heartbroken over it. He thinks we should just bury the hatchet and be friends again, because she dumped him."

"He's serious? Regardless of whatever went on between you and her, he never should have been in the middle of that. He really wants to reestablish a friendship with you after that?"

He shrugged, then set his drink down on the painted concrete. "Amazing, isn't it? Some people are legends in their own mind. Pack is one of those people."

"So... but you kept the house?"

He stood and stretched, lifting his arms to the sky. The soft, worn *Emory School of Law* t-shirt he'd changed into rolled up, putting his abs on display.

I moaned, but covered it with a cough. Gibson's head swiveled in my direction at the sound. He laughed, then tugged the hem of his shirt down.

"No sense in giving up all this Zen. I fell in love with the place and made it mine. I think the food is ready. Want to help me put it all together?"

I swung my feet to the ground and hopped up from the lounge chair, slipping my arms into the loose cover up. "Sure. I need to work off this *drank* you made me."

Gibson slid open the patio doors and waved me through it to a spacious, marble, wood and stainless steel kitchen I could only dream about cooking in. "It's not even that strong, Vanessa."

"I'm a lightweight, alright?"

"Obviously."

As soon as we made it into the kitchen, he slid the door closed, leaving it open a crack so we could still hear outside. And then big, warm hands wrapped around my waist from behind. He pulled me back against his chest and dipped his head to drop a kiss on my neck.

"I've been thinking about how to get you alone for the past hour."

"Looks like you finally figured it out."

"Mmm...seems like I did," he groaned, turning me in his arms, wrapping them around me and pulling me tightly up against him, so tight I felt... everything. His molded chest, ripped abdominals and an erection that was obvious in his swim shorts.

He dipped to kiss me, a peck at first but then I couldn't help it and opened my mouth. He tasted delicious, sweet like peaches and bourbon. He sucked my tongue and let his hands roam while we kissed, inside the cover up and then under the cups of my bikini top. My back arched and I groaned as his thumbs rasped over my nipples and he gently kneaded my breasts.

My moans must have done something him because his breath hitched in his throat and he ground himself into me, pressing me up against the counter.

"Gib, do you need a minute to yourself to take care of ... something?"

"I need a minute with *you* to take care of something."

I giggled, then kissed him and pushed him back. "We need more than a minute, baby. Maybe uhm..." I glanced out the window toward the pool and smiled, watching the girls play. "Later."

"I can live with later," he said with a sigh, moving back and pulling his hands out from under my top. I adjusted my breasts inside the cups while he openly watched.

"Seriously..." I nodded toward the lump in his shorts. "You can get these hands, if you need them."

"I have hands, thank you. I'll take care of it before I go back outside. I'll think of you while doing it."

I gasped, feigning shyness, laying a hand over my chest. "Me? Why would—you're so nasty Mr. Kincaid."

"You like it." He leaned in and gave me a long, slow kiss. "Come on here, since you wanna act shy, so we can get this dinner together."

We sat around a glass patio table, plates full to over-flowing with the most delicious smelling food. Perfectly grilled steaks, thick burgers with melted cheese, corn on the cob slathered with butter and the prettiest green salad I'd ever seen.

I glanced over at the raised garden bed that Gibson had shown us earlier. From my point of view, I could see that the dirt had been disturbed, but there was nothing flowering or growing. It was empty.

"This salad isn't grocery store salad, but your garden is empty. Did I miss the harvest already?"

Gibson shook his head and finished chewing. "Haven't even started planting yet. A bit too early for it. But there's a farmer's market about halfway between here and town. In early spring I buy my produce from them. They're sort of why I started growing my own. I got tired of driving out there every week. Now I only have to go if I want something I don't grow, or before my crop starts coming in."

"You know they sell vegetables at the store, right?"

"Yeah," he answered, tossing a playful glare at me. He picked up a cob of corn, dripping with butter. "But they don't taste good. Whole Foods will do in a pinch, but it's not the same. If I don't have to bring it home and wash the dirt off of it, I don't want it."

At that he took a huge bite of the corn cob, sending a spray of juice and butter across the table. The girls though that was the funniest thing ever.

"I guess the effort is worth it. You've got my children eating vegetables without me having to beg and that doesn't happen often." We both glanced across the table at Olivia and Jaclyn. Both had eaten about half of their burgers, but the small plate of salad and the corn on the cob were gone, picked clean.

"Everything taste good?"

"It's yummy, Mr. G. You cook better than mommy. Maybe better than Auntie."

"But not better than Uncle Sam?"

Olivia shook her head, giving Gibson an *are you crazy?* look. "Nobody cooks better than Uncle."

"Mr. G?" Gibson asked, his left eyebrow cocked toward his hairline.

"It's what we decided they could call you. I know how you don't like being called Mr. Kincaid, so..."

"Mr. G." He nodded, picking up his steak knife. "I like it."

"Can we go back in the pool now?" Olivia asked. "I'm all done eating."

"You may *sit* in the pool, on the shallow side. You need to wait a little after eating to actually swim. Do you hear me?"

Both girls nodded, then pushed their chairs back and calmly walked to the edge of the pool.

"Well, I'm floored. My kids ate all their vegetables and left half a hamburger on their plates. Children are a mystery, I tell you."

"So, Vanessa...." I nodded, shoving a piece of steak into my mouth. "You... well, you kind of outed us, back there at Sam's. Not that I mind, but are you okay with people knowing about us?"

"Oh. Mmm." I chewed and swallowed. "I consider Sam's a safe space. It's not a secret, at least between my Aunt and Uncle, that we're attracted to each other." I glanced over to the pool and saw the girls sitting on the edge, kicking their feet in the water. "People don't need to know that we're... *together*. If you know what I mean."

He leaned in, so close to me that I felt his breath on my ear. "You mean they don't need to know we're *fucking*."

My cheeks were on fire. He'd said it quietly and there was no way the girls heard him, but I still blushed at the thought that they might hear us. I giggled and playfully pushed him away.

"I'm not divorced yet. In my mind, I'm single. Not everyone agrees. Some people still have ideas about things a married woman should be doing. Even if..."

"Even if her husband is long gone. I get it. I didn't think about that."

"Plus, I have those two beauties to think about. They're

growing up fast, getting more grown up every day. I've said it before, and I know you think I'm crazy, but kids are cruel. I don't want them picked on. I don't want it getting around town that Olivia and Jaclyn's mom is..."

A whore. I wasn't going to say it out loud, but my worst nightmare is my children coming home to me, asking if I'm what all the kids are calling me. Because that's what all their moms are calling me. I'd been through that before. And that's when I stopped telling people how I met Warren.

I dropped my knife and fork in my plate and sat back in my chair, fat and happy, rubbing my belly. "Well, Mr. G, dinner was absolutely delicious."

"You sure you don't want to lick the plate? There's some butter leftover from the corn and a little juice from the steak..."

"Pardon, but you have no room to talk, Mr. Clean Plate Club." Gibson's plate was pristine, since he'd sopped up every drop of juice as he ate.

"I am a champion steak eater," he said, giving me a low chuckle. He grabbed my plate and stacked it on top of his, then reached across the table to grab the two half eaten burgers. "You think they'll finish their burgers later?"

"Probably." I pushed myself up from my chair, as comfortable as it was, to help clear the table. "But let me take care of that. You cooked, I'll clean."

"You can *help*. I'm a little picky about my kitchen, so you'll have to put up with me."

I rolled my eyes and reached for the bottles of steak sauce and salad dressing he'd brought out. "Oh, you're picky. I wouldn't have imagined that."

CHAPTER THIRTEEN

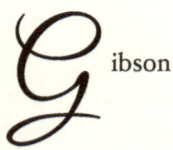ibson

A FEW HOURS OF SWIMMING, A BIG DINNER AND A twilight session in the hot tub was the magic combination to knocking two energetic little girls out. They'd put up a valiant fight, but I was quietly laughing at how they'd finally given up and were stretched out on either side of the couch in the family room.

"Look at 'em," I nodded my head in their direction. "They don't even know how to party."

"Oh, they partied. All day. They've got the day party down pat."

After the girls had fallen asleep, Vanessa moved from one end of the couch to the smaller two-seater with me. I'd made us a warm after dinner drink and she snuggled up alongside me, her long, delicate fingers wrapped around the mug. We had been watching a very kid friendly movie, but after they'd fallen asleep, switched the programming to a movie on Netflix. We were, quite literally, *Netflix and chilling*.

"So... how long do you think they'll be knocked out?"

Vanessa sighed lightly, lifting a shoulder in a shrug. "They were up early to spend the day with their dad and they've been going, going, going all day. I shouldn't have let them fall asleep here. Getting them into the car to go home is going to be interesting."

"Or you could—"

I stopped myself before letting the rest of the sentence come out of my mouth. Vanessa and I were still feeling out our relationship and I'd just met her children. I didn't want to press too hard, move too fast, make too many assumptions about how comfortable she'd be with staying overnight.

"Or we could..." She elbowed me, egging me on.

"I mean... it's past eight o'clock. It's dark, the kids are knocked out, I think you're a little loose from that seriously weak drink I made you." I stopped to give her a little side eye. She served it right back. "I don't want you to do anything you don't want to do. But it's a long drive back to town, and I would much rather you make that drive completely sober, in the daylight."

"You're inviting us to stay the night?"

"I am inviting you to stay the night. With no... expectations. If you know what I mean."

"I know what you mean," she mumbled, leaning in and tipping her face up to softly plant her lips on mine.

The sigh of relief that escaped my body was only slightly embarrassing. I hadn't touched or kissed her in hours. Having her so close was torture.

"What if *I* have expectations? Hmm?"

"Then... I probably have an obligation to fulfill them."

"Obligation? So does that go both ways?"

"Absolutely not. My obligation is to me, about me making

sure I'm readily available, should you want to make your expectations known." She glanced over at the couch, at the two slumbering beings curled up in the dancing glow of the television. "Are you nervous about doing anything with me, with them in the house? I understand, if you are."

"Not nervous," she said, fingering the rim of her mug. "More like... I'm thinking about our conversation earlier. About things married... or separated women do. Things that other people might consider inappropriate."

"Hmmm..." I mused, lifting my arm and dropping it around her, pulling her warm body closer to me. "We can chill. Seriously. It's not like we have to... do stuff... every time we see each other. But, I'll let you know... no one here, right now, in this house, thinks anything you're doing is inappropriate. Moving on is the most appropriate thing you could do."

She chuckled, leaning her head against my shoulder. "You're saying that because I'm moving on with you."

"I might be." I leaned down so I could brush my lips against her forehead. "It's still true."

I settled in, slouching a little and tipping my head back against the couch, trying to be content with just holding her, having her close to me. In my house, a place that meant a lot to me despite my original intent in buying it. I had never dated a woman with children before and I didn't know what actions or suggestions were safe, what would cross the line of something I shouldn't ask her to do.

So I did nothing. And I let her off the hook of having to even think about it.

And it was driving me crazy, to be honest.

If we were at her place, or the girls were not here, we'd have been sweaty, naked and exhausted from screaming each other's names all day. I smiled to myself, laughing a little at the mental image of she and I coming down, twisted up in high thread count sheets, pillows and blankets sitting wherever they ended up.

"What are you laughing at? And don't say the TV; that was a commercial about life insurance."

"What? Life insurance is hilarious to me."

"Mmmmm. What were you laughing at?"

"Nothing. Thinking about stuff."

"What stuff, Gib? I want to laugh too."

"It wasn't funny. Something I was thinking about, that I liked thinking about."

"Oh yeah?" She sat up a little, twisting in her seat so she could see me. "Tell me. What are things you like thinking about?"

"Uhm... Nice spring days. Good weather. Pleasant company. Short t-shirts and tight jeans on women with thick thighs and a nice ass."

"Uh huh..." I watched a sultry smile spread across her face. "Go on."

"And..." I leaned in, pressing my lips against hers. "I like thinking about doing that. And more. With you."

"More?" She whispered, leaning in to bring her mouth closer to mine. I captured her lips in a slow, heady kiss that I *really* wished could go further. But since it couldn't, I pulled away, ending the kiss earlier than I wanted to.

Vanessa laughed quietly, the sound coming from deep in her throat. "My kids are cramping your style, huh? Blockin'. Derailin'. Thwartin'. I could do this all night."

"I feel like you might. I... listen, I love your girls. They're funny, good kids, very sweet. They're always welcome here. But there are things I want to feel okay asking you to do and uh..." I eyed the two lumps on the couch and shook my head.

"You feel creepy, Mr. G?"

"A little. But I'm very attracted to their mother." I paused, then repeated, with a pointed stare, "Very. Attracted."

Vanessa laughed, one of those laughs that would have felt so good if she was laying up against me... *man, get a damn grip*.

"You want me to make the first move? Would that make things easier? Less creepy?"

"It might take the pressure off. Yeah."

"We could restart the house tour. And it could end at your bedroom."

"I LOVE THIS ROOM," SHE MURMURED, TAKING IN THE master suite inch by inch. Her eyes swept over the deep pile carpeting, the King sized four poster bed with intricate designs carved into the walnut, and the accompanying pieces — mirrors, dresser, bureau, wardrobe. I liked putting the room together and, since she was the first woman to be in it since I'd bought the new furniture, I was eager to show it off.

I opened the door to the walk-in closet and ushered her in, grinning at her loud gasp. "Gibson! This closet is the size of my bedroom!" She *ooh*'d and *ahhh*'d over the custom closet organization, done in walnut to match the bedroom suite.

"A place for everything," she said softly, her head volleying from side to side, her real estate eye not letting her miss a thing.

"And everything in it's place." I ran my finger along the wood that separated one section from another. "This was kind of a bitch to put in, but it was worth it."

"I see that. And it adds so much value to your home." She smiled, then stole a glance at me. "Sorry. I can't turn it off, in my brain. Maxine— my boss— is always talking about comps and added value. This is a good one."

"Good to know I've managed to bring up the property value."

She chuckled, stepping close to me and gliding her hands

up my chest and across my shoulders. "That's not the only thing you've managed to bring up. Why don't you show me that amazing bed?"

I backed her out of the closet, keeping a firm grip until her legs hit the mattress. I lifted her up a little, then tipped her so that she was laying on the bed. As I bent over her, she locked those long legs around me, bringing her warmth right up against me.

"Hey, sexy," I growled, lowering my head to nip at her earlobes and the side of her neck. She shuddered and let a quiet squeal.

"Hey sexy, yourself," she replied, her words slightly slurring. She gyrated her hips up and into me, grinding against my hardening dick through the sweat shorts I'd changed into. "You feel good. Ready."

"I'm always ready, when it comes to you. How are you doing?"

"I've been ready all day, Gib."

She grabbed one of my hands to guide it to the very little amount of space between us. I stroked her thigh, then lightly passed over the crotch of her jeans. She moaned. "Can you help me take these off?"

Happy to do so, I unbuttoned and unzipped her jeans and started pulling them off. They were skintight, so her thong came off with them. I tossed them somewhere behind me, then made short order of my shirt, shorts and boxers. She pulled off her t-shirt and pressed herself against me, skin to skin. She was warm, her skin was soft and she smelled delicious.

Vanessa cupped my face with her hands and brought my lips to hers, kissing me deeply with moans that sent jolts of lightning down my back. I worked my hands up under her body and squeezed her ass, then began to explore, uninhibited. I ran a hand along her inner thigh, then brushed against her pussy, moving up until I found her clit. Her hips jerked in response to my touch, so I did it again. She was... so wet. Ready.

I moaned, pulling my lips from hers, moving to her breasts. I laid little suction-like kisses across them, making my way to each nipple, a taut bud reaching out for attention. I took one, then the other in my mouth.

Above me, Vanessa whimpered, her hips moving in time with the finger stroking her. "Please. *Please,* Gibson."

I chuckled, pulling away for just a second, to reach toward the night stand drawer. Vanessa sat up a little, leaning back on her elbows. "You know I like to watch you sheath the beast," she said, laughing.

I smiled, watching her watch me rip the small foil package open, pull out the condom and roll it on. I took my time, smoothing it down to the shaft, stroking myself when it was completely on.

"So... you know this house is three levels, right? And since we're on the top floor, on the other side of the house, it's not likely they can hear you, downstairs.

"Certainly not through all that snoring they were doing."

"I want you to feel comfortable enough to make noise. Just uh..."

"Don't get crazy?" She grinned and her eyes sparkled. "I got it. No screaming like a banshee. Kind of a shame, you don't even have neighbors."

I gripped my dick by the base and stepped closer to the bed, laying a hand on her thigh and giving her a squeeze. "Something to look forward to, for next time."

She laid back and spread her legs, then reached down and spread her lips for me. "Why are you teasing me? Huh? Bring that beast over here."

I didn't hesitate to obey, pressing the tip of my dick into her pussy. She groaned, then sucked in a stream of air through her teeth. I moved slowly, thrusting until I was buried inside her, then struck up a rhythm that seemed like it felt good to her.

Vanessa was in a world all her own— eyes closed, brows furrowed, quietly moaning, holding on to my shoulders as I moved above her. Her breasts bounced with each thrust. I found myself moving faster, my body slapping against hers, just so I could watch them. Her pussy gripped me like a vise, hips worked me like a piston.

"You good?" I panted, dripping sweat already. I gripped her thighs, not missing a beat.

"So fucking good, Gibson. So fucking good; don't stop."

"Tell me when you're about to come."

She sighed, opening her eyes long enough to for me to see them roll back. "You're making me... *fuck*, I'm gonna come..."

I felt the tremble in her legs, the quiver in her belly. Her mouth fell open, her eyes slammed shut, her hips rocked up off of the bed. "Don't stop, don't stop, don't stop, I'm coming,"she chanted. I didn't dare.

She let out a loud *mmmmmmmmshit*, then I watched a beautiful flush roll across her skin, followed by beads of sweat and goosebumps. Her back arched, pointing her breasts high into the air. Her pussy clenched violently, over and over, pushing me close to my own climax.

"*Ohh*... holy shit, Gibson" Gasping, sucking in air, her body collapsed and she relaxed. "Did you come?"

"On my way, sexy. I wanted you to get yours first."

"Oh, I definitely got mine, baby. Hang on..."

She sat up, then kicked a leg up and around, until she was laying on her side, then flipped to her stomach and rose up onto her hands and knees, all without losing me. I was still inside her, dick pulsing, aching to rock my hips against her.

"I'm not even going to ask why you know how to do that. I'm just happy that you do." I palmed her hips and pulled her back against me. She yelped, though quietly, then wagged her ass at me.

"That all you got, Gib? Give it to me."

"Vanessa...woman." I shook my head, laughing out loud. "Hang on for this ride."

I pulled almost all the way out, and then grabbed her hips and pulled her back against me, quickly. Roughly. The sound of our bodies connecting sent a slapping sound into the air.

"Yeah. Yeah. That's good, do it again."

I did it again. And again. And over again, faster, rougher, louder. I pounded into her, smacking her thighs with mine until they grew pink. Vanessa tossed her head back, moaning, making sultry, satisfied sounds. Then she looked back at me, over her shoulder.

"You coming for me?"

At that exact moment, my dick pulsed and I slammed into her. Deep. Hard. One last time while it felt like everything I had poured from me.

"That was... I'm...you are amazing," I mumbled, pushing her forward so that I laid on her back. She spread her arms out; I laid my hands on top of hers and wound my fingers between hers.

"That was like three different sentences, Gibson."

"I'm having a hard time being coherent, right now."

"*Mmmmph.* Do you think we did okay, not being too loud?"

"Nobody came knocking, so..."

"Probably okay then." She sighed, sounding content. " I should check on them. In a minute."

"Yeah. Let's... let's take a minute."

CHAPTER FOURTEEN

ibson

VANESSA CREPT BACK INTO THE BEDROOM AFTER A QUICK trip downstairs to check on the girls. Or rather make sure they were sleeping and hadn't heard anything. She'd grabbed her bag and was digging through it with one hand while running her fingers through her hair, trying to comb through the tangles of curls we'd created.

"Leave it," I told her, pulling her hand out of her hair. "I like it all wild like that."

"In the morning I'll look like the love child of Don King and Nick Nolte's mug shot. It's better that I get a handle on it now." She finally tossed the bag toward me with a frustrated grunt. "I need my brush. Can you see if—"

I grabbed the bag and pulled it across the bed. I was still under the sheet and thin comforter, still nude, still high. I pulled a square-ish stiff bristled, wood handled brush out of the side pocket and handed it to her. "You know, bags have these crazy things called pockets."

She laughed and grabbed it, then pulled it through her hair, slowly re-establishing order atop her head. I laid back and watched her, sitting on the edge of the bed wearing one of my t-shirts. And nothing else. Every time she raised her arms, her breasts bounced under the thin, cotton fabric. Every movement made me wish for her to be done fixing her hair so I could pull that shirt back over her head.

And mess up her hair again.

"Girls okay?" I mumbled, trying to make conversation so that it wasn't obvious that I was staring at her.

"Mmhmm," she responded, turning her head toward me, then smiling because it was completely obvious, by the outline of my body under the covers that I'd been staring at her. "Out like a light."

"Good, that means we were quiet."

"Oh, I don't think it's because we were quiet. I think they sleep like the dead."

"So we didn't have to be quiet?" I feigned offense. "Maybe I wanted to shout your name or something."

"In the history of you and me... *together*..." She laughed, pulling her hair back to her nape and wrapping the hair tie I'd pulled off around the low ponytail. She dropped the hairbrush back into her bag and dumped it onto the floor. "You're not the loud one. It's been me making all the noise. And yes, I had to be quiet, because Miss Nosy Olivia Jackson has a sixth sense and will wake up straight out of sleep and come to my room if she hears something funny."

I laughed. "Maybe we should lock the door in case she starts to wander."

Vanessa pulled her feet up onto the bed and started scooting backward, toward me. I pulled the covers down and watched her slip between the sheets. "I think we'll be okay."

I reached for her, sliding her across the bed to me, and as soon as I felt her warmth, I slipped a hand up under the t-shirt and began roaming every inch of skin I could come into contact with— her breasts, her belly, up one side of her hourglass figure and down the other. She snuggled up close to me and buried her face in the spot between my neck and shoulder. I felt her release a little sigh, the air brushing my skin.

"You okay?" I whispered, dropping a kiss on her lips before she could even answer. She smiled, mid kiss and lifted her head to press her lips against mine.

"I'm okay. Really, really okay."

"That's like... very, very mediocre."

She laughed and laid a hand on my chest, then started lightly scratching my skin with the tips of her nails. She'd learned that I loved that— it gave me goosebumps.

"Like... things aren't perfect, not by a long shot. We have a hard road ahead of us. But life is manageable, day to day. And considering how crazy it was a little over a year ago, manageable is a miracle. I want to keep moving forward, you know?"

"Yeah. I know. And I want to help you do that, in any way I can."

Something about those words, maybe the way I said them or the way I looked as I said them brought a tightness to her expression. She pressed her lips together and closed her eyes, and seemed to stiffen in my arms.

"Did I say something wrong? Tell me, so I know to not do it. Or... say it."

"No...it's nothing." She opened her eyes, then started to say something else but her mouth opened in a wide, gaping yawn. "I guess I'm sleepy."

"Vanessa..."

I tipped her head up with my thumb under her chin. Her lids were at half mast, her eyes glossy. I felt like it wouldn't do any good to push her, not at 2AM after a full, stressful day. And some of the most amazing sex we'd had since we met. But I also didn't want her to go to sleep thinking the wrong thing.

"I'm not trying to scare you. But I do care about you and I want to spend time with the version of you that's free of all the stress that Warren causes."

"Might be a long time before you meet her. I feel like Warren isn't going anywhere any time soon. He's always going to be in my life, because of my kids. And because, for some reason, he feels like he owns me. He doesn't want me, but I can't move on."

"Why do you think he feels that way? Why's he so invested in what you're doing, when he's the one who left?"

She lifted a shoulder and smirked. "I think he feels like he raised me. He put ten years into turning me into who I am and he's not going to let someone else benefit from that."

A plausible theory. Scary, but plausible.

"I've been thinking," I told her, rolling onto my back, tucking the hand that wasn't resting on the rise of her hip behind my head. "I'm wondering how a man who claims to be close to bankruptcy was able to get a lawyer to file these motions. Not just file them, but write them. That's a couple of hours, at least $300 an hour times... I've lost count of how many I've answered, now. I mean, I looked the guy up, his attorney? He's nothing special. But it's not like he's doing the work pro bono. Warren is paying for it, somehow."

"Well, he's not paying anything else, so it stands to reason he has some money somewhere."

"Right. I just have a feeling. I'm kind of itching to look into it."

"Gibson. Don't." Her voice had gone from soft and sleepy to sharp and wide awake. I glanced down at her, surprised at the expression that met mine— tightly drawn lips, furrowed brow. "Really. Don't."

"I'm not going to make a big deal about it, but what if—"

"Leave it alone. You said his motions are baseless, and all he's doing is wasting money, right? But at the end of the day, the judge is going to see that he's crazy and he's going to grant the divorce. Right?"

"Yeah, but he's claiming to be a pauper. If there's money—"

"I'm not paying you to look for his money. There isn't any money."

"How are you so sure, Vanessa? He lied to you about everything else. Kept everything else — every*one* else behind your back. He was obviously diverting funds, funneling it into another life. Why *can't* it exist? And if it does exist, after everything he put you through, why don't you deserve a portion of it?"

Vanessa sat up, flinging the covers back, and scooted toward the edge of the bed.

"Wait... where are you going?"

"Home," she snapped, pulling the t-shirt over her head and tossing it in my direction. I watched her naked form move around the room, collecting articles of clothing that I'd enjoyed pulling off of her only hours before. "Thanks for the day, but we've officially overstayed our welcome."

"You haven't overstayed anything. Vanessa...you don't have to leave." She had gone into the bathroom and shut the door.

I pulled the covers back and got out of bed, pulling on the shorts and t-shirt I'd taken off earlier. "Look, I'm obviously saying the wrong things the wrong way. I'm sorry. I'm trying to look out for you—"

The door swung open and Vanessa stormed out of the bathroom, fully dressed. She crossed the room and grabbed her bag.

"You know..." she huffed, hands on her hips. "You have this nice community lawyer thing going on. That must feed some weird part of your ego and make you think that you have values that are totally different from anyone at Kincaid, especially Sylvia. But you're more like her than you realize. I bet that's eating you up inside so bad that you feel like you have to do good deeds to make up for it."

She tossed the handle of the bag over her shoulder and walked toward the bedroom door. "Well, you're done doing *this* good deed. I want to be divorced. You promised me that. I'm *paying* for that. I don't need any more favors. I don't need you looking out for me. You're the attorney, I'm the client. Let's keep it there."

I stood at the door of my bedroom and watched her walk down the hall, then heard her stomp down the stairs. I thought about going down there to talk to her, but thought better of it. Maybe I'd let her cool down, get her thoughts together. Realize she'd said a bunch of shit that made no sense.

So I was curious as to how Warren was paying his legal bills.

So I was interested in looking into it.

That made me a shark, sniffing the waters for blood, like my mother?

I heard a car engine revving. I crossed my arms and stared out of the window overlooking the front yard. By view of the flood lights over the garage, I watched Vanessa herd the girls out of the house, so sleepy they looked drunk. As soon as she'd buckled in one and then the other, she hopped into the front seat and backed out of the driveway.

VANESSA

I wished I could explain to myself what had just happened. I honestly, *truly*... had no idea. One minute I was luxuriously lounging between silky soft sheets in a giant bed with a handsome, manly man who seemed to like me.

The next moment I was throwing on my clothes— underwear inside out, t-shirt on backward, and stomping down the stairs. I'd planned on sacking out on the couch next to the one where the girls were fast asleep, but the longer I laid there, the more uncomfortable I felt.

Suddenly, I had to go. Just... get up and go. *Right that second.*

Thankfully the girls fell back to sleep as soon as I hit the road and sped down the highway back to Atlanta. That gave me plenty of time to think. And to figure myself out.

I blamed Sonja. She brought up good points about the Kincaids, how well connected and high powered they were, and how Judge Kincaid and his wife, the powerful Sylvia Kincaid would never approve of me, even if Gibson did.

But the way Gibson was looking at me all day was what really got to me... the things he was saying to me, especially about wanting to meet the me that I was without Warren's influence. That woman didn't exist. That woman was some fairy tale he made up in his head, someone who wasn't stressed out and consistently worried about things outside of her control. I met Warren at a critical point in my life. He'd taught me everything I knew about... anything. I wasn't kidding when I'd said Warren thought he raised me. Trained me. Taught me about how to be a respectable young woman out in the world.

How to go from a *whore* to a *housewife*.

When Gibson said he wanted to help me move on, I knew. I heard it in the tone of his voice and saw it in the softness in his facial expression. I felt it in how he opened his house up to us and enjoyed having us over a little too much. The spell had worked too well. Gibson was falling for me. For *us*. I wasn't ready to become his insta-family.

I pulled into my parking spot under Hayes Street Lofts, turned the car off and listened to the gentle snores bouncing around the interior. *I did what was right*, I thought. For them and for me, before I got in too deep and things got too complicated. I wouldn't let us get caught in another trap by another man who wanted to "save me" and "teach me how to be respectable".

And the money... I tipped my head back against the seat and released a long, low breath into the confined air of the car. Let's not even get started about the money.

Was Warren hiding some? I was almost sure of it.

Did I want to know anything about it? Most certainly not.

"Mommy..." Jaclyn's tiny, sleepy voice startled me. I sat up and turned my body so I could see her in the backseat. "Where's Mr. G?"

"Mr. G is at home, sugar."

"Oh." She yawned and I heard her shift in her booster seat. "Can I have some ice cream?"

I chuckled and twisted around again, then opened my door. The dome light came on, bathing the car in soft light. "It's the middle of the night, Jac. We're going upstairs and going to bed."

I'd just got the girls settled, promising myself I'd wash the chlorine from Gibson's pool out of their hair in the morning, when my cell phone flashed. It had been on Do *Not Disturb*, but certain numbers could get through that block. I hadn't removed Gibson yet.

I grabbed the phone and headed to my bedroom, closed the door and climbed up onto the bed, settling back against the pillows. The cheap, flat pillows at my place and not the big, fluffy ones at his house.

Gibson Kincaid: *Make it home okay?*

Yes. Just got the girls into bed.

Gibson Kincaid: *Good. Can we talk?*

Not right now, Gib. I meant what I said. Just get me divorced.

I didn't think he was going to reply again. Maybe he'd fallen asleep. It *was* nearly four am. But after a few minutes, the three dots that said he was replying lit up.

Gibson Kincaid: *I will do that. call if you need me.*

CHAPTER FIFTEEN

anessa

THE SMELL WAS THE SAME. THE LOOK, THE MOOD, ALL OF IT was familiar, ingrained in my memory, nearly burned into my skin.

Red Heels hadn't changed since the day I walked out, a bag of costumes in one hand, heels and makeup in the other. I could almost run through my routine by rote memory...

Slip onto the seat at my assigned table in the dressing room, after changing into something made almost entirely of lace or fishnet.

Talk a little shit with Sonja, put on my makeup, aka war paint.

Sneak a nip of whiskey from the bar, since I was underage, then talk *a lot* of shit with Sonja.

Once the hard driving, thumping bass that vibrated across the floor started up, I was on the clock.

The charm was on.

It was early— mid-morning, that peaceful time when the club was empty and quiet. The girls didn't start dancing until 3PM, but you could get in and have a drink.

I walked in and stood at the empty bar, my gaze fixed on the stage that stretched from one end of the room to the other, with an island strip dividing the room in half. The dark wood, though shiny from a fresh wash and wax, was scuffed and marked from years of heels clomping across its surface. The poles were where I remembered them... evenly placed from one end of the stage to the other, and two on the island.

There were a *few* changes, I noticed, now that my eyes had adjusted to the dim lighting. The bar had been expanded and it was mostly tile and granite. The floors had been refreshed, the wood areas buffed to a brilliant shine and the carpet replaced. And on stage, every few feet, a long length of colorful fabric hung from a steel pipe in the ceiling.

I dropped my bag on a bar stool and climbed the steps to the stage, grabbed one of the poles and made a revolution— one full circle in long, confident strides. Then I gripped the pole and hopped up, hooking my knee around the steel and took a spin, twirling my body around it. Slow... then faster and faster, tipping out, feeling the air whip through my hair. More memories flooded in, of living some of my most fun moments on this stage, to the beat of something raunchy. Likely by the *Ying Yang Twins*.

It was like riding a bike. Sort of. I spun faster than I intended to and tried to stop myself. The heel of my open toed bootie caught a nick in the wood and I went flying, landing on my ass a few feet away.

"Ow, shit!" I winced, trying to roll to one side so I could get up. "Damn, I'm old. I can't even get up off this floor. "

"Don't tell me you really are trying to come back here, Nessa. Not with those thighs, honey. And your pole routine needs work."

Sonja was leaning against a backstage wall, in a long black and gold caftan. Her hair was pulled back from her bare face by a wide black band. This was typical Sonja fashion. She liked to be as comfortable as possible and since she didn't dance anymore, being comfortable was a full time job.

"Shut up, Sonja," I grumbled, trying not to laugh. Also trying to move my body around so I could get up off the floor. "I need a little practice, is all."

Sonja laughed, pushed off the wall and shuffled onto the stage, her slippers flapping on her heels. "You need a lot of practice, baby. Let me help you off that floor."

I took the hand she offered. Once I was on my feet, I brushed my hands together and eyed the pole, like it wasn't my fault I'd bit it my first time back on stage in many years.

"Ya'll do aerials now?" I nodded my head toward the thin, silky strips of fabric hanging between us. Sonja rolled her eyes and turned around, heading backstage. I grabbed my bag from the bar and followed.

"Anton's idea to bring in some fresh talent," she tossed over her shoulder. "Can't just get up here and make your ass clap to the beat. Men were impressed with that when I was coming up. Twirl around on the pole a coupla times, make it look sexy. Nowadays...*hmph*."

Sonja led me to her office, a room I remembered as a storage closet eight years prior. It was stuffed to the gills with a small desk, a filing cabinet and two chairs. I sat in one. Sonja eased into the other and picked up a cup of takeout coffee.

"Girls got to do more than look pretty and be able to walk and chew gum onstage. Need to be athletic. Flexible. Strong without looking like a bodybuilder. One time this girl came in, invited Anton to come watch her on the silks. She wanted to see if she could bring her talents to Red Heels. Make some money. He was impressed, though. He had some installed, told me my new job was finding him some aerial artists."

"I don't understand. Men sit still for somebody swinging from a string?"

"Chile, they sit still for a lot if the girls got titties."

She chortled, laughing from deep in her throat. "But Anton's rule is that even if you do silks, you have to follow the rules. We don't do any of those slow, sensuous, artful performances here. You can go your kid's ballet recital for that."

She tossed back the last of her coffee and lobbed the cup toward an overflowing garbage can.

"If you want to dance at Red Heels, your routine matches the music we play, and we only play hip hop and up-tempo R&B. They make it work. We got a coupla silks artists that do well. Got regular show times and customers that come in just for them."

"And where do you find them?"

"I have my ways. I always have my ear to the pavement."

"*Mmhmmm.* Hot tip?"

She laughed. "An instructor at one of these places in the city gives me a heads up when she sees someone come through with potential. She gives the girl my card, the girl calls if she's interested. I set up an audition and let her cook. Used to be, Anton had to be in on the audition but he trusts me now."

"*Oooooh*, look who's all important at Red Heels," I crooned, laughing.

"I was always important at Red Heels. From my first day up on that stage, I knew I was a part of this gig for life. That's why I never quit. Never let nobody drag me away."

"Oh, here we go," I sighed, slouching in the chair and folding my arms across my chest. "Get it all out of your system, Sonja. Talk about how Warren manipulated me and made me quit dancing here even though he kept coming here and had other girls on the side. Tell me how I was an idiot for marrying him and bearing his children because look at what happened years later. *You told me.* You told me exactly what would happen."

By the time I'd finished ranting, the tears had come and begun to fall. She plucked a few sheets of tissue from a box and handed them to me. I took them, dabbing at the wet trails down my cheeks.

"I'm done saying *I told you so*. You get my point. Finally. But what are you crying about now? You're about to free of him, finally. And you got Mr. Superman going for you..."

I teared up again at the mention of Gibson, dropped my eyes and tried to catch the expression on my face before it changed. Didn't work.

Sonja pushed out a loud, frustrated huff. "Nessa, you didn't take all that shit I said about the Kincaids seriously, did you?"

"Why not? It was all true."

"So? Don't mean he believes it. And *he* is who matters. Did you even consider telling him everything? The whole truth? You can't start no new thing without coming clean about the old thing."

"I wasn't sure I *wanted* to start a new thing. And until I was sure, I didn't want to open myself up to that kind of judgment. I don't want any more lessons on pretending to be someone I'm not. But it doesn't even matter now. There's no more Superman."

"No more...*what* did you do?"

"Nothing. I did nothing. There are a few things I wanted him to stay away from, about the divorce. Process the paperwork. Don't go digging. The other night he told me he was getting curious about Warren's money. I mean, how is he paying for all this legal action? Gib thought he should look into it."

"And you told him not to."

I bobbed my head. "He sounded like he was going to ignore my request and do it anyway. And it pissed me off because it made me feel like all he cared about was finding this money. Everyone thinks I want Warren's money. And if they find it for me, they get some of it. Never mind where that money might have come from. What if it's dirty? I felt like I was in Sylvia's office all over again, with her looking down her nose at me."

"If he goes digging, he's going to find out who *you* really are."

"Yeah, that too. More than anything, I don't want to know what he's going to find on Warren. Lord knows what his fingers have been dipping into. I have to pretend so hard with the girls. They love him to pieces and I can't take their father away from them but I know who he is."

"You can't protect them by pretending that he won't do some underhanded shit. He already *did* some underhanded shit—"

"But I don't know about it yet." I sniffled, swiping the rough tissue under my nose. "And I don't want to. I don't want to know more about him."

"That's not going to work, baby. You don't make your way through life by sticking your head in the sand and not knowing things. If I was you, I wouldn't want any more surprises."

"Well, you're not me. I spent months learning something new about my husband every day."

I stood, pulling my light, summer weight sweater down over my hips and tossed the used tissues on top of the garbage pile. "I just stopped by to say hi. I'm showing a house, so I need to get going..."

Sonja hissed a breath and rolled her eyes, leaning to one side and playing with an earring. "Typical Nessa. Somebody say something you don't like, you run. Can't keep running, girl."

I marched toward the open door and passed the threshold, then backtracked my way through the prep area, the stage and out the front door of Red Heels. I got into my car and slammed the door shut, rolling my eyes at the enormous set of red stiletto heels that made up the marquee.

"Lord help me if I ever decide to step foot in this place again."

I shoved the key into the ignition and started the car. I couldn't escape that part of my past fast enough.

GIBSON

"In the last five years, divorces have changed," Gabriel was saying, blowing a puff of smoke into the air before continuing. "You used to have to hire a private investigator to find out if a client's spouse was stepping out. These days, people are so messy and careless, all you need is access to their social media accounts."

"Yep," Greggory agreed, bobbing his head forward and back. "They used to say Facebook was the devil; it's about to be Instagram. Or Snapchat. It disappears, but that doesn't mean nobody saw it."

"Even if you think you're careful, that woman you're with, that you think operates at the height of discretion can't wait to open her mouth and brag about who she's with. I tell these guys all the time, but..."

Gabe shook his head slowly. "They don't want to listen. And in the moment, they don't care. Do they, Gib?"

I'd been listening to the conversation, enough to follow along but not enough to be interested in what my brothers were discussing. I stirred my drink, which had been sitting so long it was warm and watered down. My cigar sat smoking and neglected in the ashtray. My mood was more than mellow, deeper than melancholy.

"In the moment," I said to Gabe, lifting my glass to the waitress as she passed. "Men don't care about much of anything. We are of singular mind, in the moment. I want what I want and damn the consequences. That's how they get themselves in a situation where they need a divorce attorney. Because at some point they said *hell yes* when they should have said *hell no*."

"You sound kinda strong right there, Gib. You've been dragging ass for weeks, the corners of your mouth all down-turned. Can I guess what you said *hell yes* to when you should have said *hell no*?" Gabe asked the question, but his near-twin Gregg wore the same quizzical expression, one that said I wasn't getting away from the table without spilling something.

"Vanessa Jackson," I said, confirming what I knew was gossip around the office. And around the table at Mink's when I wasn't there. "I was seeing her, for a while. I know, I know. You warmed me. And you were right. It got heavy quickly and... I mean, I don't know what happened but it blew up."

I was quiet about my admission, but they each responded with loud a '*Ooooohhhhh*', rearing back dramatically in their seats. "You both need to dial it back or I'm done talking."

"Okay, okay," said Gregg, pulling his chair closer to the table and leaning in. "So talk. Are things still heavy, or..."

The waitress dropped by with a fresh drink for me. I waited until she stepped away to answer. "Not anymore."

"You're still working her divorce though, right?" Asked Gabe. "You're too far into that to hand it off to someone else."

"Yeah, so things are nice and awkward now. If it's not

about the divorce, she doesn't acknowledge my messages. She said to get that taken care of, so that's what I'm working on."

"Sounds like you want to work on more than her divorce though."

I practically inhaled the fresh bourbon and set the glass to the side, nodding and wiping the corners of my mouth. "You tried to tell me. I should have just left things as they were. Like you said, there's a danger in crossing that line with a client, especially with a volatile partner that can't let go. There was a draw to her. The feeling was mutual. I thought I knew what was doing, but obviously..."

I shrugged my shoulder. "I said the wrong thing, I didn't back off when she let it known she wasn't happy. I pushed the conversation too far, and now she won't take my calls. Won't talk to me unless it's about her case. Which is going shitty, by the way. That's what our argument was about."

"Define shitty. How shitty?"

"He's picking apart the entire petition, fighting everything Vanessa asked for. Clarification here, different amounts there, re-negotiation of this, dispute of that. Never ending, stupid bullshit."

"You should be used to that, though. That's how it goes when a spouse doesn't want his wife to move on."

"I get that. The thing is... he's keeping an attorney very busy and this guy's not doing these briefs for free— not at the rate they're coming. I'm suspicious because he says, out of his mouth, that he's near bankruptcy. The IRS is after him and so are his creditors— his wages are probably being garnished for the credit cards he maxed out while he was married to Vanessa. And they're about to be garnished more for child support—"

"So there's a secret source of money somewhere," Gregg summarized. "But when you brought it up to her she said..."

"She said don't go looking for money that isn't there. Except... it kind of has to be there, doesn't it?"

"Seems like it. There's a reason she doesn't want you to find it. Maybe she helped him get it?"

I wagged my head. "I doubt that. She'd have something to hold over him if she did. It's more like..." I paused, pondering my next statement. "It's more like there's something she knows and she wants to be away from him before the shit hits the fan. I don't know. But I want to."

"Okay, hear me out, here. She's already mad at you, right? She's already not talking to you, you're already not seeing her. What's she going to do, *not* see you some more? It's unlikely she'll fire you— another attorney won't take her case for what you're charging her. So what, if she doesn't want you to look. Look anyway."

I relaxed in the soft leather of the chair and picked up my cigar. It had grown a length of ash that I knocked off before placing the tip between my teeth. I considered Gabe's point. My gut was rarely wrong about things.

My gut told me there was something to find. My gut told me that there was more to Warren than a sonofabitch who hated to lose. My gut also told me that his soon to be ex-wife had a few secrets of her own.

"Do we still use Yvette at Young Investigations?"

I pulled my phone from my pocket and scrolled the address book with my thumb, already forming a plan. Yvette was a former Army Investigator who'd opened a private agency when her fiancé died in Afghanistan just before they were both due to finish their service.

"Yup," Gabe answered. "She's probably the best option. She's quick and quiet."

"And cheap," I added, pulling up the text messaging app. "I can't bill Vanessa for this."

I shot off a quick text to Yvette, letting her know I had a

small job for her and asked her to call my office in the morning. She responded that she would and I tucked my phone away.

"Should I feel guilty about this? Because I don't."

Both of my brothers smirked across the table. "It's ammunition. She doesn't need to know that you know anything. The way Yvette works, Warren will never know he's being tailed. The more you know, the better you serve Vanessa."

"At least that's the party line," finished Gabe, bumping Gregg's fist as he said it.

"I should really know better than to follow advice from you two. Especially when you still act like frat boys. At least you aren't dressed alike tonight."

Gregg laughed. "We were, but I changed before I came here tonight. You're right, it's creepy—"

"He only thinks that now because his love interest said so. Two weeks ago, he was all *let's wear the blue pinstripe on Tuesday...*"

"Oh wait... catch me up. Love interest? That waitress you said you'd been talking to? Made a dent in her armor?"

"You didn't know? Gregg and that fine ass hon— waitress over there have been spending some time together."

Gabe tipped his head toward the same waitress I'd noticed paying him more attention than usual a few weeks ago. Just as we all turned our heads in her direction, she picked up a tray from the bar and turned to face us. And froze.

Gregg cleared his throat, the first to look away. "It'd be cool if y'all could stop staring at my woman."

"Your woman? Moving kind of quick, aren't you?"

"Says the man who was fucking his client. You have no room to criticize."

"Touché'. Just saying. Take your time, man. Know all you

can about her. I'm two for two on women I thought I knew, but I had no idea what I was getting into. Literally."

I tapped out my cigar and stood, tossing a few bills to the center of the table. "I'm out. I want to prep for my call with Yvette in the morning. Be good."

YVETTE DID MORE THAN CALL THE NEXT MORNING. AT 9AM sharp, she strolled into my office, wearing her usual uniform of baggy jeans, black boots, an ARMY t-shirt and a cap over her hair, a ponytail sticking out of the opening in the back.

Yvette had been doing private investigation work for a few years and always looked the same. Deep caramel skin tone, fit physique, no-nonsense facial expression. She was the definition of poker face and her body language didn't give away much either. It wasn't until I spent some time with her that I came to realize how witty and quirky she was, some by accident and some by design. The loss of her fiancé had hurt her deeply, so her job, which involved hiding from her subjects and the public, served both her professionally and personally. A person never *got to know* Yvette, but I felt like I was as close as a person could come to knowing her.

"I thought you were calling me this morning," I told her, releasing her from the hug she didn't want but stood still for anyway.

"I was in the neighborhood, dropping off some invoices, picking up some checks. Thought I would stop by," she said, taking a seat in one of the chairs in front of my desk.

Instead of sitting in the leather chair like it was a formal meeting, I sat in the chair next to her and kicked a foot up to rest it on the edge of the desk. "Well, it's good to see you. It's been awhile."

"Same here. I swear, you're the only Kincaid that can relax in this place."

I laughed, giving myself a once-over. It was a Friday, and though Kincaid didn't have a Casual Friday policy, I'd worn jeans and a button up shirt and the Clarks that Vanessa said she liked. "I like to keep my mother on her toes. She's already rolled her eyes at me twice this morning."

"I have to admit, I come up here to give the old bat a reason to clutch her pearls."

"Ten minutes after you leave, she'll ask me if I have to keep using your agency."

"Speaking of... your little case must be something important. I rarely get a text from you after hours."

"Oh, yeah. Now, when I say it's a small case, I mean it. I'm not looking for anything fancy, but..."

I dropped my foot and leaned across my desk to a folder that was stuffed with pages I'd gathered on Warren Jackson, anything I could find that was readily available— which wasn't much— coupled with the information supplied by Vanessa. "There's this divorce I'm working on. Husband is highly suspicious. My client, his soon to be ex, is cagey about him. I get the strong feeling that she doesn't want me to know something."

"Now you need to know what that something is." She took the folder from my hands, flipping through each page and making little noises— a grunt here, a *hmmm* there.

"Anything stand out for you, at first glance?" I folded my arms across my chest and sat back, trying to read her face. As per usual, it was pointless. The Army had trained her well— she'd never reveal her mother's secret to great lasagna, let alone military secrets. For damn sure, she wasn't going to let me know what she was thinking in that moment.

"Not really, but that's what the investigation is for. How

many hours do you want me to spend on this? You know my rate, right?"

I nodded. "Yeah, I know your rate. I guess we start with twenty and see how it goes."

"You want me to limit this to internet, or what?"

"Well, you see the history there," I said, gesturing toward the folder. "I think I've exhausted the internet search, but see what your people can dig up. I don't even know where to start, but maybe his mistress would be a better mark. We have strong reason to believe that's where he's living."

"Mmkay," she responded, flipping through more pages. "There's usually a little bit of overlap, but do you want me to dig up anything on your client?"

"No!" I hadn't intended to answer as strongly as I did. Her eyes popped up from the folder and an eyebrow crept toward her hairline. "I uh... no," I continued, quieter now. "Just him. She doesn't know I'm looking into him. She asked me not to but I can't.... *Not.*"

"Right. You need to know everything." She stood, tucking the folder under her arm. "I'll get to work on it this afternoon. Daily briefings every morning via email unless I strike gold. You want me to call your cell with any news?"

"Please." I stood, threatening to hug her again. She laughed and ducked away from my open arms.

"Go on with that touchy feely stuff. Everything good with you? You don't seem yourself..."

"They teach you that mind reading stuff in the Army? Nothing I can't handle. Getting these answers will help a lot."

Yvette leaned in and softly, so quietly I almost didn't hear her, said, "You got a thing for the client, huh?"

A blazing heat crossed my face. Obviously, I wasn't doing a good job of hiding what was going between Vanessa and me. I shoved my hands into the pockets of my jeans and shrugged, trying to control my facial expression.

Yvette chuckled, humming, "*Mmmhmmm.* You know you're not supposed to go there, Counselor."

"There's no rule against it. No hard and fast one anyway. It snuck up on me. But things are on a hiatus right now. This..." I nodded toward the folder. "Is why. So, now I want to know what I'm getting into. Is she worth going after, or is this a complete mess and I should stay away?"

"Mmhmmm," she hummed again, then turned toward the door. "Which way do I go so I walk past Sylvia's office? I feel like getting on her nerves today."

"Oh, please. Spare me her tirade, today."

CHAPTER SIXTEEN

ibson

I STEPPED OUT FOR LUNCH WITH GABE AND GREGG, ON THE promise that we could eat somewhere normal, not be served by scantily clad women. Much to their dislike, we had what was probably a very boring lunch for the two of them at a cafe on the first floor of the building.

Just as I'd made it back to my office, the interior line on my phone buzzed. The caller ID said it was Janet, Mother's secretary. I punched the button to pick up the call.

"Yes," I answered, giving my standard greeting.

"Sylvia would like to see you in her office," she said. Then added, "Now."

"'I'll be there in a minute."

There was no sense in arguing, I figured, rolling my chair back. She would come and find me if I didn't come to her, which would agitate her. Ever since my conversation with my brothers about being the favorite, I'd been more conscious of how we treated each other. I'd also been looking for clues to prove their theory wrong. So far, I hadn't found much to support it. But I hadn't found much to deny it, either.

I passed Janet's desk and gave Mother's office door a light *tap-tap*. She was seated behind the desk, the surface of which was unusually cluttered, covered in papers and files. Her iPad and keyboard sat in front of her, along with a notepad on which she'd been making a long list.

Garrett sat in a guest chair opposite her. His face bore its usual pinched expression.

"If this is another ambush about my clients, I don't need to be here. You two can drag me all by yourselves, without any help from me."

"This isn't an ambush, son. Sit." Mother gestured toward the other guest chair, next to Garrett. I dropped into it, still wary but more curious. Mother looked nervous and she wasn't her usual snappy self. For that matter, Garrett had nothing to say, when he would have normally made a few jabs by now.

"What's going on?" My gaze bounced between the two of them. They were making me nervous.

"Garrett has shared some news with me this morning and I wanted to have you in on the conversation because it affects you."

"What news? Affects me how?"

"Cheri is pregnant," he blurted. "We're finally at a point where we can start telling people."

Even though Garrett and I weren't close, I was struck with a moment of joy for him. He and his wife had been struggling with infertility for a few years. "That's great, man. That's really great. But why do you look like that isn't good news? You've been trying for a while."

"Yeah, we've been trying. We've had a couple of miscarriages that I haven't told anyone but Mother about. So, this is good news, but..."

Garrett inhaled deeply. "Cheri really misses her family down in Florida. She's always talked about not wanting to raise children here, and since it looks like this pregnancy is going to be viable, she wants to go ahead and make the move. She's been talking with her mother about renting office space to relocate her interior design firm to the Fort Lauderdale area. Her father wants to make room for me at his law firm..."

He paused, spreading his hands in a seemingly helpless gesture.

"Is that what you want? To pick up your life and move to Florida?"

"It wasn't in the plan. Not as far as I was concerned. Cheri had always talked about moving back to Florida when we had children. Honestly, I was sure we wouldn't be having any. I didn't think she was serious, but in the last month or so, it's all she can talk about. It would make her happy, and what with the difficulties we've had, that's hard to accomplish some days. I have the kind of job I can do anywhere. Since I took on that special case last year, I already have a license to practice in Florida."

"With Garrett leaving the firm, there's an open slot on the Senior team. I have a few associates that I could elevate. Your brothers, of course are eligible, but I thought it would be a good opportunity for you to dig into the business and start taking things seriously. Maybe if you see it from our end, it'll give you more of an appreciation for the cases we take, how we handle them, why we bill what we do."

"I know you have a negative view of how the firm is run, Gib," Garrett added, "but it's not like every other firm out there isn't run the exact same way. Cheri's father runs his firm this way. Clark, Peters & Jacobsen, down the street, runs theirs the same. There are entire business management philosophies based on how law firms operate. We don't do it this way because we're money hungry. We do it this way because it works, because it serves the clients and pays the bills."

"So, you called me down here to offer me a promotion if I take Garrett's place as your right-hand man. But you would want me to start doing things the way he would do them, the way you want me to do them. I'd become more involved in the management of the firm, which leaves me too busy to serve my own clients. Am I reading this right?"

"It's not a trick, Gibson. I genuinely want you to move up here, to succeed at Kincaid. But you're right; I'm not going to promote you to Senior Associate and give you managing power for you to continue serving the clients you serve."

As recently as a few weeks ago, I would have pushed myself out of my chair and walked out, giving Mother and Garrett a few choice words about the offer and what I thought of it. But recent events— this situation with Vanessa, mostly— had me reeling, thinking hard about making changes.

Maybe I didn't have to be so doggedly dedicated to a certain kind of client. Maybe I was too idealistic, too much a dreamer ,too focused on trying to change lives and help people. Maybe I wasn't focused enough on the things that mattered, letting my "manhood" dictate things I should leave to my brain to decide.

Despite wanting to walk out that door and keep walking right out of the suite and never come back, maybe I would have to suck it up and do things Mother's way— for a little while— to get what I wanted from her. I was not looking forward to that kind of personal sacrifice.

"How long do I have to think about this?"

"Cheri will be heading down to Fort Lauderdale next month. I'll follow in a month or so. Let's say six weeks. I have a few cases I need to wrap up before I can leave. Maybe I could get your help—"

"Let's not assume that I'm going to accept. You've had no problem using Gabe and Gregg in the past; let's not change that. *If* I take this opportunity, I'll need to clear my plate too."

"Six weeks it is, then." Mother tapped the wood surface of her desk like a judge banging a gavel. "But if you decide one way or the other before then, I would appreciate you talking to me about it. Agreed?"

In a stupor, I rose from the chair. Just as I reached for the knob, Mother added, "It goes without saying that Senior Associates still see clients on Friday. High profile clients. We do not have a casual dress policy, Gibson."

I almost laughed, but I knew that would start something I didn't want to finish. I ignored her and pulled the door open, uttering a low, "Yes ma'am," before leaving her office.

I suddenly had a lot to think about it.

VANESSA

I shuffled through the folders and papers stacked neatly in front of me one more time to make sure I had everything I needed for this meeting— the purchase agreement, inspection forms, my commission statement were all there. A real estate closing was nothing more than a transfer of purchase from seller to buyer, but I liked to attend every closing, just in case a selling agent decided to pull the wool over on their client. Or mine.

Dre Prescott, aka DJ Fresh Beats, sat next to me looking less like a hip hop mogul and more like a businessman in a well-fitting slate grey suit. He'd shaved, taming the wiry, wild hairs of his goatee. His hair was freshly cut, his nails clean and squared. He clasped his hands together waiting patiently for the title company representative, the property seller and his agent.

"Stop fidgeting," he mumbled, as I flipped through the folders again. "Making me nervous."

"I'm not fidgeting," I argued, closing the folder I'd been looking through and pushing the stack toward the center of the table. "Just making sure everything is here."

"Fidgeting."

I smirked. "Fine. I'm done fidgeting. I told you we shouldn't have come so early."

"I got places to be. I figured if we came early, we could leave early but uh..." He craned his neck to peek out of the open door. The staff in the office were moving slowly, with no sense of urgency. "Looks like we're gonna be sitting here for a minute."

He yawned quietly, then closed his mouth with a snap. "So what's your story?" He asked, rolling heavily lidded eyes over to me.

"My story? What do you mean?"

"Your story. You're not wearing a ring, so you're single? A woman like you should be with somebody. What's that about?"

"How do you know I'm not with somebody?"

"Recently... I don't know. You seem different. Kind of down in the way a woman gets down when she's trying to pretend nothing's wrong."

I laughed. *You're that obvious with it, huh, Nessa?*

I missed Gibson, more than I thought I would. He was the first man that I put my trust in, after Warren. Which, by the way, wasn't easy for me to do. He was also the first man that I'd felt genuinely attracted to, that I liked as a person since Warren. He gave me hope that maybe I could pick a good man.

And then he went and dashed those hopes, sending me

into a frenzy of thoughts and feelings that I didn't want to be thinking, didn't want to be feeling. It hurt to care for someone and not be able to pick up the phone and hear their voice, make a date and look forward to being wrapped up in them. He sent enough inane, innocuous text messages that I could never forget he existed. He left plenty of doors open for me to walk through. I could restore things between us by walking through one of them.

I could. But I chose not to.

Sonja said I was punishing myself for my poor choices, that I was cutting myself off from the world so that I didn't make more mistakes. That I still hadn't given Gibson a real chance. That I hadn't given *myself* a real chance either.

"Chile," she said one night, half drunk and, I suspect, a little high. "We learn our lessons by living. You don't learn the game by sitting on the sidelines. You got to get in there. Play. Mess up. Learn. Mess up some more. But play the game, baby."

I got it. I understood that, I really did. But even if I was ready to crawl back to Gibson and beg his forgiveness, what were we even doing? Having some fun, blowing off some steam? I wasn't ready to share my past with someone that was going to drop into my life, then drop back out once he picked up on a little dirt. I wasn't pristine. I had a past. I wasn't ready to put that much trust in him, to believe that he could hear about... *everything* and hold judgment. I'd seen people try, but eventually it came between us.

"I'm in the middle of a divorce." In about an hour, he wouldn't be a client anymore and I'd probably never see him again. We had time to kill, and he was asking.

"Oh yeah? That's rough. Hard on the heart." I nodded in agreement. "So... you're free, then? Single?"

"Yes," I answered with a laugh. "I'm single. You got a friend I should get to know?"

"Naw," he replied. "I wouldn't pass you off. You should get to know *me*."

I wasn't sure if I heard him right. I tilted my head and cut my eyes toward him. "What did you say?"

"You heard me," he answered, cutting his eyes right back to me. "You should get to know me. My girl is gonna be gone for a few weeks, finishing up some business in Virginia. So... we should get together."

My jaw fell open and stayed there for a few beats. "Uhm...we should get together and do what, Dre?"

He smiled, beaming a full mouth of pearly whites at me. "Don't tell me I got to spell it out for you. *Nessa*." His brows lifted and lowered and he leered in my direction. His eyes crawled my face, then my neck and the small, tasteful amount of cleavage I had on display.

I clutched at the lapels of the light silk blouse I wore, pulling it closed, in complete disbelief of the conversation I was having.

"I wondered why you looked so familiar. It came to me a while back. You got married and had some kids, got *respectable* an' shit, but yeah. I remember you from Red Heels. You got thicker. Nice ass, hips, thighs. Fuller face. You was juicy back in the day but now?" He grunted, licking his lips.

"Me and my boys used to come around to watch you dance. That one light skinned girl... Moxie, her name was, she took your spot when you left. She was aight, a little stiff but she could work the pole."

"Dre, this is inappropriate conversation, alright? I need you to stop talking. And once we get this closing over with, I don't want to ever hear from you again."

"Ay, sorry if I offended you," he barreled on, undeterred by my reddened face and insistence that he shut the fuck up. "I figured, you know... you got this real estate thing going, but do you do private shows now? Some of these supposedly "former" strippers be charging dudes to fuck on the side. Is that why you're getting a divorce? Your man can't handle other men looking at your titties?"

"You know what?" I picked up my bag from the seat next to me and pushed my chair back and stood. "I don't need to be here. The title agent has all the information she needs, the purchase agreement is straightforward. I'll have them wire my commission to Donovan. Good luck, Dre."

"Ay, where you going?" He sat up and tried to reach for me. "I said I was sorry, I just thought—"

I swerved out of his reach and backed toward the door. "You just thought you could say any old shit to me because I used to dance at Red Heels. Once you remembered where you know me from, you stopped talking to me like your mama raised you with manners and good sense and showed me what you really think of me. Well, fuck you, Dre Prescott. Should you need any further real estate assistance, don't call me. I'm not available."

I paused before leaving, turning long enough to spit, "And I hate your music!"

CHAPTER SEVENTEEN

anessa

I BURST INTO THE DONOVAN LUXURY REAL ESTATE SUITE still fuming, so angry I was shaking. If I could just get to my office, sit down and decompress before someone started talking to me, I would be fine... but no such luck. As soon as I made it to my office, Virgil sauntered down the hall wearing the signature Prada slippers he wore at work.

He was the most pretentious man I'd ever worked for, and if it wasn't for the fact that he was Maxine's right hand and that he'd helped me out immensely when I first came to Donovan, we wouldn't get along at all. As it was, I was indebted to him for his knowledge and guiding hand in building my career, so I put up with him, Prada and all.

"Hey, Vanessa. Missy from Emerson Title called about wiring the commission over. You missed a number on the form. I thought you were going to that closing?"

"Oh, I was there," I said, dropping my bag into its designated drawer and slamming it shut. "But thanks to Dre Prescott's slick mouth, I left before it started. And the next hot shit record producer, child star, *has more money than God* motherfucker that rolls up in here is going to somebody else. I'm tired of these spoiled, entitled ass brats."

Virgil blanched, then took a step into my office. "I sense some juicy details forthcoming." He pulled out a chair and slid into it, crossed one leg over the other and uttered the most classic of his phrases. "Shut up and tell me everything."

"I don't want to talk about it, Virgil. Can I get a break from the cast *of Growing Up Hip Hop*, please?"

"Well, I can go to bat for you, sure. But you know Maxine wants you working with those clients—"

"Why? What about me says I know what their lives are about? We're the same age group... so what? Their money spends the same with any other agent in this firm. And maybe another agent won't have a client hit on them at a closing."

I heard a low chuckle and looked up to find Maxine leaning against the door jamb. "Is that all you're whining about? Do you know how many clients see this rock—" She wiggled her ring finger at me; the diamonds in her wedding band glinted in the light. "And still try to say something to me? Not that you should put up with disrespect, but some of this comes with the territory. You can't just storm out of a meeting because a client has a filthy mouth."

"This was a little bit more than disrespect, Maxine. He straight up called me a—" I sighed, slumping my shoulders and dropping into my chair.

Maxine slipped into my office and shut the door behind her, taking the seat next to Virgil. "Dre Prescott said some foul shit to you?"

"Relax. I didn't punch him or anything. Though I wanted to."

"It was bad enough for you to walk out of a closing," said Virgil. "What did he say?"

"Well... first. There's something that neither of you know about me, but Dre does. And he brought it up and made some very..." I wracked my brain for the right word but couldn't find it, so I settled for "crass commentary."

Maxine seemed surprised. "I didn't realize you knew Dre."

"I don't. But he knows me. Ten years ago, I was a dancer at Red Heels Gentleman's Club, over in Bankhead. More to the point, I was a stripper. Dre, I guess, used to be a regular. I didn't recognize him, but I wouldn't. That club gets a lot of business, a lot of high profile clientele. Red Heels is where I met my husband."

Both Maxine and Virgil sat across from me, wide eyed with mouths half hanging open. Max was the first to move, clearing her throat a few times, then leaning forward, resting her arms on the desk between us.

"So... you... danced. Nude?"

"Not nude," I answered with a laugh. "At least not on stage. In the private rooms, depending on the customer..." I shrugged. "There were a lot of see through and lace and plastic costumes. I was mostly topless. But after I started dating Warren, he laid down so many rules about what I couldn't do, it wasn't worth it to stay there. All the stuff that gets big tips, he wouldn't let me do anymore.

"Eventually, he talked me into leaving. He was talking marriage and he wanted his wife to have a certain kind of image. We moved to a big house in a neighborhood of well-to-do folks. The initial reaction to my past was... not well received, among my neighbors, so I stopped telling people what I used to do and concentrated on pretending to be like them."

Virgil was still dumbfounded. "I never would have imagined that, Vanessa. And not in a bad way, just..." He shrugged, the end of his sentence hanging in the air.

"I know. That was the goal, to make sure I carried myself in a way that people never knew what I used to do. That's why I never said anything to either of you. I didn't want to be treated differently because of something I haven't done in eight years. And I didn't want you to look at me and have assumptions about me. I'm good at this, despite what happened with Dre. I want to keep my job."

"There's no danger of losing your job, Vanessa," Maxine assured me. She reached across the desk and grabbed one of my hands and squeezed it. "I wish you could have trusted us — me, at least, enough to share that, but I understand why you didn't. So... what happened with Dre?"

I heaved a long, heavy sigh. "We were talking before the closing started. He noticed that I wasn't wearing a ring. He said his girl would be leaving town for a few weeks and suggested that he and I could *get together*. And when I seemed surprised that he would think I was that kind of person, he made it clear that he remembered me from Red Heels. And that he thought I... "

I tried to be strong, but it was tough, coming clean with people who thought they knew me. I was terrified of the backlash. I dropped my gaze to Maxine's ring laden fingers wrapped tightly around mine. She squeezed my hand a few times. I squeezed back.

"He made some comments, making it sound like I had sex with my clients for money. Said my divorce must be due to my husband not being able to handle other men looking at me. He asked if I held private parties in my off-time. He was basically beyond disrespectful. But you're right, Max. I should have expected that reaction and that treatment. I should be used to people thinking—"

"Whoa, whoa, whoa. In no way did I mean that you

should sit back and let a client call you a prostitute. I'm glad you got out of there before you clocked him upside his head, because I sure would have. I'm going to call his manager and let him know—"

"Don't call his manager, Max. Dre is a grown ass man, a few years older than me. It's not like his manager can control his mouth or his thoughts. The sale is over, we got paid, and I don't have to deal with him anymore."

"Damn right, we don't," blurted Virgil. "This is Donovan *Luxury* Real Estate. He bought a cheap shack in the woods. He can take that business to another firm. Thank goodness, he decided to buy the acreage around the property. That land appraised at a high value."

"Well, I would like to work with another kind of client for a while, if that's okay. I could go for a boring transaction or two."

Maxine laughed, then tapped my hand before standing. "We don't have any boring clients, here. We can give you a break from the young and famous for a little bit, but I'm serious about making sure you corner that market. Real Estate is a great investment, likely the first sensible thing they'll do with their money. And when that money runs out, at least they'll have a home to live in. I want them to buy something from someone young, smart and successful."

I felt a blush creep up from my neck, the same blush that always washed over me when Maxine complimented me. She was a force in the industry; I was green when she took me on and I'd already learned so much from her.

"Oh, and Vanessa..." Maxine paused, her hand on the knob. "Virgil can attest hat maybe I wasn't dancing topless, but I *entertained* my fair share of men. Don't let that have you thinking less of yourself. You're beneath no one. Unless you want to be."

She winked, then walked out. Virgil stood and followed

her, tossing a "see me before you leave, so I can cut your commission check," over his shoulder before leaving as well.

I nearly collapsed in my chair, blowing out a breath so hard and heavy I almost coughed. That... didn't go as badly as it could have. I hadn't even planned to come clean, but I was afraid I'd lose my job over my temper tantrum with Dre.

Besides, if someone like Dre remembered me from not-so-long ago, how long would I have been able to hide it?

I opened the drawer I'd slammed shut and dug through my bag for my phone. I could go for it, call Gibson and do the same, since I was feeling good and bold. Maybe it wouldn't be as bad as I imagined it to be. Maybe I could say the words, since I'd already said them.

I pulled up his number, which I still hadn't removed from my VIP list, so every call, every text, every email came through like it always had. Sometimes I responded but most of the time I let calls go to voicemail and ignored anything unless it absolutely required a response. I wanted to be strong, to get through this divorce before I made decisions about Gibson.

Every time I picked up the phone, I imagined the worst possible response to the news that the woman that he was developing feelings for had a sordid past that would probably drag down his reputation and his family's good name. I groaned, gripping the phone, my finger hovering over his name.

Why was I in a hurry to open up to Gibson, just to be pushed away because I didn't meet some standard?

I moved to set the phone down and accidentally clicked on his name. The screen changed, letting me know that I was calling Gibson. "*Shit!*" I hissed, moving my thumb to hang up before he picked up.

"Hello? Hey, Vanessa," I heard from the phone. "Don't tell me you purse dialed me..."

I brought the phone to my ear. "No, I didn't purse dial you. I mean, I didn't mean to call you, but..."

"I'll take a call from you, even on accident. You okay?"

"Yeah. I'm okay. I closed on Dre Prescott's property today. Finally."

"Good. He was a picky client. Happy to get that settled?"

If you only knew... "I am, actually. And I asked Maxine to stop giving me those kinds of clients for a little bit. I could use a couple of mega rich Saudi businessmen right about now."

Gibson laughed. I held back a whimper at the sound in my ear. I had vivid memories of the last time we'd been together, before I flipped out over something I knew was silly, now. I'd been laying next to him, up against him, listening to him talk and laugh and loving how it felt and sounded through him.

"So... you didn't mean to call me?"

"I started to. But decided I wouldn't. But then I did accidentally call you."

"Oh. Well, can we accidentally talk? Or happen to be at the same place at the same time?"

"Do you have news? About the divorce?"

I heard him blow out a breath. I winced, sure that I required every bit of patience he had. "Not yet. But I was hoping to talk about anything but your divorce. I can come to Sam's if that's easier. I haven't been there in a few weeks. I'm going through lemon pepper wing withdrawals."

"It's not that I don't want to talk to you. I want to finish one thing before I start something else."

"So, you're going to keep us on hold until your divorce is settled, no matter how long it takes? You want to give Warren that much power, to keep you from moving on, from being happy? You were happy with me, weren't you?"

"Yes," I admitted. There was never any pretending that I

wasn't happy with Gibson. "I've never been alone, you know? Never had to depend on me, fend for myself before. I need to find me, I guess. Figure out who I am outside of Warren. I know that doesn't make sense."

"I respect your decision. I don't have to like it, but I respect it. You need to do what you need to do. Will you call me when you've... found yourself?"

I chuckled. "You don't have to make it sound like some new age thing I'm doing. I want some time to stand on my own two feet. Is that okay?"

"Yeah," he answered, after a moment. I could hear the disappointment in his voice, the way it rumbled low across the line. "I respect what you're doing. Just remember that I care about you. Those two things don't have to be at war with each other. When you're ready, all you have to do is call. You hear me?"

"I hear you, Gibson. Thanks. You'll still call me if anything happens with Warren?"

"Of course. Listen...I hate to cut this short, but I'm late for a meeting. I'll talk to you soon, alright?"

I said my goodbyes and held the phone to my ear as the line disconnected.

GIBSON

I hung up the phone after my call with Vanessa, feeling strangely encouraged by it. We hadn't made any steps forward — she wouldn't agree to see me and wouldn't talk to me for longer than a few minutes and that was by accident. But she wasn't ignoring me anymore.

It was a start.

I locked my phone and popped the door latch on my Jeep, grabbing my bag from the passenger seat as I got out. I jogged across the parking lot to the front entrance at East Side Community Center.

"Hey, Gibson!" Diya called out, as soon as I walked through the double doors. She wore a short sleeved polo with *ECCC* stitched on the sleeves A little boy with deep walnut skin and chubby cheeks sat on her lap, playing with a small, red fire truck while Diya fed him from a plastic container. "This is Daniel. They brought him over so I could feed him lunch. He's almost done."

"Take your time," I told her. "Are we meeting in here?"

I pointed toward the small conference room we'd used the last few times I'd come to the center to meet with her. She nodded, so I headed across the hall and got settled in the room. A few minutes later, Diya walked in, closing the door behind her.

"Thanks for coming to meet me. I hate going all the way downtown."

"I don't mind at all. What did you want to talk about?" I had my notepad and pen ready to take notes so I'd be able to itemize my bill.

"So... I want to terminate Armando's parental rights to Daniel."

I dropped the pen and scrubbed my fingertips across my forehead. "Are you sure about this? Why, suddenly?"

"It's not sudden. Ever since I got arrested and Daniel was taken away, he didn't seem like he cared at all. Not about me, not about our baby. It was all me, trying to get him back—"

"Diya, what was he supposed to do, from jail?"

"There was a lot he could do!" Her bright eyes lit up like flames of anger. "His other baby's mother gets money, her child is taken care of, even though he's away. She's got his people watching over her, over her son, making sure neither of them go without. What do I have?"

She sucked her teeth and shot her eyes toward the

window. "Nothing. I was in jail and I had nothing. My mom had to get me a lawyer. He doesn't send anyone around to check on Daniel. Not even an extra dollar here and there to help pay for food, some diapers. I'm still paying off court fines, plus fees for taking my GED and doing everything the judge said I had to do. Me and my mom did that. All by ourselves, and don't get me wrong, I'm proud of that, but he's had nothing to do with me getting Daniel back and he obviously doesn't give a shit about his welfare. He doesn't ever ask about his son."

"Diya, be honest. Is this something your mom is pushing for?" If I remembered right, her mother had been staunchly against Diya ever having contact with Armando again.

"No, Gib," she answered, rolling her eyes and heaving a loud breath. "This is something I want. Because if it's going to be me and Daniel, then I want it to be just me and Daniel. When Armando gets out of prison... *if* he gets out, because he's already been in trouble for trying to sell behind bars— I don't want him coming to us demanding to be treated like that boy's father. Not when he hasn't been *acting* like his father."

I picked up the pen again and began writing, though reluctantly. I wasn't sure a judge would go for Diya's reasoning, but sometimes a client got something in their heads and, despite my trying to save them the legal fees, they had to see it through. It was a drastic measure, to remove a parent's rights to a child. But, for all I knew, Armando would readily agree and sign the paperwork.

Of course, it was rarely that easy.

"Tell you what. I'll draw up the paperwork and send it to you to review. But then I want you to sit on it, for at least thirty days. I'm not trying to talk you out of anything, but once you do this, it's done. If you're upset with Armando, this isn't the way to get back at him. If you're ready to file after the waiting period, I'll do it for you. Also..."

I set the pen down and leaned forward, clasping my hands together. "I'll always be here, if you need me. But there's a chance I won't be as available as I have been. Nothing's been decided yet, but some things are changing at the firm, from the top down. It might affect me. It might not. I wanted to give you a heads up."

"Oh." She stared, wide eyed. "You're not leaving, are you?"

I chuckled, landing a hand on her shoulder and giving her a squeeze. "If I left the firm, it would be to start my own gig, and I would take you with me. Don't worry about that at all, okay?"

"Okay. Sorry I panicked for a second. That was very self-centered of me."

I laughed. "What's that about? Are you in therapy?"

"Yeah." Shyly, she smiled. "I've been going twice a month. It's going to my head, I think."

"As long as it helps." I slid my notepad off the table and stuffed it into my bag, along with my pen. "So listen, like I said, I'll send you the paperwork, which will start the clock. And then in thirty days I'll call you and see what you want to do. Deal?"

She nodded, beaming a warm smile. "I'll still be sure, in thirty days. Waiting won't be a problem. I want no connection to Armando and the only thing he can hold over me is my son."

My phone buzzed on the table. I had a text from Yvette.

"In time, we'll deal with that," I told Diya, snatching up the phone. I stood, pulling the strap of my satchel over my shoulder. "Something just came in, so I'll let you get back to work. I'll be in touch, and call me if you need me."

I PICKED UP MY ORDER OF ICED TEA FROM THE BAR AT Drip, a mid-city coffeehouse, then slid into a booth across from Yvette. She wasn't in her usual t-shirt, jeans and ball cap uniform. She wore her hair down, a form fitting blouse splashed with pastel colors, a pair of slacks and, if I wasn't mistaken, her lips were shiny with gloss.

I must have stared long and hard, because Yvette laughed. "My mother had an appointment and she wouldn't let me go with her unless I dressed like a grownup, so..." She spread her arms wide, splaying her hands. "You get grownup Yvette today."

"Well, I like her. She should show up more often."

"It's not practical in my line of business. I can't hide in some bushes in this getup with all this... hair." She blew a breath, which moved a lock of hair out of her eyes. "Anyway, thanks for meeting me. I have a report for you."

"Great. I'm a little nervous. Whatever you have to say could change a lot of things."

"Well," she drawled, pulling a folder from the bag sitting next to her. "Things are about to change. Let's start with the easy stuff. I confirmed that he is indeed living with a woman. Her name is Andra Mitchell. According to Facebook, she's new, as in the last six months or so. The woman he left your client for is a different woman. I don't think he's seeing them both right now. Maybe she wised up and kicked him out.

"He does still work at Service Software. When they downsized three years ago, they converted him to a contract consultant. He got to keep his laptop and his clients, but he lost his office and his expense account. We can safely assume he is working out of Andra Mitchell's home. I trailed him to a Mailboxes Plus location, so he's not getting his mail there, but he's definitely living there."

"Wait a minute..." I grabbed the printout and tracked the words with my finger to make sure I was reading right. "As far as Vanessa knows, the change with his employment happened recently, like within the last few months. He's not had an office for *years*? So, when Warren was leaving on business trips and staying gone, he wasn't even leaving town. He was going to... whomever he was seeing at the time."

Yvette slid a set of photos over to me, two side by side shots of slim, lighter toned black women, each with long hair and gentle curves but one seemed much younger than the other. Neither of them seemed worth leaving Vanessa.

"The woman he was with when he left Vanessa is Jasmine Simmons. No idea when he stopped seeing her, but I'm almost positive there was overlap with this gal here..." She tapped the second photo. "She's older than him by at least ten years, on a good day. I guess the young ones were too hip to his game. He decided to go a for a cougar. And she.... well..."

"What's going on, there?"

"I don't know how he finds these women. She does alright for herself, an Executive Assistant for a brokerage firm. She owns her home; paid off the mortgage after her husband died a long while back. Maybe she seemed lonely or something. At any rate, she's a pretty good mark. He seems to have her completely convinced that he's in love with her. He lives there, works out of the house. I observed them for a few days. Went over the limit on my hours, but I knew it would be worth it."

"And it is. It *is*. What else?"

Yvette grinned, flipping through pages, pulling out a full page printout. "*This* was a little harder to find. I told you my team was gifted, didn't I?"

At my nod, she beamed even brighter. "First thing we did was find his email address and do a little key logger trap. You know, send an innocuous email, he opens it, now we can see everything he types. Our boy has been busy, mostly padding his Cayman Islands bank account." She drew her finger down the edge of the printout, which was a screenshot of an online account. She stopped at what appeared to be the current balance. My eyebrows shot up.

"So, you see that the balance is substantial enough to disappear for a good long while, if not forever, when the time is right. It's more than he'd reasonably be able to save, given his salary, which makes me think he didn't come by it honestly. He's looking to relocate, somewhere near Spain, if his email is any indication. He's got a contact there."

"What a conniving son of a bitch. I wonder if this has been going on since before Vanessa? Maybe she was the original mark—"

"But she got pregnant?" Yvette finished. "Could be. They ended up in what appeared to be marital bliss, which was a good cover for whatever he was doing, I suppose. His type always has someone that believes every word that comes out of his mouth, and is willing to do dirt on his behalf."

"Vanessa admits to being very naive. She was young and he was persuasive. I could see it happening. But then she woke up, and he took off."

"Sounds like Jasmine too. My... *hacker* has been working on tracking down how old this account is. We're not billing for that," she made sure to add. "I need to know."

"Let me know, when you find out. I need to know too." Yvette agreed. "So...it doesn't make sense for him to fight the divorce so strongly when he's planning to leave. He's hounding Vanessa about seeing his children, contesting every request for any kind of support."

"Well, his macho reaction to filing the divorce is what tripped him up. He's been funneling money from his secret account to an account he and Andra share, then from that account to his. We watched him make two transfers from that account to his, and then he sent some checks to his attorney."

I sucked down a mouthful of tea to give myself a minute to think. Then an idea struck me. I pushed my glass to the side and propped my elbows on the table.

"I haven't studied tax law since my second year at Emory, which is too long ago. But I remember enough to know that you can't tell the government that you don't have any money and have a sizable amount stashed somewhere. And you can't *not* pay your taxes while being secretly— albeit illegally wealthy. If your team can prove that account is his— which, if we follow the paper trail, it looks like you can— this could be big. He could go to prison."

"Yup. And the IRS is definitely investigating him."

"You can see that?"

"From his email, yes. He's panicking. Whatever plan he had is falling through."

"So... why doesn't he just run?"

"It takes a lot of guts to leave everything and everyone behind. Maybe he's not ready. Trying to save more money, maybe? Or he's completely consumed with the divorce and he's trying to win."

"The divorce seems to be consuming him. He's fighting it pretty hard. I met this guy. Well, his shoulder met my gut when he rushed me. He's intense. And very much attached to Vanessa, even though he left her."

"So, aside from a few other bits of information, like where he hangs out when he's not at home, that's it. Where do we go from here?"

I smoothed my palm over my freshly cut hair, exhaling slowly and thinking fast. My next step could be huge. It could bring everything to a close.

"Can you get me a report of his hangouts? And something that shows we're doing more than guessing at this money he has stashed. I'd like to see if I can use it to get him to back down on the divorce. If I can call in a favor, I have some leverage."

"Sure. And then?"

"Keep working him. Send the bills. I'll tell you when to stop. His major activity is going to be online, I think. But watch him, and if it looks like he's jumping, I want to know about it."

"You got it," Yvette said, closing the folder and sliding it over to me. "These are your copies. I have my own. I'll email you a list of his most frequently visited places. Please tell me you don't plan to confront him."

I pulled my phone from my bag and scrolled through my contact list. With a sneaky, wry smile, I glanced up at Yvette. "Can't tell you that. I'll be safe, but I have every intention of confronting him."

"You *do* have a thing for your client. Look, I know you have a license to carry; take your piece with you. And if you don't want to, call me. I always have mine on me."

I laughed. Warren didn't come across as the type to carry a piece, but she could be right. I didn't think he'd make a run at me at Sam's, and I paid for that. I made a note to pull my Glock from the safe I kept it in. In my current line of work, I very seldom needed a weapon for protection.

Pulling the gun out of the safe? What are you doing, man?

I pressed the button on the contact I'd located and pressed the phone to my ear. "Pack. Gibson, here. Yeah, I know you're surprised. So am I. Hey uh...there's something you can do for me and you owe me, so I'm not trying to hear 'no'. Can we meet?"

CHAPTER EIGHTEEN

anessa

"One gin and tonic, one Jameson on the rocks. Food will be out in a few. Anything else I can get you while you wait?"

Both patrons shook their heads, reaching for the drinks I'd set on the bar. I tucked the order pad into my apron pocket, smiled and bounced away. I had an endless list of things I could be doing— refilling condiments (and wiping off the lids, because gross), wiping down tables, sweeping the floors, even dusting.

I'd talked Uncle into sprucing the place up a little. We now had new china dishes to serve on, new silverware and cute little silver baskets to hold all of the sauces, which were now at each table and not behind the bar. Auntie and I had pulled out her old sewing machine and made plastic backed table cloths and curtains, which really helped to upgrade the appearance of Sam's.

The inside, anyway. Over the summer, Uncle said he would consider having the exterior painted and hang a new sign. "Can't let Gladwell over there outdo me," he'd grumbled one evening, when I showed him the difference between their new paint job, patio tables and window etchings and Sam's drab, faded appearance that hadn't changed in twenty years.

It was early evening on what had been a beautiful, almost summer day. If it wasn't for the usual dusting of pollen at this time of year in Atlanta, it would have been perfect. Mostly perfect.

I was going on three months of attorney bills and I still wasn't divorced. And I didn't see it happening any time soon. Gibson and Warren's attorney had been battling each other with paper. Motions against this, motions against that, disputing everything else. Once one thing got settled, something else popped up.

I was *tired*. Tired of being married to this maniac, this narcissistic, selfish, mean fool. Tired of keeping my life on hold, waiting to start a new chapter until the last one had ended.

Then set on fire.

Aside from being frustrated at still being married, I still wasn't seeing Gibson. I fought with myself about it every day. Every morning, I woke up and the other side of my bed was empty, with no chance of it being occupied by anyone other than a 7 or 8 year old. My text inbox wasn't full of funny jokes and sweet compliments and sexy proposals. What I'd had with Gibson wasn't much and wasn't long, but I'd had a glimpse of what real relationship was supposed to be like. What being somewhere in the vicinity of love was supposed to feel like.

I thought I'd had that with Warren, until I took the blinders off and saw that love, to him, was manipulation. Love was using me and our daughters for who-knows-what, for as long as possible, then leaving us to sift through the pieces of the life that we'd built together, that he'd destroyed and left behind.

I propped my hands on my hips and stretched, turning one way and then the other. It loosened up the tension in my neck and back but also got my mind off of this mental tug of war between Gibson and Warren. Behind me, Uncle's office door opened.

"Lil' Girl? Where are you?"

"I'm right here," I answered, to his bellowing summons. "And stop opening doors and yelling for me like I'm the cow that got out of the barn. This place isn't big enough to lose me."

"How I'm supposed to see you behind the door? Come on in here." He opened the door wide enough for me to step through and closed it behind me. "Have a seat," he ordered, sinking into his desk chair.

"What's up? Am I in trouble?"

"Naw, you ain't in no trouble. I just ran a report and I wanted you to see it."

He handed me a sheet of paper, which I recognized. It was the original contract between him and I about working at Sam's. The total amount of money he'd lent me to get my car fixed and take care of a few things was listed at the top, then every week the hours I'd worked ran against that balance. I noticed, at the bottom, that the number had dipped into the negatives.

"Uncle...does this mean what I think it means?"

"If you think it means you worked off your loan and now I got to cut a check for you, then yeah. That's what that means."

"Wow... I didn't even... I guess I thought it would take longer."

"Well, these long days you been working, trying to avoid

dealing with that lawyer probably helped. I don't like to gossip, but your Auntie ain't had no news to pass along lately."

My lips bent into a sideways grin, despite my best efforts to not smile. "Ya'll talk about me, then? You're admitting to that?"

"We been talking about you since before you was born. If we should go get you, because your mama wasn't doin' right. What we should do with you, after your mama died. What we should do with you after you took your narrow behind over to that strip club and started taking your clothes off for money. What we should do when you met Warren, knowing he should have been a better influence on you. And then when those babies came along, there was a lot of talking."

Uncle rubbed the patch of grey hair under his lip. "Yeah, I'd say you've been a favorite topic of conversation for... going one twenty-nine years. And nothing you have to say is going to change that. We have grand-nieces to talk about now too."

This speech, though heartwarming, wasn't something I'd never heard. I was aware of the obstacle course I'd put my Aunt and Uncle through. Making things right was my primary goal. That's why I rented a condo near them and I worked in Sam's bar. Besides my daughters, Sam and Marilyn were all I had in the world.

"So... you done chased the boy off, or what happened to him?" He leaned back, propping his feet up on the edge of the desk. "His table has been empty for weeks."

"We had a disagreement. About Warren and how he should proceed in removing him from my life."

"I disagree with your Auntie at least once a day, on general principle. A disagreement don't mean nothin' if you can work through it."

"True. But we were complicating things. You know... trying to date, with him being my divorce attorney."

"Sounds like you realized that you got it bad for him and that scared the wits and wisdom out of you, because dropping him don't make no sense."

"There's so much more to it than that, Uncle." I stood, then began pacing the small office. "It's not as simple as being brave because maybe I feel something for someone. You know where I've been and what I've been through. Warren is enough without throwing in Red Heels. He has family and friends and a reputation to protect. In the blink of an eye, it went from having fun to.... he started hinting at taking care of me and the girls, at being together. *Really* being together.

"And he's a Kincaid, so he has money. What do I look like, getting swindled by my husband and immediately hooking up with a wealthy attorney? Who's to stop someone from saying I got with him for that? I mean, if you could have seen the look in his eyes every time we—"

I stopped myself before I actually uttered the words *we had sex* but I had the feeling Uncle knew where I was going, because he dipped his head into the palm of his hand.

"I don't want to get into your business—"

"But you're about to."

"But maybe, I was gon' say before you got rude, you should think about what would be so bad about *really* being together. All that other stuff you talkin'... it's just excuses and you know it."

He waved off my protests with a hand in the air. "Now, I heard you and I'm sure those are points to consider, but those aren't reasons to not be with someone. *Warren* was reasons to not be with someone. Gibson seems like a nice young man. Got his stuff together. Can take care of himself. Dedicated. Young men don't come sit in this spot, ordering two baskets of wings to keep me happy, leaving here smelling like chicken strips every day for no reason. You got that man hooked. You gonna lose him if you don't get your act together, Lil Girl."

I nodded with my lips pressed together so I didn't argue with him. Because I knew he was right.

"Take some advice from an old man," he added, speaking softly. "People say life is short all the time. But it's real, real long when you ain't livin', when you feel like you have to punish yourself for mistakes you made. You got two little girls who want to see their mama happy. And you got an Auntie and an Uncle who want to see the same. This mess with Warren isn't settled yet....*it will be*. In the meantime, you got to live your life. This train don't stop for nobody."

"And if he can't deal? What if I decide to keep living but the person I want to keep living with doesn't want that with me?"

"I heard him tell you one time to not worry about *what if*. Nothing you can do about a *what if* situation. Work with what you got and what you know. Deal with the fallout later. That's how the rest of us have to live. He pushed his chair back from the desk and stood. "We best be heading back out there."

"Yeah, we've been missing for a minute. And since I'm working for actual money now, I won't even give you any lip about it."

"Okay, now," he said, grabbing my arm. "You're welcome to help out as long as you need to, for the money. But come summer, I'm gon' need a full-time waitress. Summer is coming and my grandnieces want to spend time with their mama. So, you need to plan on hanging up those apron strings soon."

He wasn't much for touchy feely shows of affection, but I reached out and wrapped my arms around his neck anyway. He let out a nervous chuckle, then let his arms circle my waist for the briefest of moments.

"You always find a way to rescue me, Uncle. Thanks for that. And for the good heart to heart that I know you didn't want to have, but you just can't help yourself." I giggled and he laughed. "When the girls get out of school in a few weeks, I'll be done with Sam's. But I'm close by if you need me. Unless—"

"Unless you're with the lawyer at the big house with the pool and the garden."

I blushed, pushing away from him and reaching for the doorknob. "You need to get some business to mind, Uncle."

"I got plenty of business," he argued playfully behind me. "I mind it so well, I can mind yours too."

We stepped out of the office together and went our separate ways, Uncle to the kitchen and me to the dining room.

"Well, it's about time someone showed up out here."

I whipped around to find Sonja seated at a table in a darkened corner of the bar. "Thought I might have to serve myself."

I grinned, heading for her table. "What are you doing here? Shouldn't you be harassing some young dancer that looks younger, prettier, thinner than you?"

"You got a big mouth on you, girl, 'bout as big as your thighs. I take days off now and again. I came to check up on you."

"Well, thanks for that. It's nice to be missed, I guess. You want something to drink?"

"Naw, I came into this bar and sat down for the atmosphere and ambience."

I snickered. "A simple yes would have sufficed. But come out of this dark corner and have a seat at the bar; I don't pour like they do at Red Heels, but I'll take good care of you."

"Uh... Nessa. If it's all the same, I'd rather sit here." Then I noticed it. The dark ring around her eye, bigger than the oversized shades she was wearing to try and hide it.

"Sonja? Girl, what happened to you?"

"It's just a little something. Looks worse than it feels. It's nothing."

"Nothing? This is big enough to take you out of the club on a Friday night. Don't sit there and tell me it's nothing!"

I reached for the huge, dark shades, pulling them away from her eyes, then wincing at the raw, multicolored skin that had been hidden. The sight of her made my heartbeat speed up to a near unmanageable level. I was hot all over and starting to shake in anger.

"Who did this to you? Tell me, right now!"

"Nessa, it's not—"

"Stop saying it's not a big deal! Was it Anton?"

"No! You know he don't hit his girls. Don't even think that."

"Then who?"

Sonja was quiet for a few beats. She sniffled, swiped a Kleenex under her nose, then looked up at me. "You don't know him. He's a... uh, he's a regular."

My brows nearly shot off my face, I was so surprised. "A regular, as in a customer? Sonja, are you joking right now? You've been telling us for years not to date out of the club and—"

Sonja glared at me, her dark eyes becoming beady little orbs in the of middle red and purple swollen flesh. "Now look here. I didn't come down here so you could pay me back with *I told you so's*. I know what I said. I know what I did. I went into it with my eyes all the way open. I thought."

"You didn't ask old boy to beat up on you, though. I'm going to go pour you something stiff. When I get off in an hour, I will join you, so you can tell me who this man is that put his hands on you. And then you can try to talk me out of rounding up the Red Heels posse to beat *his* face in."

GIBSON

Warren's muscle-bound physique, folded into a black Mercedes coupe was easy to spot, even easier to follow. He roamed around town, stopping at several Mailbox Plus locations, then a few banks and retail shops before hopping onto the freeway that would take him south of the city.

It was dusk, the remnants of sunlight casting a glow across the horizon. Warren seemed oblivious to my Jeep several cars behind him, but I never lost sight of him. I trailed him for a few miles, then followed as he exited the freeway and began to wind his way through southwest Atlanta. Traffic was thick, but eventually he pulled into the valet lane at a parking lot and got out of the car.

There was no subtlety to the place. The enormous neon sign and flashing images of dancing girls made it clear that this was a strip club. I pulled away, finding a parking spot a few blocks away from the club and doubling back on foot. I stood in line, paid the $20 entrance fee, endured the scrutiny of not only my ID but my person with metal detectors and pat downs.

Aside from a drunken frat boy escapade on my twenty-first birthday I didn't make a habit of visiting Atlanta's plethora of strip clubs. Gabe and Gregg, however, were entirely more well-versed. I should have asked them to set my expectation.

By the time I made it inside, the place was jumping, packed wall to wall with men in casual gear and suits, women in skintight, colorful ensembles. The music thumped loud and hard and the lighting flashed from red to blue. I felt like I was at a rave... a very loud, hip hop themed rave.

"Hi, handsome. You looking for some fun? I'm available."

A dancer sidled up to me, so close I could smell her perfume, her shapely figure covered in what seemed to be thin pieces of fabric to cover essentials, secured with nothing more than string. She seemed young— exceedingly so, with a heart shaped face and long, straight hair.

She stepped in front of me, grabbing one of my arms to slide it around her slight waist. Then she hooked her arms around my neck and stepped in close. "What do you want to start off with? A lap dance is only twenty. If you're looking for more than that, we could book a room."

Her eyes rolled up to mine in what I was sure was supposed to be a seductive gaze. "Tell me what you want and we can get started."

"I'm actually looking for someone."

She frowned. Then the look melted away, replaced by a sultry smile. "Oh, another dancer? You want me to find her and we can tag team?"

She seemed to have more arms than humanly possible. I withdrew mine from around her , then pulled hers from around my neck and shoulders. She was clinging for dear life, teetering with me step by step on super high heels as I tried to walk around her.

I finally freed myself of her and stepped back. "Thank you. I'm not interested, but thank you."

She frowned for real this time, folding her arms over her ample chest. "If you change your mind, ask anyone for Luxury. They'll come find me." She whirled around, sending her long hair out in a fan around her.

I inched further into the club, scanning the room for Warren. I spotted him at the bar, chatting it up with a pretty Tamron Hall look alike, wearing a sparkly, silver strapless dress that hit her mid-thigh. I wasn't close enough to hear them, but he said something that made her toss her head back and laugh. He slipped her a few folded bills. She smiled and stepped away.

I took this as a sign that this was my chance to get near

him. Warren looked like a bag of money—nothing like he'd looked when he busted into Sam's that day. His hair had been freshly cut, his goatee edged nicely. He wore a collared shirt and dark jeans but his wrist bore a watch encrusted with diamonds and a silver and diamond chain hung from his neck. He appeared to be handing out cash left and right, so it wasn't likely that he would be alone much.

I wound my way through the crowd to the bar at the other end of the club and pulled out the bar chair next to Warren. I chose not to say a word. Rather, I waited for him to recognize me, which took a minute, but after a few double takes, he focused his glossy eyes on me.

"You don't strike me as the gentleman's club type." He accepted a short glass of dark liquor from the waitress in the sparkly dress, then leaned over to whisper something in her ear. She nodded, then walked away. "Sorry, did you want her to bring you something?"

I shook my head. I didn't want to chance that he'd have something added to my drink. "I'll order from here, thanks." As soon as the bartender came around, I ordered a bourbon and sat quietly. I wanted Warren to get nervous about my presence. I wanted him to wonder how I'd found him.

"So…" He finally muttered, after downing half of his drink and licking his lips. "You gonna sit there all night? Or am I gonna call my attorney and tell him he's not keeping you busy enough?"

"I'm plenty busy, Warren, thanks to your attorney. I know you think you're holding up this divorce, but eventually it will go through."

He huffed a low laugh, then sipped from his glass, while surveying the full club from our vantage point. "That's what she pays you to think. Once I drain her of whatever little money she has, she'll give up."

The bartender brought my bourbon and I sipped slowly. Calmly.

"Regardless of how much money my client has, this divorce will go through. I promised her that and I'm going to see to it."

"Promised her?" His laughter was a thick, a sticky gurgle from his throat. "You don't sound like any lawyer I ever heard of. Lawyers don't make promises. I pay them and they do what I tell them to do."

"Well, maybe I'm not your typical lawyer. My clients count on me to keep my word and that's what I'm going to do for Vanessa. So that begs a question..."

I sipped my bourbon and took my time picking up the rest of the sentence.

"Why are you fighting this so hard? Why are you trying to drain her? You know the more she spends on this, the less money she has to take care of the children you don't support. And like I said, all of this paperwork is a waste of time and money. This divorce is going through."

"Why am I fighting? Because Vanessa thinks she's smart. Thinks she's slick. Thinks she's getting over on me."

His lip curled as he turned his glare on me. "She thought she could go out and get a job and make her own money, then come home talking to me about empowerment and shit, like she was *somebody*, like I wasn't taking care of her, paying all the bills, making her life easy. I got to talk to her a certain way, treat her a certain way or I don't respect her—nah, fuck that. I'm not bowing to a bitch. She got what she wanted. She can make her own money and stay out of my pockets."

"She's doing that. You left. You haven't lived in the same house in two years. Why not let her go?"

"Because she's still *mine*. Nessa don't know what she wants. A few more months of struggling, living in that little shit place she thinks I don't know about, paying her own bills, buying clothes for those kids, she'll be begging to get back with me."

He chuckled and tossed back the last swallow of his drink before he lifted his glass to the bartender to demand another one. Then his eyes narrowed and he looked at me. *Really* looked at me.

"Hold up, though. You're supposed to be her lawyer but you're way too interested in her. You want her, huh? Bad enough to be up in my face about it. You let her wrap them long legs around you and whisper sweet words in your ear and now you're making promises like you matter to her, like she's not using you to get what she wants."

"Vanessa's personal life is her business. I'm here to talk about the divorce. "

"That ain't happening, so you can swagger your square ass outta here."

"You sure about that?"

"Damn sure. As sure as I am that you don't know Nessa like you think you know her." He looked me up and down and sneered. "You're too straight edge, too Wall Street to know about her and still want to be with her."

"Enlighten me, Warren. What are we talking about? What do you mean?"

He chuckled, low and slow for a few seconds, a hand covering his mouth. "*Bruuuuh*. She didn't tell you how we know each other, did she?"

"She said she met you through work."

"Yeah. Work." He smiled, a wide grin full of teeth. "I met her when she *worked* those chocolate titties in my face. Nessa was stripping at a club over on the north side of town. Red Heels. The spot is still open, but I ain't been allowed in there for a minute."

I thought my hearing was going out for a few seconds. I could have sworn that Warren said... "Stripping?"

"She was real nice when she was younger," he regaled, licking his lips. "Long legs, big titties, round ass. And dumb. Believed everything I told her, if I put some money in her pockets. Not like these girls today; they been through too much to believe the average lie rolling from a nigga's lips. But her?"

He shook his head, pursing his lips. "Nessa was right out of high school, straight from Sam's house, had something to prove. Snapper tight, ripe for the picking, in more ways than one, if you know what I mean."

My face flushed hot and suddenly I was sweating. I reached for my drink and sucked down a few gulps while he chortled next to me.

"As you know, I managed to secure all of that for myself, for a while. And now here you come, looking for sloppy seconds, I guess."

"Yeah, uh..." I quickly recovered and tried to set this nearly derailed train back on track. "Like I said, Vanessa's past is her business. She'd like to be divorced from you. I came to talk to you about that."

"Boy, you don't give up, do you? Pussy's good ain't it? I don't know why I'm asking. I've had it."

"So long as we're spilling secrets and personal business, there are some things that I know about you. Things that, if I were to report them, would put you in a world of hurt."

"Oh yeah? Like what?"

"An offshore bank account that you think no one knows about, in the Cayman Islands. The IRS might be interested in that. That's just for starters. I don't know, I have a vivid imagination. I could probably make anything sound like a reason to investigate."

Finally, I'd started to get a reaction, the kind of reaction I wanted from Warren. Less cocky, self assured and in control.

More wary, quiet, restless. He tapped the bar with the tips of his fingers and stared into his glass.

"I see I've caught you with nothing to say, so let me fill in the blanks. I happen to have records, obtained easily, in fact, that you're being investigated for tax evasion. I know you're in arrears, almost a hundred grand. I know that you're trying to tell the IRS and other creditors that you don't have any money or a way to pay it. I also know you're at a strip club peeling off twenties and that you're poised to disappear, when the time is right.

"I know a few other things, Warren. First, I'm not your attorney, so there is no privilege. I'm obligated to disclose what I know, if asked. And believe me, I'll make sure I'm asked. I know you could go away for a long time, if you're convicted. I know the white collar, country club prison doesn't exist for a black man. They could seize your accounts. The accounts of anyone connected to you, including your girlfriend. *If* you get out before retirement age, you won't have that little nest egg you've built. Again... that's only the beginning."

Warren was buying every word that fell out of my mouth. Most of it was true. His nervous taps sped up and so did the blinking of his eyes.

"Okay. So... what? You came up in here to tell me you think you know something. I'm talking to a lawyer. So?"

"So, I have a proposition for you. If you want help— *real* help, not an attorney off the internet, I'll hook you up with a buddy of mine. His specialty is cases where people are in deep shit with the IRS. Which, I believe, is about to be you, if I walk out of here knowing what I know and not getting what I want."

"You trying to blackmail me, now?"

"I'm trying to strike a deal. My contact takes your case, does his best to keep you out of prison and your money intact. In exchange, you stop fighting this divorce. You withdraw all your motions. You sign these papers—"

I pulled a stack of pages from my back pocket, unfolded them so that he could see that it was my original Petition for Divorce.

"You let the divorce go through. In forty-five days, your marriage is over. There's no provision for spousal support, no demands to pay back any monies Vanessa paid to credit card companies on the joint accounts you held. She doesn't *want* your money. You forfeit custody of Olivia and Jaclyn—but you *will* establish and maintain visitation and take care of those children."

"And if I don't agree to any of this?"

I grinned, feeling cocky now. "Don't forget what happened at Sam's a while back. There are cameras in that bar. You attacked Vanessa, then you attacked me. The minute I get back to my car— hell, the minute I step outside this club, I could make a phone call and have you arrested. *Tonight.* And then somebody might ask me about you and I might not be able to keep my mouth shut about what I know."

Warren sucked his teeth and shook his head, waving me off. "You playin' me , man, trying to get me to sign them damn papers."

"Am I? Did you know that you've been under surveillance? How do you think I know this information? How do you think I found you? Does Andra know you're at a strip club, spending up money you say you don't have? Do you know I can tell you the balances of the three bank accounts you have here in Atlanta and I can ballpark the Cayman Islands account? I'm not playing with you, Warren. Far from it."

Warren had no answer. I didn't figure he would.

I signaled the bartender and when he made it over to us, I asked for a pen. He supplied a simple stick pen with the club's name emblazoned across the side. I handed it to Warren and flipped the contract to the last page, with the signature block.

"How do I know you're on the up and up about your contact that can help me? What if I'm signing this for nothing?"

"Contrary to popular belief, most attorneys are bound by a Code of Ethics. I know that's not something you're familiar with." I leaned to the right and pulled my wallet from my pocket, then flipped through a collection of business cards. When I found Pack's card, I slid it over to him. "Kent Packard is your man. He's not taking new clients, but I've already spoken to him and he's expecting your call. You two have a lot in common; you should get along well. He's good at what he does. Tell him *everything*. He can't help you with what he doesn't know."

Warren signed his name on the line where indicated, a loud, furious scratching of pen against paper. As soon as he finished, I snatched up the pages.

"Like I said..." I got up from the bar stool and stepped aside, leaving the seat next to Warren vacant. "This divorce is going to go through. Eventually."

I paid for my drink and left the bartender a healthy tip, then fought my way through the crowd and back out the front door. The entry line was long, winding around the building and down the street. I glanced at the people trying to get in— folks of all shapes and sizes, men and women paying money to see women like Luxury writhe and gyrate to a loud thumping beat.

Then I thought about Vanessa, and about the same line of people clamoring to get into a place with neon lights and smoke haze and overpriced, watered down drinks, just to see her titillate and tease... probably topless.

The thought made me a little bit sick. Not because of the choice of occupation. There was no doubt in my mind that

Vanessa wouldn't have been dancing if it wasn't what she wanted to do.

I couldn't imagine her doing those moves, up on that stage in a skimpy, tied on costume. Well, actually I could, and the mental image was... stimulating, to say the least. The thought that someone else, *many* someone else's had enjoyed the sight of her was enough to make my heart burn.

It also made me wish I'd known that this life was part of her past, before I went and confronted her sooner-than-anyone-thought-he-would-be ex-husband.

No wonder she didn't want me to dig. It wasn't Warren's dirt that she didn't want me to find.

CHAPTER NINETEEN

anessa

HOW. *UTTERLY.* EMBARRASSING.

I was sitting in the second row in the auditorium at the girls' elementary school, watching the spring choir and band production. In a few weeks, school would be out and this performance would close out the year for the arts programs. Auntie and Uncle were next to me, beaming with pride at Olivia on flute and Jaclyn in the choir. Jac's blouse was a little too small— I hadn't even thought to check to see if she'd grown any since the last time she wore it— and she was clawing at the collar, itching to unbutton it.

During a quiet piece, a raunchy Beyoncé lyric about good sex and Red Lobster rang out from my cellphone, so loud I'm sure people in the parking lot heard it. I reached under my chair for my purse, hissing, *"Shit!"* as I pressed the button on the side to quiet the phone.

I was actually trying not to laugh, as was everyone around me.

"You didn't put your phone on silence?" Auntie whispered, not even trying to hide her laughter.

Uncle was confused and leaned across Auntie. "What she say about the Red Lobster?" He whisper-yelled.

"Nothing! Shhh!" I grabbed my purse and the phone and tipped out of the auditorium to the lobby. That ring was Gibson's tone. I *still* hadn't taken him off VIP, so though the phone was on Do Not Disturb, his calls and messages came through.

Gibson Kincaid: Call me as soon as you can.

He picked up almost immediately, the sound of road noise loud behind him. "Hey, thanks for calling me back. Sorry for the short notice, but I wondered if you could meet me in about an hour?"

"Why? Is something happening?"

"You could say that. I'd rather discuss it in person. I have to get on a conference call in two minutes."

"Uh.... okay. I'm not working today, but I could go to Sam's."

"That's fine. I'll see you in an hour. Gotta run." He hung up before I could ask him anymore questions. Confused, I powered the phone down completely and shoved it into my bag, then re-entered the auditorium to catch the last performance.

Twenty minutes later, we stood outside the school on the sidewalk.

"Well, I believe that was right nice, lil' girls. I loved seeing my babies up there giving us some good music and good singing."

Uncle smiled and gathered Olivia and Jaclyn to his side. They looked adorable in the black and white band and chorus outfits. Aside from a missed note here and there, they did a great job. They beamed with pride under Uncle's arm, Olivia clutching her flute case and Jaclyn pulling at the tight collar of her blouse. I bent to unbutton it for her.

"Vanessa, why don't you and the girls come over to the house? I fried some chicken and made some macaroni and cheese and green beans...and I even have some ice cream and pound cake for my favorite nieces."

My mouth started watering at the mention of fried chicken. I'd been going nonstop since I dropped the girls off at school. Asking to be assigned to some different clients at Donovan had me wishing for the young, black and fabulous set that I'd dropped like a hot potato. Raja Al Haber, managing director for an international investment group, had kept me on the tips of my toes for over a week. Her must-have list for a sprawling estate no more than thirty minutes from her mid-city office was nearly impossible to satisfy, but I'd finally nailed down a property that *might* work for her and her sons. As soon as I'd arranged for Ms. Al Haber to tour the property, I had to rush out of the office for the 3PM program at the girls' school. I hadn't even had a spare second to eat lunch.

"That sounds good," I told her, straightening again and moving my purse back to my shoulder. "I need to run an errand first. Do you mind taking the girls with you?"

"Sure. They love riding in Uncle's Cadillac. Come on here, girls." Uncle ushered the girls toward Cherry while Auntie hung behind.

"Was that your lawyer, that called you?"

I blushed, then nodded. "He asked if I could meet him. He sounded excited. I hope it's good news about the divorce." I crossed my fingers and kissed them to the sky.

"Me too. Don't be too late for dinner, now. And tell him he's welcome to come by. There's plenty to eat and I cook as well as your uncle does."

I grinned, giving her a hug before I headed off to my car. "You're sweet, but there's no way am I letting him be interrogated by the two of you. I won't be late. Thanks for taking the girls."

I beat Gibson to Sam's by a minute. As soon as I slid into "our" booth, I saw him come in the front door. The puzzled expression at not seeing Uncle behind the bar made me laugh.

"Where's uh..." He thumbed in the direction of the bar. "Where's Sam?"

"The girls had their spring program at school. He and Auntie went with me. That's where I was when you called me. Got me in trouble too."

"Me? How'd I get you in trouble?"

"You know the song I picked out as your ringtone? Well, my phone rang in the middle of the program, loud as hell. I had to leave to call you back, then the music teacher wouldn't let me back to my seat until I promised her that I turned my phone off."

Gibson laughed, albeit quietly. "Sorry about that. Those people don't know good music." He flipped over the front flap of his satchel and dug through a few folders before pulling out a stack of pages that looked familiar. Very familiar.

"That's the Petition for Divorce." Suddenly, I was nervous. Hot and sweating so much I felt the beads popping up along my hairline and my top lip.

"It is," he answered, annoyingly calm. He flipped to the back page and set it in front of me. I recognized Warren's large, hard scrawl. He always wrote like he was trying to rip through the page. "I need you to sign it. When you do, I'll file it, and then the clock starts. In forty-five days, you'll be a free woman."

"Wha... wait, what? You talked to Warren? And got him to sign it? Did you have to hold him at gunpoint?"

"Not at all," Gibson answered, splaying his hands. "I met him in public. We had a talk. I convinced him to sign them."

"But... how—"

"Vanessa," he interrupted, his tone going low and soft. "Does it matter how? Just sign them. I'll run to the office and scan a copy and email them to you for your records."

My eyelids fluttered closed. *Ten years*. Ten years of dealing with Warren, fighting him tooth and nail, being under his thumb would be over, disappeared with the stroke of a pen.

"When I met Warren, I was a child, looking for a way to show my family that I was grown and they couldn't control me. I wish I could go back in time and talk to that girl and tell her that he isn't who she thinks he is. A few people tried to tell me. I refused to listen."

"We all have those moments, when we should have known better. Sometimes we have to learn our lessons the hard way, right? It's almost over, though."

As soon as I signed the page, Gibson took it and stuffed it back into his bag. "I've gotta run. Thanks for meeting me. I'll get this filed right away. I'll call you when the process is complete. You'll get a copy of the divorce decree in the mail, but for all intents and purposes, you can consider yourself divorced."

"Music to my ears!" I almost shouted. Then almost cried. "I feel like doing a cartwheel through this restaurant right now."

"I wouldn't stop you if you tried."

"I know you have to run, but you're invited to dinner tonight. My aunt cooked. Uncle's not the only one that can put a hurtin' on some chicken."

"Thanks. I can't." Gibson was quiet and curt as he slid out of the booth. "I'll be in touch," he said, backing away from the table and offering me a little wave as he walked toward the front door.

I slid out of the booth and followed him out of the front door. He was dogged, directed steps heading for his Jeep. "Gibson... wait! What's going on with you? Why are you so... why are you like this?"

He stopped, turned on his heel and gazed at me. "Like what? I got you what you wanted. I'm happy for you. Honestly."

"Like my *lawyer* and not my *friend*. I thought that now that this is all settled, we could talk." I shoved my hands into the pockets of my skirt and inched closer to him. "I've been thinking that maybe I... okay I *definitely* overreacted at your suggestion of looking at Warren's finances. I was so stressed out and I wanted it over with and I knew that would drag things out even longer."

I expected him to grab my hints and run with them, pick up the conversation. Weeks ago he'd been begging to see me and I'd been holding myself back from running into his arms.

Tonight... nothing. He stood mere inches from me and didn't reach for me, didn't attempt to touch me, to kiss me, to let me know that he still missed me. Maybe he didn't. Maybe I'd waited too long. Maybe he— *shit*.

"Gibson..."

His gaze wasn't hard but it wasn't soft either. Something about the way he looked at me made the hair on the back of my neck stand up.

"You know, don't you?"

"Know what?"

"About Red Heels."

His expression said everything. Yes, he knew. And he was angry that I hadn't told him.

"So you did it anyway, when I asked you not to? You went digging and found out some things?"

"Actually, I did go against your wishes. I needed to know more than I knew. I uncovered some things, found a way to leverage that information and get him to sign the divorce papers. He was all about helping himself. But I didn't find out about your past by digging. Warren was too happy to tell me where he met you."

I was amazed and agog and... a little light headed. I stepped back from Gibson, planting my hands on my hips. "Wow," I finally said, laughing a little, but not with joy or mirth.

More like... I *fucking* knew it.

"This is his last jab at me. He wants to make sure we never work out, that you're so disgusted with me that you come at me with this... cool, calm, cold attitude. I told you— if he thinks I want something, he's going to make sure I don't get that. He wants me to know he's still powerful, that he still controls my life. That *son of a bitch*."

"Except I'm not disgusted, not about your previous line of work. I'm not cool, calm and cold, I'm... "

He dipped his head, stared at the pavement for a beat or two, then looked up. I saw the struggle in his eyes, the tension in his jaw, the furrow of his brow. If I could have reached out and smoothed it away, I would have, but I was sure he wouldn't allow me to touch him.

After a few moments and hard swallows, Gibson tried again. "As much as you and I have shared, you couldn't have told me? You thought I would react in some way, or treat you differently or make assumptions... I don't know. All I know is that you didn't trust me enough to tell me. I get that it's hard to open up, Vanessa, but we talked about everything except the things that mattered the most. I had, literally, half the story."

"Gibson, I'm so sorry I didn't tell you. I wasn't—"

"Don't. It's... we don't need to rehash it. You had your reasons, I guess. " He shook his head, then started to back away. "There's a lot going on in my life right now. I don't want to complicate things. I guess I need to sort myself out, too. I wanted to file your divorce and get Warren off your back. I did that. I wish you the best."

I wanted to throw things. To pick up one of Gladwell's patio chairs and hurl it into traffic. To punch my fist into the brick wall. Instead I just stood there, slack jawed watching the muscles in Gibson's back as he walked quickly toward his Jeep.

"Son of a *bitch*!"

GIBSON

That hurt.

A lot.

Walking away from Vanessa was not something I wanted to do, but I couldn't stop my feet from carrying me further and further away from her. She was hurt by how I'd treated her— I could see that, plainly. But I didn't have the capacity to deal with it. Not right now. Maybe soon.

Maybe not ever.

Maybe I had learned my first, very hard lesson about getting involved with my clients. I should have listened to Gabriel— there was an entire iceberg of drama underneath the cute little ice cube that bobbed on the surface.

I headed to my office, planning to scan the papers Vanessa and Warren had signed and put it on my paralegal's desk to file in the morning. Then... maybe off to Mink's for a drink and a smoke. Maybe home to do a little digging in the garden. Or maybe I would sit in my office, close the door, turn off the lights, bust into the office stash of Knob Creek and try to forget about the last few days.

I tossed my bag to the floor next to my chair and dropped into it, propping my elbows on the desk and burying my face in my hands. No sooner than I'd had a quick chance to catch my breath, I heard a booming voice in the hallway.

And then the owner of the booming voice darkened my door way. "Son? Everything okay in here? I heard something heavy fall."

"I'm fine, sir," I answered, standing to greet Judge, as was my habit. He swept into my office, still bearing the wide shoulders and broad chest from his days as a linebacker at Alabama State. He was graceful, though, as quick on his feet as if he was a hundred pounds lighter. "I dropped my bag; that's what you heard. What are you doing here?"

Judge paused, looking at me sideways. "It's your mother's birthday. We're all meeting here to go to dinner. Did you forget?"

"Ahhhh....shit!" I hissed, smacking my forehead. I glanced down at my casual attire— jeans and a polo shirt— and cursed again. "Dammit! I did forget. The last few days have been..." I sighed, loudly. "Wild. That's the only word I can think of to describe it."

"Well, throw on a jacket. We're going to Chops. You know how she loves that place." I did remember that she loved the high price steaks and upper class atmosphere. "We're also celebrating Garrett and Cheri tonight. You cannot miss this dinner, Gibson."

I brushed a palm down my face, sure that I looked haggard and unkempt. I couldn't put on a jacket and roll into Chops with the rest of my family, who were sure to be wearing their designer everything and dressed to the nines.

"Why don't I meet you all there? I can call my personal shopper at Neiman Marcus, have him pull something for me and I'll change before I get to the restaurant."

He nodded, satisfied with my compromise. I'd be a little late but I knew Mother would prefer late and well-dressed over on time, looking like the low-rent attorney she thought I was.

"Son..." he eyed me, stopping on his way out of my office. "Need a minute?"

That phrase was our code for *talk to me before your mother knocks your block off*. When I had reached my most rebellious stage with Mother, it was often Judge that talked me off the ledge. *Need a minute* was a way for me to grab his ear, complain, de-stress and decompress. I hadn't taken the option in a long time but right now, I could use the ear and advice of a wise man.

"I don't want to make you late..."

"Don't worry about that. Your mother is on a conference call. I got bored listening and I started roaming. That's how I heard the thump in here." He pulled out one of the tufted grey guest chairs and settled into it, then tapped the other, inviting me to sit. "Take a minute," he said.

So I did. I sat next to Judge and started with Vanessa. Meeting her, feeling the instant, magnetic, unavoidable and mutual attraction. Finally answering that attraction, thinking shit was good, getting a little cocky in how well I was strad-dling the line between lover and lawyer. Then losing her. Finding out all I had about her and her ex and having to play investigator and negotiator.

And doing all that because *I still wanted her*.

I talked about Mother, and her attitude about how I did my job, my clients, the work I'd dedicated myself to.

I talked about Garrett, and the opportunity that loomed in front of me, one that I considered accepting, because clearly what I was doing wasn't working.

"For a while now, you've had stars in your eyes about doing your own thing, only sticking with Kincaid until you got on your feet. What happened to that?"

"Your wife happened to it," I answered dryly, walking the

very edge of disrespect. With Mother, I could push buttons. With Judge, I didn't dare. "She won't live up to her end of the deal. No seed money to start my own firm, no word of mouth..."

"And this is a problem because you would be the first attorney ever, in the history of law, to start a new firm with no money from your mommy?"

Judge's lips bent into a hint of a grin to soften that crushing blow. I'd been telling myself the same thing. I had savings, stock options I could sell, had even made a few contacts with other attorneys to share office space. But I'd been weighing those options against doing what I didn't want to do to get what I wanted.

"Seems to me like you're considering taking steps where you have to be a man that you're not. You're not, have never been, and could never be Garrett. You really think you could fill those shoes? The man wears a size fourteen. *Ships on dry land*, my great grandmama used to say." He smiled at a distant memory of a woman I never knew but often heard quoted at family gatherings.

Judge inhaled deeply, then tipped forward, leaning thick arms on his knees. "You're at an age where the hard decisions come, where you have to do some breaking away from the norm, the expected. These choices you need to make— this young lady you seem to be taken with; the job here at Kincaid; moving on to your own thing— all of it comes down to knowing who you are and what you want. If it's within your grasp, reach for it. If you miss and fall, your family's behind you. Even your mother, though I know you don't believe that."

"Yeah, I heard some nonsense about how I'm her favorite. I don't see it."

He laughed hard, from his chest. "Then you're not looking. You've got two older brothers that should be considering a Senior appointment at this firm, and yet she chose you."

"Because she wants to control how I practice law."

"Because she is afraid of losing you, son. She's just trying to hold on."

I would never in my life believe that Sylvia Kincaid was afraid of anything. But if everyone else wanted to believe that... well, okay.

"I feel like..." I paused, rasping my tongue over dry lips. "I feel like no matter what I do, there's a serious chance I'm going to fail. I've never been in that position before. I'm not in a hurry to fall on my face. You know what I mean?"

"I do. But what I hear is... *I've never taken a risk before*. I've never stepped out on a limb before. I've never done exactly what I want to do, my way, and not given a shit what people think about the outcome. You haven't even begun to live your life, son. Don't you think it's time you got to it?"

I heaved a long sigh, emptying my lungs. A lot was clearing up for me, in my mind. But a lot was still muddled. It was the muddled part that was stressing me out.

"Thanks for the minute, sir. I appreciate it." I stood, offering him a handshake, which he took. "You'd better get going before she comes storming down that hallway. I don't want to get caught in the crossfire."

"I heard that," said Judge, rising from the chair and heading for the office door. "You think about what I said, though. And let me know how things work out."

CHAPTER TWENTY

anessa

"ARE YOU SURE YOU DON'T WANT ME TO COME WITH YOU? I showed a house and it went so well, I don't want to ruin my good mood. I'm not going back to the office."

I chatted with Sonja while plugging an earbud into one ear and trying to maneuver the circular, paved driveway in front of an old-style brick southern home—columns and porch swing and all, located in North Atlanta. Ms. Al Haber had *really* liked it, and it fit her budget perfectly at just under $2 million. She wanted to think about it for a day or so, however, so I didn't need to rush back to Donovan to write up a contract.

"I don't need a chaperone. Besides, that Sheriff's Deputy I talked to sounded cute. He said my voice was *smoky*. So no, I don't want you there, with your pretty ass and them thick thighs fuckin' up the vibe and cock blockin'."

I'd finally talked Sonja into pressing charges against

Franklin Bell, the man that had assaulted her. He hadn't returned to Red Heels, at least not since Sonja had gone back to work; Anton had made it clear to the bouncers that he was banned from entry, should he even try.

The next step was *reporting* the assault. If it was one of her dancers, I'd told her, she would insist on it.

"You gonna stop talking about my thighs, heifer. Call me if you need me. And don't act thirsty; you have options."

"I'm about to go in there *parched*. Watch me." I snorted and laughed, with zero doubts that she would do it, cleavage and all. "Before I let you go, lemme serve you some tea right quick."

"On who?"

"Your friend Karen, aka Moxie, aka *I don't know what I want*. Guess who she's back with?"

I almost dropped the phone. "*Shut up*. Shut the whole hell up, Sonja. Didn't she just divorce Dennis and take *all* of his money?"

"I guess he learned that it's cheaper to keep her. And not to piss her off." She hacked out a loud laugh that made me laugh too. "She moved back into the penthouse last week. Talkin' about how they realize they're meant for each other and other bullshit sayings that amount to *oops, I accidentally thought I could live without this person*. I knew it would end up like that."

"Well...." I sighed, glancing up at the house. "If they're happy, more power to them."

"Yeah, I guess. So... when you gonna realize you *accidentally* thought you could live without Gibson?"

"Don't start with me, Sonja. It's not up to me, this time. I tried to talk to him, but he walked away, so..."

"So..."

"So.... what?" I spit back, rolling my eyes, though she couldn't see them. "What words are you looking for?"

"I'm not looking for words baby. I'm looking for action. Do you want this man, Nessa? I mean, do you want him in your life? For real."

"Yes. For real, I want him in my life, but— "

"Then do something besides sitting around pouting. *Go get him*. I got to go, I'm about to pull up at the police station now."

Sonja hung up before I could even say goodbye. Lord, that woman got on my nerves. Action? What the hell was I supposed to do about a man that didn't want me?

I pulled the earbud from my ear and started to tuck the phone away. But then I changed my mind, reinserted the earbud and scrolled through my contacts list. The VIP list.

I clicked on Gibson's name and crossed my fingers, but it rolled straight to voicemail. "Damn." Then scrolled to a different number.

"Kincaid Family Law, how can I help you?"

"Good morning. Is Gibson Kincaid in the office? Or reachable? I'm a client." I winked, at no one. Until my divorce was final, I was still a client.

"Mr. Kincaid is working from home today. May I take a message?"

"No... no. Is he for sure at home?"

"I spoke with him about an hour ago and he told me that he was at home. Shall I connect you to his home office?"

"No, thank you. I'll speak with him later."

I hung up with the receptionist at Kincaid and switched apps on my phone.

It was the last day of school, so Auntie and Uncle were picking up the girls to take them to Wild Water Theme Park and keeping them overnight.

I had no afternoon appointments.

Google Maps still had Gibson's address stored.

I bit my bottom lip and pressed the button to begin navigation. "Here I go," I mumbled to myself. "About to make a fool out of myself because Sonja said she wanted to see some action."

THE GPS DIRECTED ME TO TURN OFF THE ROAD AND INTO Gibson's driveway much sooner than I anticipated.

I was already halfway to his place anyway, so it didn't take as long as it had before. I didn't have nearly enough time to rehearse my speech in my mind, figure out what I was going to say to try to convince him that I hadn't meant to keep things from him so much as I wasn't ready to tell him *everything*.

But now I had arrived, parked in the driveway next to Gibson's Jeep, and had to get out of the car or risk looking like a crazy stalker. I popped the door latch and got out, admiring the cool breeze and the bright sun. The lake was stunning, the small, choppy waves carrying from one end to the other in an endless loop. It was just as beautiful as the first time I'd visited.

I climbed the front porch steps and rang the bell. I heard it echo and reverberate through the house, but I didn't see any movement, hear any footsteps. After a few minutes, I went back down the stairs, across the driveway and around the side of the house.

I found him, headphones on his head, shovel in his hands, in a sleeveless t-shirt and a pair of shorts. The muscles in his arms and legs, rippling smoothly in symphony with every movement, glistened with a thin sheen of sweat. He was turning the soil in the vegetable garden, forming rows with each dig into the dirt.

I intended to move around so he could see me, so I didn't scare the shit out of the poor man, but he twisted around at

the end of the row and caught a glimpse of me. He looked...
and then looked again.

I waved and smiled, feeling stupid. *Action, though.*

"Hey," he said, pulling the headphones down and hooking
them around his neck. "Is everything okay? You and the girls,
you're okay?"

I nodded, shoving my hands into the pockets of my
slacks. "Mmhmm. Thanks to you, we're great."

"Okay." He nodded a few times, glanced down at the dirt
he was standing in and looked back up. "I wasn't expecting
company today. Sorry I'm so... dirty."

"I tried to call, but your phone went straight to voicemail.
Your office said you were working from home and I was
showing a house about twenty minutes away and uh..."

I swallowed, hard. My throat was so unbelievably dry.
"Things between us ended rather abruptly. But I feel like
there's still a lot hanging in the middle of... us. I was hoping
we could clear the air."

"Clear the air," he repeated, with flat affect.

"Or... fight. Or let you tell me how hurt you are that I
didn't tell you I used to be a stripper. Whatever will make you
say words to me; whatever will make you stop ignoring me."

"I wasn't ignoring you, Vanessa. You told me you needed
some time, you wanted to stand on your own two feet. I
thought that was a good idea. I backed off. You came all the
way out to my house to ask me to talk to you?"

"When I tried to talk to you, outside Sam's, you said you
didn't want to complicate things. Which, I get because who
needs complication, but honestly, Gibson..."

I took a few steps toward him, hoping he didn't back away
from me. He didn't move, except for his eyes, which never
left my face.

"I'm not going to be dramatic and say that I'm worthless
and miserable without you, because I'm not. But for a little

while, I got to be with someone that genuinely cares about me. To wake up in the morning and smile at a text or talk with him on my way to work. I had sex that wasn't greedy and selfish. I felt pleasure at being touched and wanting to give that back. My world right now is... fine. But maybe *fine* doesn't cut it anymore. I've been great. Spectacular. *Really fucking amazing*. I came all the way out here to ask if I have a chance at getting that back."

"Hmmm..." he mused, his lips pursed, then gave a low whistle. "Did you write that speech last night?"

I grinned, running my tongue over my teeth. "I practiced it in the car, thank you very much."

"I especially like the part where you're not worthless and miserable without me. I'm touched by that; it was romantic."

"Okay, so I don't know how to do this, obviously. But you haven't kicked me off your property yet so you must be thinking about it. About us. About me." I shrugged, then added. "About the benefits of dating a woman that can hang upside down from a pole by her ankles."

Gibson smiled, staring at some point above my head. "Hang on a sec...I'm imagining how that might come in handy."

"I could tell you, but I'd rather show you."

Gibson raised the shovel, stabbing it into the dirt so it stood on its own. Then he took my hand and led me to the patio where we had eaten dinner and watched the girls swim. I sat down in one of the patio chairs; he grabbed another and dragged it close to me.

"I want to be clear that I wasn't judging you, Vanessa. I would never— it would make me a hypocrite, considering the clients I work for. You've told me enough about that time in your life to get where you were coming from, what you thought you would gain. I understand a lot now, about Warren, about that connection you had with him, about the hold he tried to have over you. And how, when you began to come into your own, and he should have been proud of you, he didn't like losing control over you. I get all of that.

"So, me being upset wasn't about you *being* a stripper. It was about *not* knowing that you used to be a stripper. I was blindsided by information I should have had. I couldn't even defend you right, because I didn't know."

He paused, squinting in the sunlight before he brought his attention back to me.

"The last thing I want is to pressure you, but I thought we had something. There's ten years of history that you share with Warren. He knows everything about you. I was *much* nicer to you, but I didn't rate knowing everything."

"Gib," I sighed, hoping the leading look in my eyes was working. "Part of me wanted to come clean, to share everything with you. The other part of me never wanted to sit across from Sylvia Kincaid at a family dinner and have her thinking ugly thoughts about me. I could just hear her telling you that you're too good for me, that I want you to spend all your money on me. And let's not even start with my children — how I'm looking for a replacement baby-daddy—"

"Vanessa—" he interrupted, but placed two fingers over his lips to shush him.

"I know you think it would never happen, Gibson, but I've been here before. People have surprised me. People I thought I knew."

"Okay, so my mother might have some choice thoughts and she might say something. I wouldn't put it past her. But it's not like I don't have your back. It's not like I wouldn't defend you with my last breath. I'd never toss you to the Kincaid wolves and not be in that pit with you. Hell, I live half my life in that pit. I need you to trust me, Vanessa. Trust that I'm not Warren."

"I realize that now. That's why I'm here. Aside from a few

funny stories and a couple of not-so-flattering ones, you know everything. I *want* you to know everything about me. I'm not a perfect person. I've been through a lot of shit in the past couple of years. I have some work to do, on me, and I know that. But...I also know that I deserve to have love in my life. Real love. And I deserve to feel the way I feel about you. I mean... I'm trying to tell you that I love you."

I expected a bigger reaction to those three words. I expected *any* reaction to those three words, but Gibson didn't flinch. *Blink. Blink*, and then, "You do, huh?"

"Yes, I love you. And I miss you. And the kids miss Mr. G's corny jokes and his pool. And I miss damn good fucking."

"I miss that myself."

"I don't want to be pushy. I'm not making any demands or putting out an ultimatum or anything. I just wanted to apologize for keeping that information from you. You said when I was ready, to let you know, so I am. But if you still have a lot going on, I don't want to feel like a complication."

Gibson laughed. "Too late. But I like your kind of complication."

"What complicates things, Gibson? I'm not a client anymore, technically. I'm all paid up, as of yesterday, so there's not even any financial weirdness. And thanks to you, Warren will be out of my life in three weeks and counting."

"Honestly, I'm the least troubled by what's happening between you and me. Other stuff... firm stuff, is what made me take the day off and get in the garden. My oldest brother is leaving Kincaid. My mother wants me to take his spot."

"Oh." I grinned... then it faded when I realized he wasn't smiling back. "Isn't that good?"

"No," he said, wagging his head. "It's not. I'd have to stop serving the clients I want to serve. I won't have time to sit at Sam's and wait for you to take a break. I'll be serving my Mother's interests, which I can't do. I'd refuse to, even if I could, but I can't. So... I'm out here working the dirt and trying to figure out how to hang a shingle and become an *actual* community lawyer. It'll be rough at first, but it'll be mine, so it'll be worth it."

"I think that's great. And I know you'll disagree but I think it's commendable that you'd walk away from what I'm sure was a lucrative offer to stay true to your clients. And to yourself."

"I hope it's commendable a year from now," said Gibson, with a nervous chuckle. "And beyond. Who knows, I could crash and burn."

"So, Sonja, one of my friends from Red Heels, used to always say, 'you can't get good on the pole if you sit on your ass every time you fall off of it. Get back up and try it again until you stop falling on your ass.' Or something like that. But I feel her advice applies to your situation."

He laughed, softly. "Thank her for me. I agree, it's actually applicable. I don't plan on spending a lot of time on my ass." He leaned over and oh-so-casually dropped a kiss on my lips. "I missed you."

"I missed you too. Can we... can we maybe stop missing each other?"

"Mmmm... well, that depends. I have a question for you."

My eyebrows rose. "Okay..."

"How do you feel about gardening?"

"Like... planting things? Digging in the dirt?" Not the question I was halfway expecting. "I don't think I have ever gardened before. I can't keep a cactus alive. If it wasn't for my aunt, I wouldn't know how to take care of my kids."

He stood, grabbing my hand and marching us back over to the bed of dirt. "This is how this is going to work. Take off those prissy real estate agent shoes and roll up your pants. I'll teach you how to plant snap peas. You'll show me that *hang from a pole by your ankles* move. You give a little, I give a little. Deal?"

I started laughing, but Gibson was completely serious, even bending to roll my pant legs up for me. "I feel stupid," I said, giggling at myself in a blouse and slacks rolled up to my thighs, in the dirt in my bare feet.

"You look beautiful," said Gibson, then leaned in to kiss me. He was dirty and I didn't care. I stepped in closer to him opening my mouth to deepen the kiss. It was blissful, having gone without it for so long, but familiar too.

"Don't think I'm glossing over that *love* thing. I'm waiting for the right time to say it back."

"Take your time, Gib. I'm not going anywhere."

"Good. Because I bet you're actually pretty good at gardening."

I side eyed him, pursing my lips. "And I bet you're actually pretty good on the pole."

SWEET. *HOLY*. DEITY I WOULD NAME, BUT MY AUNTIE would pop right out of the woodwork and bop me upside my head for taking the Lord's name in vain.

It would be worth it. I was in *pain*.

We'd spent most of the day out in the vegetable bed, tilling the soil, digging rows, planting seeds and marking them so we'd know what was in what row, then covering up the seeds. A long while after sunset, we limped into the house filthy and stinking... but happy.

We spent the day chatting. Not deep and introspective, meaning of life type talking, but "who was your favorite teacher" and "what's your favorite color" type of talking. I clowned Gibson roundly because his first car was a Range

Rover. Never mind that it was a hand-me-down, and he hated driving it.

Gibson learned about my special talents— not shaking my ass for a crowded club, but that every Halloween, I carved a fantastically artistic pumpkin. Freehand, no stencils. I couldn't draw, but I was excellent with an X-acto knife. I made him promise to plant pumpkins so I could show off my talents in the fall.

After we came inside, Gibson made me strip at the door, since I was caked with mud and barefoot. Then he ran a towel over my feet and sent me upstairs to the master bathroom to get in the shower.

Now I was moaning, standing under the hard spray, letting it pound into my shoulders and knead my muscles. I heard the bathroom door open, but since the shower was dark tile encased in opaque, smoky glass, I couldn't see what was going on.

The door opened and Gibson stepped inside to join me, clutching a small device and a set of shower pods. I grinned, giving him a playful side eye. "You got one of those aromatherapy shower things!"

"I told you, you had me at shower," he said, grinning. I stepped back and let him clip the device to the shower head, aim it and install an aromatherapy pod. In minutes, the scent of lavender and eucalyptus wafted over us.

He stepped back and let me get in front and hog all the spray. Then took the towel I had been using and a bottle of body wash, squirting a generous amount and building a frothy lather. Without preamble or even me asking him to, he began to scrub the dirt from my arms, legs and feet, then guided the cloth along my shoulders and back, over the curves of my hips and behind, down the backs of my thighs.

"I might never get out of this shower, Gibson."

He chuckled behind me. "Well, then I'd have to serve you dinner in here. That could get messy. Turn around."

I turned to face him. "But we're *in* the shower, so that would be easily resolved."

"Eventually, you're going to run out of hot water."

"Oh," I pouted, watching him lather up the towel again, then begin scrubbing my neck, making his way down my chest, soaping up my breasts and nipples before moving down my body to my stomach, over my hips, to my thighs and legs.

I was about to mention that he'd missed a spot when he hooked an arm around me and pulled me close, then grabbed my thigh and hiked it up around his waist.

"I'll do this part by hand."

His fingers gently probed, exploring my folds before locating my clit and teasing me with long, languid strokes. He dipped his head to trap my lips in a sensuous, heady kiss. I was feeling good... loose and wet, in more ways than one.

Just when I thought I couldn't feel any better, a thick finger slid inside me. And then another. It was a good thing Gibson held me firmly in his arms, because the sensation was enough to make me weak in the knees.

"*Mmmmph!*" I whimpered, loving how the sounds of my pleasure bounced off the tile. Gibson had no response, but he didn't really one; he just needed to keep those fingers moving.

The pressure in my pelvis built steadily; tremors shook my body. I was close... so close. I rode Gibson's fingers like it was the longest, thickest dick I'd ever had. When I came, it was furious and loud and thrashing and oh my... *deity*.

"You... are seriously so good at that," I panted, trying to get my bearings as he set me down.

"One of those talents I can't put on my resume. Like pumpkin carving."

"Oh, shut up." I hooked an arm around his neck and brought his lips to mine for a long, hard, moan filled kiss.

"So... it's been awhile. I was hoping for more than fingers tonight."

"Were you?"

"Mmmm."

"I might be able to work something out. Or in." He wiggled his brows at me and I giggled at the double entendre. "First, I have to ask you something."

"What, Gibson?"

"Were you planning to come back out here to harvest all that stuff you planted?"

I laughed, loud. "Well, I *am* tempted to make you do it by yourself, for having me out there in the mud and manure, but... I hoped that spending the day with you, and taking a shower with you... and letting you finger fuck me in said shower might mean that I was welcome to come out and help you with your gardens. And... other stuff."

"Other stuff?"

"Yeah." I stretched up onto my toes and kissed him, this time softly, with as much emotion as I could muster up. "Other stuff. If you'll have me."

"I'd like that, Vanessa," said Gibson. "I don't want to pressure you, like I said. If things are moving too fast, I can slow down. But I meant it when I said I wanted to help you move on, get your life back. I know you can do it on your own. I just want you to know that you don't have to. I want to be a part of that effort, as much as you'll let me."

"I have no intention of fighting you, Gib. You can help me move on as much as you like. Right now, I'd like to move on out of this shower and into your bed so I can show you how much I missed you."

"And you owe me a move."

"You don't have a pole."

"Give me a couple of weeks; I can fix that."

I reached behind me to turn off the shower, since the hot water had cooled to lukewarm. We stepped out and toweled each other off, then tossed the towels in a corner of the bathroom.

When I entered the bedroom, I stopped short at the arrangement that had been set in the middle of the bed— a tray with two plates of Uncle's wings, an array of sauces, and glasses of what looked like Gibson's bourbon lemonade.

"Never let it be said that I'm not romantic. Your weakling glass is on the left, by the way," he said, making his way around the right side of the bed "Wouldn't want you to get too drunk."

He opened a drawer and pulled out a t-shirt, then another and pulled out a pair of shorts. He tossed both at me, then pulled out a set for himself.

I pulled on the items of clothing he gave me. "How you manage to insult me while being so sweet is a gift." Gibson laughed while dressing, then gestured for me to join him on the bed. "So, we're going to sit on the bed and eat chicken wings and drink liquored up lemonade?"

"And maybe Netflix & Chill. Cool?"

I shrugged, and climbed up on the bed. "Sounds like a perfect Friday night to me."

"Truth is," he said, as we were getting settled, "I stopped in at Sam's last night. This was actually going to be my lunch, today. He mentioned that he and your aunt would have the girls tonight, so I was going to come by your place and bring TaKorea and ask if we could talk. I was going to tell you that uh...well, that I love you."

My mouth fell open and eyesight blurred from the tears I was, for some reason, trying not to shed. I reached for him, cupping his face in my hands and planted a kiss on his lips. "I love you too. Especially for thinking chicken wings are romantic."

"All those nights I sat at Sam's eating chicken wings and watching you work? That's real life romance, right there."

I laughed, nodding. "Okay, it's romantic. I guess. I'm sorry for ruining your plans for tonight."

"You didn't. You made them better. One more thing..."

He leaned over to the bedside table and slid something small and metal off of it. "This is yours. It's a key to this house. I want you all to be here as often as you want to be here. I want you to feel at home. And if you're with me, know that no one will ever have anything slick to say about you as long as I'm around. Deal?"

"Do you know how happy I am that I ran smack ass into you that day at Kincaid?"

Gibson leaned over to kiss me, drawing the kiss out to a long, lingering romantic smooch.

"Not half as happy as I am. Now, eat up. It's almost like we're having dinner at Sam's."

EPILOGUE

ibson

It was an eerie, end-of-an-era feeling, to be packing up my office at Kincaid.. I'd done a lot of growing up, a lot of changing. I'd learned a lot. I'd rebelled a lot and done things my own way... a lot.

But I'd also had the unique opportunity to remain in the safety of the family cocoon much longer than most. I had access to Mother's legal brilliance, Garrett's work ethic, and Gabriel and Greggory's camaraderie. I would miss that... walking into Kincaid felt like walking into my second home.

It wasn't like I'd never step foot in that office again. The building I'd rented to house *Gibson Kincaid Law* wasn't more than fifteen minutes away, so I wouldn't be far—I could still meet my brothers for lunch some days. And I'd offered my services if they came across a client they felt they couldn't help. As a member of the family, I was still on the letterhead, my photo still hung on the wall, and I was still a de-facto member of Kincaid Family Law.

But walking around my office with a box, carefully depositing the last of the little things I'd put up to combat the drab color scheme and make the place feel more mine just felt... like an ending.

A tap-tap sounded at my door. I turned to find Mother standing in the doorway in a smart white suit, her hands clasped and grasping an envelope.

"On my last day, you actually knock on the door before coming into my office."

She smiled and stepped in, taking a long, slow look around at bare walls and empty bookcases and the clean surface of my desk.

She cleared her throat. "I'm leaving for court in a few minutes but I wanted to see you before you left. I can't make the ribbon cutting at your new office building, but your brothers have assured me that they'll be there to represent the family. And Judge may stop by. You know, you just have to mention cake and he's a guarantee to show."

I chuckled, nodding. Judge did love cake.

"And... well, I wanted to give you this, and say goodbye."

I grinned. "Goodbye? A card? I'm not leaving town, Mother. I'm going to see you at the house for dinner on Sunday. Gregg's excited to introduce us to this woman he's been seeing."

"It's just a little something."

She handed the envelope to me. It was much too thin to be card. I flipped it over and stuck my finger under the flap, ripping it open. Enclosed was a check. For... much more than I was expecting, which was *none*, so I was floored.

"It's not for the full amount that I would have given you, had you done what I asked you to do. But I didn't want you to leave Kincaid and go out on your own without knowing that I— *we* support you. Your family will always be here for you. Please don't hesitate to call if you need us. Mkay?"

A big, goofy grin crept from one corner of my mouth to the other. "I am your favorite aren't I?"

She sighed, rolling her eyes. "Don't be ridiculous, Gibson. I have no favorites."

"Except me. I'm the favorite. This check proves it."

"It proves that I don't want you to fall on your face. At least financially."

"Mother. Mom..." I stepped closer to her, opening my arms wide. "*Maaaaa!*" I wailed, loudly, capturing her in an embrace and holding her close to me.

"Gibson! Let go of me, boy! You're wrinkling my suit!"

I loosened my arms and stepped back to get a good look at my mother. She was smiling... somewhere on the inside. On the outside, that pink glow was creeping up from her neck and the purse of her lips told me she was not pleased.

It was an act. I was sure of it.

She pulled at the waist length jacket and brushed imaginary dirt from her ensemble. "I swear, I give you an inch and you take a mile. Now..." She sniffed, holding her head high. "I'm due in court. But uhm... you'll be bringing Vanessa to dinner on Sunday, won't you?"

I'd been holding off on folding Vanessa into the family. She and I— and the girls— were doing great, rock steady. We spent weekdays at Vanessa's condo, though for the last month we'd been talking about looking for a bigger place in town. Eventually. Weekends were spent out at my house—in the garden, in the lake, in the pool. The girls had picked out and decorated their room, and the house that I had originally bought to surprise one woman was taking on the personality and feminine touches of another.

We threw a party at Sam's when her divorce was final. The

decree came in the mail and I could tell that she wanted to cry with relief. But she held it in, slid it back into the envelope and slipped the envelope into a drawer. I took her to dinner and we had what was probably the best sex we'd ever had, that night. It was like it was her way of letting go of him. Finally.

And Pack was, so far, successful in keeping Warren out of prison, which was good for his daughters. He'd been abiding by the visitation schedule and the child support checks began arriving from the state. He was still in deep shit, but Pack was earning his paycheck.

When it came to the Kincaid family, though, the pace was slow and steady. I didn't want to have to disown any of them for disrespecting her.

"Yes ma'am, she'll be there. Are you ready for that?"

"Yes. Yes, I am."

"I mean it, Mother. At the first snide comment or rude remark, we take off. I know how you can be, and I'd like it if I didn't have to make a scene. Pick on me all you want, but Vanessa is off limits."

"I understand, Gibson. You love her and you trust her, so... what choice do I have but to do the same? Besides, you act like she is the only woman you know that ever worked a stage. See some world, son."

She stormed out of my office, leaving me puzzled and trying to decipher her riddle.

"Only woman that... what?! Mother! Come back here!"

THE END... OF THE BEGINNING. I HOPE WE'LL SEE VANESSA AND Gibson again when we next visit Decatur, Georgia and Ruby's Soul Food Cafe!

THANK YOU!

Without readers, there's only me typing words into a vacuum. Thank you for your interest in this not only *this* novel, but the ones that came before it and the ones that are yet to come. It is my deepest hope that you enjoyed it thoroughly!

I'd like to give a shout out to those who helped me with important plot details on this book, the Betas who read and gave much needed feedback and the friends who cheered me on— especially the ones who gave me good skrippa names.

I love to hear from readers, so please reach out! You'll find my social media, website and email information on the following page.

ABOUT THE AUTHOR

DL White is an emerging author of black women's fiction and romance. She lives in Atlanta, Ga and has been writing for most of her life, but seriously began pursuing publishing in 2011. Dinner at Sam's is her sixth release, and her fifth full length novel.

For more information about her and her books, please visit
BooksbyDLWhite.com
authordl@booksbydlwhite.com

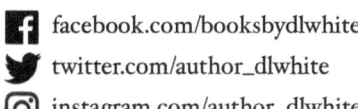

facebook.com/booksbydlwhite

twitter.com/author_dlwhite

instagram.com/author_dlwhite

ALSO BY DL WHITE

If you enjoyed Dinner at Sam's, I hope you'll pick up another title by DL White

BRUNCH AT RUBY'S

BEACH THING

LESLIE'S CURL & DYE: POTTER LAKE #1

UNEXPECTED, A HOLIDAY SHORT

SECOND TIME AROUND: A POTTER LAKE HOLIDAY SHORT

THE GUY NEXT DOOR: A POTTER LAKE NOVEL

Don't forget to leave a review, and tell a friend (or two)!